BEAUCHAMP HALL

Danielle Steel

Beauchamp Hall

A Novel

RANDOM HOUSE
LARGE PRINT

Published in the United States of America by Random House Large Print in association with Delacorte Press, an imprint of Random House, a division of Penguin Random House LLC, New York.

Cover design: Eileen Carey
Cover photograph: © Shutterstock

ISBN: 978-1-64385-197-6

Printed in the United States of America

This Large Print edition published in accord with the standards of the N.A.V.H.

To my wonderful children,
Beatrix, Trevor, Todd, Nick,
Samantha, Victoria, Vanessa,
Maxx, and Zara,

May you always have the courage
to pursue your dreams,
and may all your dreams
come true!

I love you with all my heart and love,

Mom/d.s.

BEAUCHAMP HALL

Chapter One

Winona Farmington opened one eye and saw through the window the white wonderland she woke up to for most of the winter in Beecher, Michigan. It was a small town, almost two hours north of Detroit, with a population of ten thousand. Beecher's main claim to fame was that it had been hit by the tenth deadliest tornado in U.S. history in the 1950s, long before Winnie was born. Nothing much had happened there since.

The other side of her double bed was cold, which meant that Rob had gotten up at least an hour before, and left for the meat processing plant where he worked. She guessed even before she glanced out the window that he hadn't bothered to shovel after last night's snow. The house she lived in had been her mother's, and she owned it with her sister, Marje. Marje was already married with kids when their mother died, and she and Erik owned their own house, so Winnie stayed in the family house and they agreed that if they ever sold it, they'd split the proceeds equally. But for now at least, Marje didn't need the money. Her husband owned a busy plumbing company, and the house was a good investment and likely to increase in value, so she'd never asked Winnie to sell it.

Rob stayed with her almost every night. He had his own apartment, but rarely went there except when they had a fight, or if he stayed out too late and got too drunk when he went out with the boys and didn't want to hear Winnie complain about it the next morning. The rest of the time he slept at Winnie's, did no repairs, felt no great attachment to the place, and only helped her with something minor when she asked him. He kept some clothes in her closet, but nothing too personal, and none of his favorite items to wear.

Winnie had once escaped Beecher to attend the University of Michigan in Ann Arbor, and had loved it for the three years she'd been there. She had big dreams then, and wanted to work in publishing in New York after she graduated. She'd even visited the city a couple of times with her roommates and loved it, but then her mother got sick at the end of junior year, and by the end of the summer, it looked as if she only had a few months to live. Winnie didn't want to miss being with her mother for her final days. They'd always been close, particularly after Marje moved out after she graduated from high school when Winnie was eight. She had her mother to herself from then on, and their time together was precious. Her mother had shared with her her passion for books, the delight of Jane Austen, the Brontë sisters, her favorite authors, biographies of famous people, history, and current novels.

Winnie took the first semester of senior year off to be with her. But she was no better by Christmas, and Winnie took spring semester off as well to nurse her. It had been hard to come home to a small, quiet town, where nothing ever happened, after the excitement of the university. Coming back to Beecher was like returning to her childhood, and her whole focus was on her mother. She had no life of her own. Her friends had married right out of high school, or gone to Detroit to find better jobs than they could find in Beecher. A few had gone to college, but not many. Some even had babies by then, and Winnie suddenly had nothing in common with them. She was busy with her mother's care.

It was never spoken, but Marje simply assumed that Winnie would be there for their mother. She had a husband and a child by then and made it clear she had no time. Winnie was single, still in college, and Marje saw no reason why Winnie's plans couldn't be deferred, and her dreams put on the back burner. Winnie was the obvious choice of caretaker, and she didn't want to let her mother down. She had always given up so much for them. And Winnie didn't want to abandon her mother in her final months. She loved her and wanted to spend as much time with her as she could.

Miraculously, and despite the doctors' dire predictions, her mother had hung on for seven years, and even rallied several times, but never long enough for Winnie to leave again. She fought a noble battle, and finally died when Winnie was twenty-seven. By then it seemed too late to go back to college. She had a job, a house, a life, and New York and her dreams seemed as if they were on another planet. She was working as a cashier at a restaurant, and got a better job at the local printing company after that. She met Rob four months after her mother died, and the time had drifted by like a river from then on, carrying her along with it. She didn't need a college degree for the job she had. Her own natural organizational skills and common sense were enough.

It was hard to believe she and Rob had been dating for eleven years. She wasn't madly in love with him, but he was familiar and comfortable. They never talked about marriage or the future, they lived in the present, had dinner together on most nights, went to the movies, bowling with friends sometimes. It wasn't what she really wanted, but there was no one else more interesting around, and suddenly she slipped from twenty-seven to twenty-nine, then turned thirty at dinner one evening with Marje, Erik, and Rob. Then just as quickly she was thirty-two and then thirty-five. They'd been together for ten years when she turned thirty-seven. And now she was thirty-eight and couldn't figure out where the years had gone. Eleven of them, with Marje reminding her constantly that she needed to get married and start having kids before it was too late. She conveniently forgot that Winnie had spent seven years, crucial years, taking care of their mother, while Marje claimed she was too busy to help. Winnie wasn't angry about it, but it was a fact of her life. She had sacrificed a big chunk of time, which she'd never get back.

She couldn't see herself having kids with Rob either, and he wasn't eager for kids or marriage. He was thirty-nine, and most of his friends were getting divorced after fifteen and twenty years of marriage. Marje and Erik had a good marriage and seemed happy enough. She knew her sister had had at least one affair, maybe two, which Marje had never admitted to, but Beecher was small, people talked, and Winnie had guessed. She didn't know if Erik knew or not. He was a good breadwinner and a terrific father who coached Little League for their two boys. Winnie couldn't imagine Rob doing that. He had nieces and nephews of his own who didn't interest him much, and he referred to all of them as the "rug rats."

Winnie had read in **Cosmopolitan** magazine once that women couldn't afford dead-end relationships after the age of twenty-eight, or they ran the risk of getting stuck in them for years, and missing opportunities for marriage and children, possibly until too late to have them. The magazine had warned that you turn forty before you know it. Her mom had always cautioned her to try to find the right man and settle down before the bloom was off the rose. She wasn't there yet, but she was getting close, with a man who didn't set her heart on fire, took her for granted most of the time, and never told her he loved her. It wasn't exactly a dead-end relationship, it was more of an open-ended one that just kept limping forward through the years without arriving anywhere. She wondered if he would marry her if she made a fuss about it, but she didn't because she wasn't sure how she felt about it herself. It was a no-frills relationship: a box of candy on Valentine's Day if he remembered, and he almost always forgot her birthday but would take her out to dinner a few days later, if he had time. She couldn't see the point of getting married, unless they wanted kids, and they didn't. She wasn't ready to have babies, she wanted to figure out what she envisioned for her future first.

"Well, you'd better figure it out pretty damn soon," her sister scolded her. "Or you'll wake up one day and be forty-five or fifty, and it'll be too late, for kids anyway. It happens faster than you think." Marje was ten years older than Winnie.

"I'm only thirty-eight," Winnie reminded her.

"Yeah, and it seems like just last week you were

twenty-eight. You won't be young forever, Win." Marje always liked reminding Winnie that she was getting older, it made her feel more comfortable about being middle-aged herself. It had taken Marje and Erik a long time to get pregnant, and their boys were now fourteen and seventeen. They were good kids, who had no ambition to leave Beecher. Erik expected both of them to come to work with him at his plumbing company someday, and neither of them objected. They already helped out there after school. The company was a good moneymaker, and neither boy was planning to go to college since their parents hadn't. Winnie's three years at Michigan, as an English major with a creative writing minor, were considered an aberration for her family. She'd gone to college before her nephews were even born, so she wasn't an example they could relate to, and she had done nothing special with her life.

She kept herself busy with the things she loved to do. She still read voraciously and was first on the list at the library for every bestseller that came out. Her mother had been a volunteer at the town library on the weekends and instilled in her a love of books. Winnie wrote short stories from time to time, and had done well in her writing classes in college. And when her mother had gotten too sick to continue working, Winnie had taken over one of her favorite duties. She read stories to children every Saturday morning. It was also a volunteer job and she loved it. Her mother had been "The Story Lady" to the local children, and Winnie happily stepped into her shoes. She had done it at first to help her mother, who didn't want to disappoint the children who expected her to be there on Saturdays. It gave Winnie a chance to share the gifts her mother had given her with the children. She introduced them to "The Red Shoes," **Charlotte's Web, Stuart Little, The Little Prince, The Secret Garden, Little Women,** and Nancy Drew for the slightly older girls. The children loved her and Winnie got to read her favorite childhood books again. She had a gift with the children, like her mother had, although she didn't think so. Marje always said the books their mother read to her had bored her, while Winnie devoured them, much to their mother's delight. Every Saturday morning, Winnie spent two hours at the library, and was "The Story Lady," carrying on her mother's tradition and following in her footsteps. It was Winnie's only contact with kids, other than her two nephews, who were as uninterested in books as their mother.

Winnie's other passion had always been horses, ever since she was a little girl. She'd had a chance to ride at a friend's father's farm, and had had a few lessons. She was a decent rider and her friend's father said she was a natural. She liked to ride, but what she liked best was watching them. She had an instinctive sense for what a horse seemed to be thinking or feeling. She had walked into the corral once where they were keeping a horse that had been mistreated before they bought him. No one had been able to ride him, he was wild-eyed and terrified, bucked off anyone who rode him, and kicked anyone who came near. The men at the stable said he was hopeless and they were planning to sell him again, or worse. Winnie felt so sorry for the horse that she let herself into the corral where he stood alone. She spoke softly to him, as he eyed her in terror but didn't move. He let her stroke him, and pawed the ground next to her, as one of the men watched, afraid to call out to her to stand back, stunned by what she was doing.

In time, Winnie was able to ride him, bareback with only a bridle. They called her "the horse whisperer" after that. She had a talent for taming abused horses, and people in Beecher knew it, and called on her once in a while to help them out. As far as they were concerned, she had a gift. She didn't get a chance to use it often, but it was there. It was as if she could get into a horse's mind and still its fears. They trusted her, and calmed down whenever she was there.

Winnie peeled off her flannel pajamas and got into the shower. She had a long, lean body, in contrast to Rob's heavyset frame with a paunch. He liked drinking beer when he came home from work. Marje had put on weight, and was a different body type from Winnie, who had always been tall and slim. Winnie had dark hair, pale blue eyes, and creamy skin. With better clothes and somewhere to wear them, she would have been pretty. Their mother had been, though she had let herself go once she was widowed at thirty-three. Her husband had died in a hunting accident. Marje remembered him slightly, Winnie didn't. Marje looked more like him, sturdy and rugged, with a tendency to put on weight after she had her kids. She envied Winnie's slim figure, but ate too much of what she cooked for her family to lose the weight she'd gained. She'd been the prom queen in high school, but looked ten years older than she was while Winnie looked younger than her age. Winnie had never been a prom queen and didn't care. She was always lost in the books she read.

While drying her hair, Winnie looked out the window again, trying to assess how long it would take her to shovel the driveway. She did it nearly every day since there was new snow almost every night this time of year. Rob could have, before he left for work, but never did. When she asked him to, he reminded her that it wasn't his house and that was why he parked his truck in the street, and suggested she do the same.

She made a bowl of instant oatmeal and had a cup of coffee, bundled up in her parka and snow boots, grabbed the shovel from the garage, put on gloves, and went to work on the driveway. It took her half an hour to get the snow pushed aside and packed down enough to drive over it in her SUV, but she was only ten minutes late when she got to the printing company where she worked as the production manager. She kept all the big projects organized and on track. She had exceptional organizational skills, and thanks to her, they met all their deadlines. It wasn't a creative job, but vital for the smooth running of the business, and she did it well.

Hamm Winslow, her boss, came out of his office and glared at her. She hated the job, and her boss, but it was decent money. He owned the printing company, and had been her boss for the last ten years. Her best friend, Barb, worked there too. She had a more menial job than Winnie, but was good with layouts, and very visual.

"Nice of you to come in before lunchtime," he said snidely. He always had something unpleasant to say, and had no respect for his employees, or anyone for that matter. He was a miserable person.

"Sorry, my driveway was iced up," she said blandly.

"Whose isn't? You expected to wake up in Hawaii, maybe? Get up earlier, don't come in here late again. Got it?" He was even nastier to the women who worked for him than the men, and he got away with it.

"Sorry." He was always angry and complaining about something. Nothing was ever done fast enough or well enough for him, and he took pleasure in pointing out publicly the mistakes they made. "He's in a great mood," Winnie commented under her breath as she slipped into her seat at the desk next to Barb's. They'd gone to middle school and high school together, and Barb had gone to junior college and got her two-year associate's degree, which didn't seem to make much difference. She'd been dating Pete for four years, they'd gotten engaged a few months before, and were planning to get married next summer. Her future husband was a dentist and a nice guy. She spent all her spare time now planning the wedding. They were going to have the reception at the local hotel. Barb wanted to work in his office after they were married and quit the job she had, which would leave Winnie to face the ogre alone. She wasn't looking forward to it.

"Somebody screwed up a big order for the bank," Barb whispered to her. "You should have heard him yelling ten minutes ago."

"Glad I missed that," Winnie whispered back, shot a smile at Barb, and turned on her computer. It felt just like high school, and middle school before that, when they sat next to each other in class. Barb opened a drawer and pointed to three bridal magazines in it and Winnie laughed.

"I'm throwing the bouquet at you, you know. You'd better be ready to catch it," Barb said, smiling.

"I'll be sure to duck," Winnie said, checking on an order she had on her screen. It wasn't ready yet, and they were getting close to deadline. She was going to get on the production department about it immediately. Hamm never realized how vital her services were to him, or never showed it if he did. He never praised her or thanked her.

"Rob is a great guy, you should marry him. It's time, Win," Barb said as a follow-up to her comment about the bouquet.

"Who says?" she said, looking unconcerned.

"We're getting old!"

"At thirty-eight? You sound like my sister. She got married right out of high school. Thank God we didn't do that. She could be a grandmother by now, for God's sake. Now there's a scary thought."

"You'll be old enough to be one by the time you start having kids, if you don't hurry up." There was nothing else to do in Beecher except marry, have kids, go bowling, and play softball in the summer. She didn't say it, but Winnie wanted more than that, much more. Barb had been engaged once before, after years of dating the same guy, and it hadn't worked out. He'd cheated on her constantly. Now she was ready to settle down, and in a hurry to have babies. Winnie wasn't. "Who are you waiting for? Bradley Cooper? Send him a map. You've got everything you need right now." That wasn't how Winnie saw it, but she didn't say it. She didn't know what she wanted, but she knew this wasn't it, working for Hamm Winslow for the rest of her life. And she wasn't sure Rob was it either. After eleven years, she knew things weren't going to get any better than they were now. Their relationship was lack-luster at best, but not bad enough to walk away from either. It wasn't exciting, or romantic. Rob said only women, and men with low testosterone, were romantic and liked all that mushy crap. That was one way to look at it. She didn't expect him to throw roses at her feet, but a little more attention might be nice. Like shoveling the driveway for her once in a while, so she wouldn't be late for work and didn't have to start the day cold and tired. He could have done at least that for her, particularly since he slept there most nights. He bought gro-ceries occasionally, which he thought was a big deal. He always said she owned the house after all, and she wasn't paying rent, so she could afford to pay for her own food. There was nothing gallant about Rob.

Both women got busy at work then, Winnie went to push the production department. At the end of the day, Barb turned to her with a question.

"How about dinner at my place tonight? Pete is going to a dental conference in Detroit."

"I'm having dinner at my sister's," Winnie said with a sigh.

"That should be fun. Not."

"Yeah, but she makes a big fuss about it when I don't see her for a while. She claims the boys miss me. I know they don't. They don't even talk to me when I'm there. I wouldn't have at their age either."

"Have a good time," Barb said with a smirk, and

they both left work and got in their cars. It was already dark, bitter cold, and the roads were icy. But it was only two miles to Marje and Erik's house and Winnie was a careful driver. She let herself in the back door when she got there, and the boys, Jimmy and Adam, were watching TV in the basement playroom. You could hear it all the way up to the front door. And as usual, the house was a mess. No one ever cared. Marje's strong suit was not keeping house, and she made no apology for it. Erik was used to it and didn't seem to see it. Whenever the mess got to him, he cleaned it up himself.

She found Marje in the kitchen, getting dinner ready. It was pot roast, which seemed like a hearty meal for a cold night. Her sister was a good cook, and her family were all big eaters, Winnie wasn't, but it smelled good anyway. Marje was lucky, she hadn't had a job in years. She was a stay-at-home mom, thanks to Erik's business, and she got a new car every two years. She drove a Cadillac Escalade, which was a lot nicer than Winnie's six-year-old SUV.

"How was work?" Marje asked, as she checked on the pot roast and smiled at Winnie. They were very different, but there was a sisterly bond between them. Marje blamed their mother for encouraging Winnie to be a dreamer. Marje had made fun of her when Winnie had written a paper once in high school about why Mr. Darcy from **Pride and Prejudice** was her favorite hero of all time and she wanted to marry a man like him. Winnie loved stories from another century, preferably set in England, which her sister thought was ridiculous. Marje loved watching reality shows, and still never read a book. Their mother had given up trying to encourage Marje to read in her teens, and shared her love of books with her younger daughter.

"Work was okay," Winnie answered. "Hamm is such a jerk. He's not happy unless he's beating someone up and humiliating them in front of everyone else. It gets pretty old." But they both knew the money was good, and Winnie had seniority now. She didn't want to start over somewhere else, which was part of what kept her with Rob too. What if she never met anyone and never had another date? It was easier to stick with "the devil she knew," at work and with Rob.

They talked for a few minutes about Erik and the kids while Winnie set the table and Marje slid into her favorite subject.

"So what's happening with you and Rob?"

"Nothing. Don't start that, please. We both go to work, he comes over at night, we fall asleep, and go back to work the next day."

"Sounds very exotic," Marje said, "and a lot like marriage. You've had years of practice. You might as well just do it one of these days."

"Why are you so hot for me to get married?" It always annoyed her. It was the only thing they ever talked about.

"I don't want your life to pass you by. Trust me, at your age it starts to fly. I don't want you to miss it."

"I'm not missing anything. I'm happy."

"Really? You don't like your job, your boss is a horse's ass, you're not crazy about your boyfriend, and what else is there in your life?"

"What's in your life?" Winnie volleyed back. "Erik and the kids. That's no more exciting than mine."

"It suits me," Marje said, and Winnie knew it did. "You've always been such a dreamer, I'm just afraid you're going to dream your life away, waiting for some kind of magic to happen. There's no magic, Winnie. This is all we get." It sounded sad to Winnie.

"You mean I don't get to be Cinderella when I grow up? Mom always said I could be anything I wanted to be. That's why I went to college and wanted a job in New York." It would have been so much more than what she had here.

"Well, that didn't happen, so you've got to work with what you've got. 'Bloom where you're planted,' as they say." That was very philosophical for Marje, and Winnie smiled.

"Very profound. Don't I look like I'm blooming?" she teased her sister. She knew Marje meant well, or thought she did, although she could be a pain in the neck at times. And there was a wide chasm between them. They were so different and always had been. That hadn't changed.

"Actually," Marje said, narrowing her eyes to

study her, "you look depressed. Why don't you get highlights or something, or change your hair color? Rob might like it." It was always about Rob and what might make him propose. Marje had dyed blond hair with three inches of dark roots. Winnie's was her natural dark brown, almost black, color. Their mother used to say she looked like Snow White.

"He likes me the way I am," Winnie argued. "And I'm not depressed. I accept my life as it is." But she thought about what she'd said again on the way home. Did she accept her life? Had she made her peace with it? Did she still want more? Did she have a right to it? She was no longer sure. Dinner at her sister's had been the way it always was, always the same conversation between the adults, about work or the kids, brief chaos when the boys joined them at the table, and then Winnie went home to her empty house. Rob was bowling with friends that night.

She turned on the lights when she got home and sat in front of the fireplace in the living room for a few minutes. She remembered when she used to sit there with her mother, in the last years of her life, talking about the books they read, and the dreams the stories spawned. She still thought she was going back to college in those days, but they never talked about that because it would only happen after her mother was dead. And then she didn't go back anyway.

She heard the front door open behind her and turned to see Rob walk in and shake the snow off his boots. He was a big, burly guy with lumberjack looks, and didn't talk a lot. His family was originally from Norway, and there was a raw, hearty look to him. She had expected him to come home later, he usually did.

"You're home early." She smiled at him. "I just got home from Marje and Erik's."

He went to get a beer, popped it open and took a sip, and sat down on the couch next to her with the can in his hand. "Everyone was tired tonight, and two of the guys were sick. We called it a night early, and went to Murphy's Bar for a while." She could smell it on his breath. He wasn't an alcoholic, but he drank a lot. He said it was the Scandinavian in him. Her brother-in-law drank just as much. Most of the women she knew didn't. "What are you doing in here?" He looked around the room they never sat in. They either sat in the kitchen or her bedroom. There was an old-lady quality to the living room. She hadn't changed anything since her mother died. It was full of her mother's things, and some antiques she'd inherited from her grandmother. Winnie kept the room as a kind of shrine.

"I was just thinking of my mom when I got home, and the books we used to read. At the end, I used to read aloud to her. **Rebecca** was one of her favorites." She didn't know why she was telling Rob, she knew he didn't care. Just the thought of reading a book put him to sleep.

"That sounds maudlin," he said matter-of-factly, chugged his beer, and got up. "I'm beat. I'm going to bed."

She turned off the lights and followed him upstairs. He turned on the TV in her bedroom, dropped his clothes on the floor, and climbed into bed while she took a shower, in case he wanted to make love. Their sex life was pretty good, despite his lack of romantic sensibilities. He was great in bed when he was in the right mood. It had been part of the glue that held them for the last eleven years, the strongest thing between them.

She started talking to him when she got out of the shower, and he didn't answer. She walked into the bedroom, and he was sound asleep on his back, snoring loudly. The beers on his bowling night had caught up with him. She looked at him for a moment, put on her pajamas, and tiptoed downstairs to her mother's bookcase. She knew exactly where the book was that she wanted, she hadn't read it in years. **Jane Eyre.** She ran back upstairs with it and got into bed, smiling as she held it. It was like a visit with her mother, and a trip back in time, as she opened the familiar book. There was always something comforting about holding her mother's books. She loved the familiar feel and smell of them. The pages were yellowed, and it was like meeting up with an old friend as she began reading, and

Rob continued to snore next to her. She knew that when she woke up in the morning, he'd be gone again, and he wouldn't have shoveled the driveway for her if it snowed during the night. Nothing was ever going to change. But as she read the book her mother had given her as a young girl, nothing around her mattered, and her real life faded away. That was one of the best things about reading, she could just disappear and forget everything she didn't like about her life.

Chapter Two

The printing business where Winnie worked was always busy in December, with calendars and Christmas cards, and end-of-the-year reports to deliver. They could hardly keep up and Winnie and Barb had to work late almost every night. Winnie was planning to spend Christmas Eve and Christmas Day with Marje and Erik and their boys as she always did. And Rob went to relatives in Detroit. They never spent Christmas together. His mother was in a nursing home in Detroit. Winnie had never met her. She had Alzheimer's so there wasn't much point. He'd never invited her to meet his other relatives. They didn't have that kind of relationship, he said. With the exception of his bowling league, they spent most of their time together alone, in a kind of bubble suspended in time. She had promised to make dinner for him the night before Christmas Eve, and hurried home from work to do it. He brought venison he'd shot with a friend. Winnie cooked it from a recipe she found on the Internet, and it was delicious. Rob was impressed. She had poured him a glass of red wine with dinner, and he said he'd rather stick with beer.

"That was a damn fine meal," he said, smiling at her. "I didn't think you could cook like that."

"Neither did I. The recipe was easy."

"What are you doing for Christmas?" he asked, as though he expected it to be different.

"I'll be with Marje as usual, same as every year." The holidays always made her miss her mother, but she didn't want to tell him that. He wasn't the kind of man you exposed your soft side to. It would have made him uncomfortable, and Winnie feel too vulnerable.

"Well, save New Year's Eve for me. We can go to Murphy's for dinner, and hang out till midnight, and then come back here." It was his favorite bar, and she knew he'd spend half the evening shooting pool with his pals who hung out there too. She had nothing else to do. They'd been going to Murphy's on New Year's for eleven years. Her life with him was one long déjà vu, but she never met other single men.

She brought out her presents for him then, a heavy cobalt-blue sweater, a black knit cap, and some thermal gloves with a heated panel that you could put in the microwave to warm them up. He said he really liked them. The sweater fit him perfectly, the hat was warm, and he said the gloves were great.

"They'll keep your hands warm while you shovel my driveway," she teased him, and he grinned.

"Then I guess I should have gotten a pair for you," he shot back at her, and then went out to his truck to get his gift for her. It was a medium-sized box in silver Christmas paper with red ribbon. She opened it and found another sweater. He gave her one every year, this year's was yellow, and when she took it out of the box, she saw that there was a black lace G-string in the box too. He loved seeing her in sexy underwear and bought it for her himself, since she never did. "Why don't you put it on and show me," he said. She reached for the sweater, surprised he wanted to see it, and he stopped her and handed her the G-string. "Not the sweater," he said, laughing at her with a lustful look. There was something about the underwear he gave her that always made her feel cheap. It usually had rhinestones on it, or tassels, or an arrow pointing toward the crotch, but to keep him happy, she disappeared and came back wearing it with the sweater she'd had on, and high heels.

"Come on, baby, take off the sweater." He was leering at the G-string, and with her long legs, she looked sensational in it. She peeled off the sweater, pretending to strip for him, and she was wearing a black lace bra that almost matched the lace G-string. "Now that's more like it!" He grabbed her as soon as she got near him, and lifted her off the ground in his powerful arms and laid her on the couch. He had his own clothes off and was on top of her immediately, making deep guttural sounds. Everything about him was familiar to her. He was an adept lover and knew what she liked best, but there was nothing tender about his lovemaking. He was too aroused by the thong he had given her to wait for long, and he came with a shudder and a fierce shout, then lay still on top of her.

"God, I love you in that underwear," he said, as she looked up at him. It always had the same effect on him. The gift was more for himself than for her, but she always went along with it. She knew it meant a lot to him. They went upstairs then and made love again, and it reminded her why she stayed with him. She couldn't imagine the sex being as good with anyone else, and finally, exhausted and happy, he rolled over and fell asleep. She got up, put a bathrobe on, and went downstairs to clean up the kitchen. She picked up the G-string from the living room floor and put it in her bathrobe pocket, and then went back upstairs and slid into bed next to him. She knew there should have been something more with him, but there wasn't, just hot sex when she wore the right underwear and a warm body in her bed. He still hadn't told her he loved her. He never did. And when she woke up in the morning, he was gone. He hadn't stayed to wish her a merry Christmas, or left a note to say so. He figured he had given her his best gift the night before, on the couch and in her bed. She knew it was all he had to give and all she'd ever get from him, other than a sweater once a year and sexy underwear.

She shoveled the light snow from her driveway and left for work. Everyone was in a festive mood. Their office party was set for noon, with a buffet from an Italian restaurant, and after lunch, they could all leave. The office would be closed for a week. No one needed to have anything printed between Christmas and New Year's Day. Even Hamm, the original Scrooge, was willing to give them the week off.

"Did you bring your present for the game?" Barb whispered to her, as she took hers out of her desk right before lunch. The whole office played the white elephant game every year. Each employee bought a gift that cost roughly twenty dollars, wrapped it anonymously, and put it in a pile. They all drew numbers and took turns in order picking a gift. The other employees could steal any gift they wanted twice, from whoever picked it, and after that they were safe and could keep the gift they had. And the person a gift was stolen from would get another turn. It usually led to jovial screams of protest as a gift someone wanted was taken, and shouts of victory when someone else got to keep it or stole it back. Some of the gifts were really fun, most weren't. Winnie thought that she should put Rob's Christmas G-string in the game one year. She was tired of getting them, but she had bought something respectable for the game, a good-looking cheese platter someone could use over the holidays. There were bottles of wine, and an assortment of odd-shaped gifts people were eyeing, trying to guess what they were.

"Of course I brought a gift," she said to Barb, went out to her car to get it, and put it in with the others. "I never get lucky with this game," she said to Barb in a whisper as they each picked a number. "I've gotten a set of coasters three years in a row, and I never have guests over. I've had a jeweled tissue box, a leatherette pencil cup, and a pair of mittens with reindeer on them."

"I hope you get mine," Barb whispered, and pointed to where it was. "Trust me, you'll love it." Winnie smiled at how excited she was, and indicated which one was hers.

The game had begun and their coworkers were already stealing bottles of wine from each other by then, and a bottle of vodka. There was a nice-looking plaid shirt, three pairs of wool socks, a wool hat that looked like a polar bear, an Italian cookbook, a pair of light-up Christmas earrings that three of the women wanted and kept stealing. The game started getting loud and boisterous halfway through. Barb got Winnie's cheese platter and loved it, someone else stole it, and she got it back, and Winnie decided to trust her and picked Barb's gift, opened it and found two DVD sets of a TV series she'd heard of and never seen. The actors in the photograph were wearing clothes from the 1920s, there was a castle in the background, and it was set in England. The series had been a big hit and was still on TV. Barb had given her the first two seasons, and knew from veiled inquiries that Winnie had never seen it.

"You're going to love it," Barb promised her. "They're in their sixth season now." It was called **Beauchamp Hall,** which Barb said the British pronounced "Beecham," and was about a fancy family. Winnie was a little disappointed, she never watched TV, and would rather read a book, which was why she'd never seen it. She hoped someone would steal it from her, so she could pick something else, but no one did. The game ended, and Barb clutched the cheese platter, saying Pete would love it. Winnie put the DVDs in her purse and told Barb that she was thrilled and could hardly wait to see the show, which wasn't true.

They all enjoyed the buffet lunch of lasagna and pesto ravioli after that. They'd been allowed to drink wine to go with it since the office was closing after lunch. Hamm was feeling very expansive, and even gave Winnie a flirtatious look after a glass of wine. Everyone was careful not to drink too much since they had to drive home on snowy roads. There was eggnog without alcohol too, and Winnie opted for that. Barb had two glasses of wine since Pete was picking her up.

"What did Rob give you for Christmas?" she asked Winnie as they ate tiramisu for dessert.

"A yellow sweater and black lace underwear. He gives me the underwear every year, it's for him."

"I wish Pete would give me something like that," she said, giggling.

"It gets old after a while."

"Well, I know what you'll be doing on Christmas night," Barb said with a gleeful look.

"No, he's visiting his relatives in Detroit like he does every year. And staying to see friends afterwards. And he's going to visit his mother in the nursing home there. Besides, we did that last night," she replied, laughing at her friend's comment, and Barb shook her head.

"No! I meant you were going to watch the DVDs of **Beauchamp Hall.** You've got to watch it, Winnie. The way you love period stories, you're going to die. The costumes are gorgeous and the characters are fantastic. And they shoot it in a real castle in England, I forgot what it's called."

"Oh . . . of course . . . I'll watch it before we come back to work," Winnie promised, feeling as though she'd been given homework. She'd never gotten involved in watching a series, and for some reason the idea didn't appeal to her. But she didn't want to offend her friend, and now she felt she had to see it. She wished again that someone had stolen it from her. Another set of coasters would have been better.

"You have to call me the minute you've seen it. I want to know what you think," Barb insisted. "Believe me, you'll be hooked after the first episode. They're starting to shoot the seventh season now in England. Pete loves it too." Winnie knew one thing was sure, she wouldn't be watching it with Rob, he'd have a fit and laugh her out of the room.

"What are you giving Pete for Christmas, by the way?"

"An espresso machine. It's what he said he wanted. He's giving me a really fancy new Cuisinart. I already know. I saw it in his car." She looked faintly disappointed. "What did you give Rob?"

"We have a sweater exchange every year. And I gave him heated gloves so he could shovel my driveway. He didn't take the hint."

Pete came to pick her up, as expected, and the two women hugged and wished each other a merry Christmas, and agreed to talk during the week. Barb made Winnie promise she'd watch the DVDs as soon as she could. They were in her purse and she forgot about them when she got home. She picked up **Jane Eyre** for a while, and then dressed for dinner at her sister's, and put her gifts for them in her car. She had autographed basketballs from the Detroit Pistons for both boys. She had bought a dress that Marje had said she wanted that she got on the Internet, and the same heated gloves for Erik that she'd gotten for Rob, since Erik did shovel their driveway.

She arrived just as Marje was putting the finishing touches on dinner, and the Christmas tree was lit. Winnie had a small one at her house, which Rob said was silly, since she didn't have kids and it just made a mess. But it smelled delicious and Winnie loved having a tree every year, even if it wasn't big. The one at her sister's house touched the ceiling, with an angel on top that had been their mother's and reminded them both of their childhood. Winnie had agreed to let her have it, since Marje had kids.

Erik served her a glass of spiked eggnog, and then they sat down to dinner. Marje had made turkey and it was delicious, and they all had second helpings of the stuffing until it ran out. It was the perfect Christmas meal. Afterwards they sat in the living room, listening to Christmas carols and opening their gifts. After they got their basketballs, the boys went downstairs to the playroom to play video games. Their parents had bought them a new, bigger flat screen TV. Marje had given Winnie a new pair of red Uggs, which she always wore around the house on cold nights. Marje gave her a pair every year. Like the sweater from Rob, it wasn't a surprise. But Marje loved her dress from Winnie. Marje always said she didn't have time to shop and didn't enjoy it anyway.

It was a cozy family Christmas. They asked where Rob was, and she said he was in Detroit with his relatives, as always, and would be back later in the week. At midnight they all went to mass. She got home at one-thirty in the morning and slipped into bed, thinking about Rob. He hadn't called her, but she thought he might on Christmas Day. He didn't like holidays as much as she did, and didn't always call her. He thought holidays were for families and married couples, not for people who were just dating. After eleven years, she was just a "date," but he wasn't much more than that to her. And as she thought about it, she fell asleep.

Winnie woke up to bright sun on the snow on Christmas Day. It looked like a Christmas card. She lay in bed reading for a while, and dressed in time for lunch at her sister's, which was casual and would be a meal of leftovers from the night before. Erik and the boys would watch football on TV all day. It gave the two sisters time to talk.

"Have you heard from Rob?" Marje asked with interest and Winnie shook her head.

"I don't expect to. He's not big on holidays, and he's probably busy with his family, or his mother at the nursing home." He was good about that, which Marje always said was a good sign, but of what?

"How depressing," Marje said sympathetically.

"Yes, it is. He doesn't talk about it much. He says she doesn't recognize him anymore. He goes a few times a year, but she has no idea who he is."

"The poor guy needs a family," she said meaningfully and Winnie laughed. Her sister was never subtle.

"He has one, and so do I. You're all I need, big sister," she said warmly.

"That would be pathetic. Don't you want to be more than just Aunt Winnie? Don't you want to be a mom one day?"

"To be honest, I'm not sure," she said seriously. "I've been thinking about it. Maybe I'm just not the marrying kind, or meant to have kids." She enjoyed the children at the library for two hours a week but never longed to have her own, at least not yet.

"What would you do for the rest of your life without children?" Marje couldn't imagine it. Erik and the boys were her whole life and her job.

"Maybe I'd be happy. I'd still like to do some writing one day. I always wanted to do that after college, but I never got the chance. I'd love to try, short stories like I used to write, or something." She had published several in a magazine in college, and their mother was very proud.

"Mom always said your stories were good." Marje had never read them.

"She was prejudiced." Winnie laughed. But their mother was also well-read and intelligent, even though she hadn't gone to college. She had inspired Winnie and encouraged her to write. It had just never happened, except in her creative writing classes, which didn't really count.

At the end of the day, Marje switched on one of the reality shows she loved, and Winnie watched it with her. It was a group of housewives in Las Vegas, who all looked like hookers, had set up a Christmas meal together, and were joined by their husbands at the end of the show. The men looked like gangsters and the women were squeezed into tight, sexy dresses with big hairdos, too much makeup, and tons of jewels. The dining room the show was shot in looked like a bordello. Winnie was mesmerized and couldn't believe what she was seeing, and Marje was glued to it with delight. She told Winnie which ones were her favorite women on the show.

"You watch this regularly?" She was amazed.

"I never miss a show. Today is their Christmas special." Winnie couldn't imagine watching it again, or caring about the women involved, but Marje felt as though they were her friends. And she said the dress Winnie had given her that she had wanted was vaguely inspired by the women on the show. Winnie had already noticed that all of them looked as though they had breast implants, their breasts were huge, and their lips were puffed up with collagen. Nothing about them was real.

At the end of the show, Winnie got up to leave. She went downstairs to see Erik and the boys, thank them for her gift, and wish them a merry Christmas again, then she hugged her sister. It was snowing outside again, and she wanted to get home before it got too deep.

When she got home, she made herself a cup of tea and sat in her kitchen, watching the snow falling. Rob called her from Detroit.

"How was your Christmas?" he asked her.

"Really nice with Marje and Erik and the kids. What about yours?"

"It was great. We went to a bar to shoot pool for a while last night, then we came home. I haven't stopped eating since I got here."

"How's your mom?" she asked carefully, not wanting to upset him.

"I'm seeing her tomorrow. She doesn't know it's Christmas anyway." But what if she did, even if she didn't recognize him? It seemed so sad to her. "We're going out for dinner tonight with some cousins I haven't seen in years. They're here from Miami." It all sounded foreign to her, since she didn't know any of the people. He only had one brother and he hadn't seen him in years. The people he visited in Detroit were aunts and uncles and cousins, but Winnie could never keep any of it straight. "I'll see you when I get back. You'll have to model your Christmas gift for me again." She wasn't sure why, but he made her feel cheap when he said it, like a hooker he was hiring for the night. She loved having sex with him, but not by masquerading as a stripper, or pretending to be a whore, even if just for him. She didn't answer and changed the subject.

"I hope you have a great dinner," she said vaguely.

"What are you doing tonight?"

"Going to bed, I'm exhausted. Too much food, and I was up late last night after church. I'll probably read in bed."

"My cousin gave me a couple of great porn films for Christmas. We'll watch them when I come home." His saying it made her think of the DVDs she'd won in the white elephant game. She hated porn films and didn't want to see any more of his. But Rob loved them, they aroused him, and he always wanted to have sex with her while they were watching, imitating what was happening on the screen. She avoided watching them with him whenever she could. There were still things about him that gave her the creeps, even after eleven years. At least he wasn't addicted to porn, but he liked it a lot. She had let him know as often as possible that it wasn't her thing. Rob was more about sex than about love. He was good at sex, but love wasn't in his repertoire. "See you when I get back, Win," he said and they hung up. No **I love you,** no **Merry Christmas.** Same old Rob.

She went up to her bedroom then, got into bed

and reached for the copy of **Jane Eyre** on her night table, and remembered the DVDs again. She had no interest in them, but thought that if she watched one, she could fake it to Barb about the other ones when she asked her. She decided to get it over with. She had nothing else to do that night. She looked at the boxes when she took them out of her purse. Each season had eight episodes that were each an hour long, and a two-hour Christmas special at the end. Barb had given her two seasons. Twenty hours of TV, way too much, but if she watched an episode or two, maybe Barb wouldn't care about the rest.

She dutifully got the first disc out, and put it in the DVD player attached to the TV in her room. It was Rob's. He had brought it over so he could watch porn videos with her. She dreaded it when he came over with a new one, and she tried to find an excuse not to see it: tired, sick, headache, busy, early day tomorrow. Sometimes he couldn't be put off, but she always tried.

The screen sprang to life with the first season of **Beauchamp Hall,** and she hopped into bed, pulled up the covers, and turned off the light as the first episode began. She was struck by the beautiful costumes, all historically accurate, and the incredible décor inside the castle, with enormous paintings and elegant antiques. It had an **Upstairs Downstairs** feel to it, with a fleet of servants, and a family composed of all the important players on the show. Three of them were famous actresses, several of the men looked familiar to her, even though it was an English production, but she had seen them in movies. And the manners and mores of the players were authentic to the period. It was everything she loved about English books and movies. The behavior of each actor was exquisite, the performances flawless, the dialogue brilliantly written, the story engaging, the characters perfectly defined in their roles as good or bad people. Their position in the world was clear, bound by tradition, whether noblemen or servants. It was an absolutely gorgeous show, as she got engrossed in the story for the first time. Predictably, by the end of the hour, several of the storylines were left hanging, and she wanted to see how they turned out, so she watched another hour. And a third one after that. She had to put another disc in for the next two episodes. At the end of it she had binge-watched five hours of **Beauchamp Hall,** and she wanted to watch more. But it was midnight by then. She looked at her watch, and like a naughty child past curfew, with no parental supervision, she grabbed another disc, put it in, pressed Play, and watched the intricate stories unravel. She was in love with the characters by then, and fascinated by the castle, the family, and the staff. It was a perfect replica of English aristocracy in the 1920s, when grandeur, opulence, and the upper class still prevailed. She felt as though she had been pulled into a different world, where her own life ceased to matter, only theirs did.

It was two in the morning when the third disc finished, and she still had another episode and the two-hour Christmas special to go, and she decided to watch them in the morning. She could hardly wait to wake up and see more. It was snowing hard and had been all night, and she hoped she'd get snowed in so she could watch the rest. She didn't have to go to work all week. She wanted to savor it and enjoy each moment of the story, and the costumes and the sets, but once she started, she couldn't stop. It was exactly as Barb had said. It was totally addictive, and she had had a fantastic evening watching it all alone.

She woke up the next morning and watched the rest of the first season, and the cast felt like old friends by now. It was lunchtime when she stopped. She ran downstairs to the kitchen, grabbed something to eat, and went back upstairs and started the second season, which was even more exciting than the first one.

She spent another three hours watching it in bed, and it was dark when she finally got up, and had another seven hours left to enjoy. She took a shower, put on fresh pajamas, and watched another four hours that night, and woke up again the next day to watch the last three hours of season two, and felt bereft when it ended. It was as though she had lost her best friends, and had been exiled from their magical land. She watched two of her favorite episodes for a second time that night. She had spent two full days and nights, and Christmas night, watching **Beauchamp Hall,** and as Barb predicted, she was totally hooked.

She called Barb that night. "What did you do to me?" she said when Barb answered.

"What do you mean?"

"It's like a drug! I can't stop! I've just spent two days in bed watching it, and all I want is more."

"Well, there are four more seasons for you to watch, including the one playing in England now. And they're filming the seventh season as we speak, or they will be, starting next week. You can order the others that have already been shown on the Internet. I'm exactly like you. I binge-watch it when I get it. And Pete is just as bad. We love it."

"The castle is incredible. Is it really like that in real life?"

"Haversham Castle. Apparently it is. It's owned by a British marquess, and he lives there with his sister, a lady, but he owns it because of the laws in England, which give the land and the title to the oldest son, and traditionally no one else inherits anything. They looked pretty cool in the article I read, they're about our age or a little older. The show saved them from losing the castle apparently, they were out of money, and they make a fortune from renting it for the show. The whole town gets involved and watches them film it."

"The man who writes the show must be brilliant," Winnie said with open admiration.

"It's his first big success. It's a huge hit over there. I knew you'd love it, Win. I'm so glad you watched it."

"It's the best Christmas gift I got. I've never been addicted to a TV show before."

"Neither was I, until **Beauchamp.**" Barb sounded thrilled that Winnie loved it.

"I'm going to order the other seasons tonight." She went straight to her computer after she hung up, and ordered them all. The sixth season wasn't available yet, since it was still playing in England, but she put in an advance order, which she'd have in four weeks. She had three more seasons to look forward to for now, as soon as they arrived. She could hardly wait.

She had just pressed the send button with her order when Rob called her.

"Hi, I just got back. What are you up to? I missed you." It was nice to hear that and surprising coming from him, he rarely admitted it.

"I've been in bed watching DVDs for the last two days. The ones I won in the elephant game at work. It's a fantastic show."

"I've got a pretty fantastic show for you too. Can I come over?" He usually didn't ask, he just showed up.

"Sure. I don't have anything to eat in the fridge, I haven't been to the grocery store in days. I couldn't tear myself away from the TV."

"I'll pick up something on the way," he said, and walked in half an hour later with a pizza box. He bounded up the stairs after he left it in the kitchen, walked across the room to her bed, and kissed her hard. She'd been watching an episode from season one again, and enjoyed it just as much the second time. "What's that?" He noticed it on the screen, and looked unimpressed by the costumes and the main drawing room of the castle.

"The show I told you about." She smiled.

"Never mind that." He ejected it and tossed it on the dresser, took a DVD case out of his pocket, put a disc in, and hit Play. And within seconds she could see what it was, the porn film his cousin had given him, and it was one of the roughest ones he'd brought over yet. She looked at it, uncomfortable at how extreme it was, and it was a shocking switch from the genteel show she'd been watching for three days. Before she could comment, he tore off his clothes and grabbed her, and started re-enacting what they were doing on the screen, trying to force his fist inside her, until she pulled away and made him stop.

"What's wrong?" He looked annoyed and was violently aroused.

"That's kind of a rough hello, isn't it?" She was unhappy about how brutal he wanted to be. There was nothing loving about it, it was the rawest kind of sex.

"Since when did you get so prissy? Come on, babe, I missed you. I've been thinking about this for three days."

"I missed you too. How about we just make love, that works pretty well for us. We don't need to play porn games. Those guys are pros." She wasn't prudish, but there was something disgusting about it, and she didn't want to participate. But he wanted more than just making love. He looked angry as he grabbed her again, and made love to her more roughly than he usually did. It frightened her a little, and wasn't fun for her. But he came like a rocket, and within minutes wanted to make love again. He had come home starving to the point of being crazed. And after the second time, she wanted him to stop for a while.

"What's wrong with you? Most women would beg for a guy who can make love to them like that. I've got the cock of a twenty-year-old." **But a heart of stone,** she wanted to say.

"I like it better when you're more tender and sensual."

"I like it better this way," he said angrily. "I'm not gay." He looked furious.

"You don't have to be gay to be gentle, Rob," she said quietly. She didn't like his homecoming style at all. And out of the blue, she suddenly wanted to ask him a question. "Are you in love with me, Rob?" It broadsided him completely and he didn't answer for a minute.

"What the hell have you been watching on TV while I was gone? **Desperate Housewives**? What kind of question is that?"

"An honest one. You never say it. Do you love me?"

"What do you expect, for me to throw flowers at you or burst into song? Sure I love you. Do you think I could make love to you like that, if I didn't? That's how men express love."

"No, that's how men express lust. That's different."

"I love your body," he said, ignoring what she said. "I like being with you. We've been together for eleven years. That must mean something." It could also mean habit, fear of loneliness and of being alone. They had great sex, but all of a sudden she wondered what else they had, and what he felt for her. And even what she felt for him. The love interests on **Beauchamp Hall** were so intelligently expressed, the characters really cared about each other, and despite their upper-crust manners, they fell in love and found elegant ways to demonstrate it, nothing like the porn film he wanted her to re-enact. She felt violated by everything he had done that night.

"Eleven years together means a lot. I just wonder what we're doing sometimes."

"We're having great sex. Unless you want to go all virginal on me now."

"I don't just want to be made love to, I want to be loved and respected too."

"Oh, for chrissake," he said, leaping out of bed, and pulling on his clothes. "I don't know what you've been watching since I've been gone. **Little House on the Prairie** or **The Sound of Music.** I'm not a kid, Win. I'm a man. And this is how I am. If you don't like it, then maybe we need to think about this. I'm going home. Call me when you're normal and ready to act like an adult again."

"I don't need to act like a whore to be an adult, Rob. I'm a woman and a human being. I'm not some hooker in a Tijuana bar."

"And I'm not some namby-pamby guy who wants to beg you to have sex like a fifteen-year-old. You know what I like, and how I like it."

"I don't like watching porn with you," she said bluntly, "or how it makes you act."

"And here I just told my cousin you're a great woman and will do anything I want."

"Actually, I won't," she said firmly. "Is that what you like about me?" She looked shocked.

"I don't like how you're acting now. I can tell you that." And with that, he stormed out of the room, thundered down the stairs, and slammed the front door behind him. She could hear his truck start a minute later, and then drive away.

Shaking at everything that had been said, she rescued the DVD of **Beauchamp Hall** where he had tossed it, took his out, and put the **Beauchamp** disc back in, pressed Play, and climbed back into bed. Within a few minutes, she felt calm again, and as though she had entered a world of noble gentlemen and ladies, people who knew how to behave and how to treat those they loved. She watched three episodes in a row, and felt as if all was right with the world again. And she had the answer to her question. Rob was not in love with her. It hit her like lightning. And she was not in love with him.

Chapter Three

Rob didn't call her for three days after the night he came home from Detroit. She didn't call him either. She didn't like the way he had treated her, and her realization that he didn't love her and her own doubts about loving him had shaken her. They were great sexual partners, but not much else. They had no common interests, no shared friends, except for a few of the men in his bowling league. They went to work, came home, slept in the same bed on most nights, and made love when he felt like it. She realized suddenly that he hardly talked to her, and it had taken her eleven years to notice. For years, she had told herself that all men behaved like that. But what if they didn't? The men on **Beauchamp Hall** didn't, but it was a TV show, and set nearly a century earlier. And Erik respected her sister, although she knew their marriage wasn't exciting, and she knew that her sister had had an affair he probably didn't know about a few years back, but she'd stayed with Erik.

What did she have with Rob, other than predictably efficient sex? She wanted more, she wanted real conversation, someone to take walks with, to share good times, and to learn things from each other. She wanted what the players at **Beauchamp Hall** had, but that was a fantasy and she knew it. Now she was dissatisfied with her life and a man who wanted to re-enact a porn video with her, who said he loved her body, but not much else. She wondered if he even knew her, or asked himself if he did, or cared. She would have talked to Barb or Marje about it, but she knew she'd sound crazy if she told them she wanted her life to resemble a TV show. Marje especially would have gone nuts over that and accused her of being even worse than a dreamer.

Rob called her the morning of New Year's Eve. She'd been watching season one of **Beauchamp Hall** again, and assumed she'd be watching it that night if Rob didn't call or take her out, and that was beginning to look like a serious possibility. She wondered if it was over between them and didn't want to ask.

"So, are we going out tonight?" He sounded awkward.

"Do you want to?" she asked cautiously.

"Yeah, I do. I don't know what got into you the other night, but let's forget about it, and have a nice time at Murphy's like we always do." She had just watched the Christmas special from the first season with everyone in white tie and tails on New Year's Eve, as they danced around the ballroom. The reality of her own life was laughable compared to that, but it was also almost a hundred years later, and even in British aristocratic circles the world had changed dramatically since then. She would be spending New Year's Eve watching her boyfriend play pool at his favorite bar, drinking beer instead of champagne. And she'd been spending New Year's Eve with him that way for eleven years. "I'll come pick you up at seven. I have some things to do before that."

"That would be nice," she said, sounding subdued. Despite her epiphany, she wasn't ready to end it with him yet, and not on New Year's Eve. That was more drama than she wanted with him. She wanted to be sure of what she felt for him, or didn't, before she reacted to it.

She was wearing jeans when he picked her up. There was no point wearing anything else. No one at the bar would be dressed up. A few of the younger girls might be wearing halter tops, but she felt stupid wearing one in the dead of winter, and freezing in the drafty bar all night. Instead, she wore the yellow sweater he'd given her for Christmas, and he looked pleased when he saw it.

"You wearing the thong I gave you too?" he whispered in her ear when he kissed her, and she laughed.

"No, I'm not."

"You can put it on for me later, to start the year off right." She didn't comment, and they drove to the bar in his truck. He started playing pool with his friends as soon as they arrived, and they had burgers at the bar around ten o'clock. He started another pool game half an hour later. At midnight, he was winning, and she walked over to him, tapped him on the shoulder and kissed him at the stroke of twelve, while his friends hooted and whistled. Then she went back to sit at the bar, and he went back to the game. She found herself wishing that she were at home watching **Beauchamp Hall.** She was living vicariously through the actors and the show. Their dialogue was so perfect. They said everything she would have wanted them to say. Even their hair looked impeccable in the style of the period, their jewelry, their clothes, their manners, the way they moved and behaved and reacted to each other. The restraint they used when dealing with difficult situations. She watched it at every opportunity, it had Winnie in its thrall. It had become her guilty pleasure. She was already depressed that in two days she had to go back to work, and wouldn't have much time to watch it anymore. It had been perfect in the past few days, because Rob was working and she wasn't, so she sat at home in her pajamas all day and watched it. But in two days that had to end.

Rob drank too much beer that night, while playing pool, and Winnie had two beers early in the evening, and had eaten since. She was totally sober at 2:00 A.M. when they went home, so she drove his truck, and she had to help him into the house.

"Come on, baby . . . put the G-string on for me. . . ." He was staggering and slurring. He leaned on her heavily and she could barely get him up the stairs, and the minute he hit the bed with all his clothes on, he passed out.

He woke up at eleven o'clock on New Year's Day with a pounding headache, and went downstairs to find her. She was sitting in the kitchen, watching an episode of **Beauchamp Hall** on her computer, when he walked into the kitchen and sat down.

"Not that crap again. Why are you watching that? I can't even understand what they're saying." She turned it off so it wouldn't bother him, and poured him a cup of coffee. "I won a lot of money last night," he said, looking pleased. "I had a great time." She nodded. She hadn't, but didn't want to complain. It was no different from all the other New Year's Eves they'd spent there since they met, and she'd put up with it before. She knew he wouldn't understand why something had changed. She wasn't sure she understood it either.

He went back to his place after she cooked him breakfast. He said he was going to meet up with some of the guys, and would be back that night.

Barb called. Pete had some work to do in the office, and she came over to watch two episodes of **Beauchamp Hall** with Winnie. They had just finished the last episode they'd been planning to watch when Rob came home early and saw Barb in leggings and a tight exercise top that showed off her figure. He looked her over with a practiced eye, as though Winnie weren't there. Winnie pretended not to notice, and Barb said she'd see her at work tomorrow and left.

"She's hot," Rob commented when the door closed behind her. She had a good figure, but always complained about her big breasts and what an encumbrance they were.

"She's getting married next summer," Winnie said, putting the DVD away.

"To the dentist?" Winnie nodded. "He's a wimp. She deserves better than that."

"He's good to her," Winnie said and walked to the kitchen to cook dinner, and Rob followed her.

"Are you okay?" he asked and she nodded. "You're acting weird these days."

"I'm trying to figure some things out." She didn't look at him as she said it.

"About us?" He could sense that something was different, but he didn't know what or why, and neither did she.

"Maybe."

"Maybe what you need to figure out is why you watch that stupid show all the time. I think it's making you a little crazy." She wondered if it were true. Suddenly she wanted to be with the people on the show, and live among them, as though they were real and not actors speaking lines someone had written for them. She was starting to believe it was real. Maybe Rob was right. She felt as if she might be losing her grip on reality. And her own life seemed off-kilter. Rob was part of it. The relationship they'd had for eleven years didn't seem like enough compared to what she was seeing on the show, but the universe of **Beauchamp Hall** didn't exist. Yet her life seemed so inadequate compared to it. Even the servants seemed more eloquent and more polished than Rob, who acted like a boor most of the time.

She didn't say anything to him about it. They ate dinner without talking, went to bed afterwards, made love without his putting any exotic demands on her, and he fell asleep five minutes later. When she woke up in the morning, he had left for work. She managed to shovel the driveway after the night's fresh snow and get to work on time. Winnie looked serious when she sat down at her desk. Barb didn't say anything for the first half hour and then looked at her intensely.

"Are you okay? Something wrong?"

"I don't know. All of a sudden, my life doesn't fit, like it shrank in the wash or something."

"Uh oh, sounds like **Beauchamp**-itis to me." Winnie smiled at what she said. It felt that way to her too. "You know they're just actors, right? They're not real people. They don't live at the castle. And they're not waiting for you to show up."

"Yeah, I know," Winnie said sadly. "But everything used to be so great back then. So elegant, so polite, so right. It puts a whole new perspective on my life."

"It's a fantasy," Barb reminded her. "We'd all like to live like that, but even those people don't anymore. They all lost their money, and they look like you and me. There are not many grand lords and ladies around these days. How are things going with Rob?"

"Not so good," Winnie said. "We had a couple of bad fights last week. He gets a little crazy sometimes. I don't think he loves me, Barb. I'm some kind of sex object to him. And what's worse, I'm not sure I love him either. We just stay together out of habit, and because we have nothing else to do. I asked him if he loved me a few days ago, and he told me he loves my body. I think all he wants is sex most of the time. I don't think he even knows who I am, or cares." Barb looked surprised to hear it.

"Do you know who you are?" Barb asked her pointedly.

"I thought I did. Now I'm not so sure." It had been troubling her a lot lately.

"Because of **Beauchamp**?" she asked, worried about her.

"No, because of everything else. What am I doing with a guy who never talks to me?"

"He's hot," Barb said admiringly. She liked his looks, and he emanated a kind of virile sex appeal that had always seemed attractive to Winnie too. But now he seemed like a Neanderthal at times, compared to the aristocrats on **Beauchamp Hall.** And he'd been acting like a sex addict recently.

"He says the same thing about you, that you're hot," Winnie told her with a look of surprise.

"It's the breasts," Barb said, looking embarrassed. She had hated them all her life but was scared of having a breast reduction, and couldn't afford one anyway. "Guys want to meet them before they even want to meet me. They have an identity of their own because they're so damn big. They think I'm the goddess of fertility or something, except for Pete. He loves me, not just my tits."

"Rob acts like I'm a hooker he picked up in a bar somewhere and kept around for eleven years. It freaks me out sometimes. And scares me. He thinks it proves he loves me because he wants to have sex with me all the time. All it proves is that he's a horny guy."

"There are worse things." Barb looked anxious.

"I don't think I'm a person to him," Winnie said. "I'm just a piece of ass. And I'm not even sure what he is to me."

"Have you said all this to him?" Barb looked concerned. Winnie was being so intense, which was unlike her. She always went with the flow, even with Rob. But now she was questioning everything.

"I've said some of it. But I still need to figure it out for myself. Maybe we're the wrong people for each other."

"After eleven years?"

"Could be. Maybe this is all we'll ever be. A guy who sleeps over at my place because my house is bigger than his apartment, and he can get laid before he falls asleep at night, if he's in the mood."

"That's a little harsh, don't you think? He cares about you a lot more than that."

"I'm not so sure. Now he thinks I'm weird because I'm watching the show. He wants to watch hard-core porn and that seems normal to him. He thinks I'm a freak."

"He's into porn?" Barb looked surprised, as Winnie nodded.

"The worse it is, the better he likes it. He wants me to try everything they do. We had a fight about it when he came back from Detroit after Christmas. I don't think a man who loves me would ask me to do some of those things. It's demeaning. I don't know. All of a sudden everything feels wrong about us. Maybe it's some kind of midlife crisis for both of us." She was being earnest about it and Barb didn't know what to say.

"Pete would have a heart attack if I put a porn video on. He's pretty straightlaced." She sounded disappointed as she said it.

"It's better that way, believe me," Winnie said with feeling. "I feel like a cheap trick with some of the things he wants me to do."

"I feel like the Virgin Mary with Pete. He thinks I'm some kind of saint."

"Aren't you?" Winnie teased her. She knew Barb's history and all of her secrets since high school. There had been a number of men other than the two she'd been engaged to.

"It's probably better if he believes that, instead of the truth. I was pretty wild for a while after high school. He doesn't need to know that. He keeps referring to me as the future mother of his children. A little porn might do him some good. His maternal grandfather is a minister."

"I guess nobody's ever happy with what they've got. I just want to figure out what Rob and I feel for each other, after eleven years."

"Maybe he'd respect you more if you got married."

"I don't think that's the issue. Honestly, I don't know what the issue is. Maybe we're just bored with each other, and he needs the porn to spice it up. But if that's true, where will we be in ten or twenty years? Cheating on each other? I don't want that either. And I'm not going to marry someone to make him respect me, if he doesn't already."

"Have you ever cheated on him?" Barb was curious.

"Never. If I want to cheat on him, I'll break up with him. What's the point of staying with him if I want someone else?" Barb nodded, thinking about it, and didn't comment for a minute.

"I guess that's true," Barb admitted. It reminded Winnie of her sister, who had cheated on Erik, but their marriage seemed to be solid in spite of it. And maybe Erik cheated on her too. Relationships were so damn complicated. And getting married seemed so extreme. She wondered if she ever would.

"Do you ever feel trapped here?" Winnie asked her then.

"I never think about it. We grew up here. It's home." She'd never wanted to move away from Beecher, and had always had smaller dreams than Winnie. Getting married was enough for her.

"All I wanted when I went to college was to leave and never come back. I couldn't when my mom was sick, and then I gave up on the idea," Winnie confessed wistfully. "Sometimes now I think about it again. New York, even Chicago. Wouldn't that be exciting?" Barb shook her head.

"No, it would scare the hell out of me. I wouldn't last in New York for a week, or Chicago, or Detroit. What would I do there? I don't know anybody. I'd be terrified to walk down the street." Winnie still loved the thought of it, even though she knew she'd never do it. Rob was more like Barb and her sister. His universe was defined by Beecher. It was all they'd ever known, and they didn't want anything else. If Winnie could have flown away on eagle wings, she would have in an instant.

"I think about it now again when I'm watching **Beauchamp.** I'd give anything to turn the clock back and be part of that world."

"It's just a TV show, Win. It seems real, but it isn't."

"I wish I could write something that seems that real." She was full of dreams suddenly, about places and things and people, and the writing she used to love doing. The series she'd been watching had ripped the lid right off the tiny tin can of a world she'd been living in, and now nothing seemed to fit. Everything in Beecher felt too small for her. The show had changed her, just in the space of a week. She felt as though she had come loose from her moorings. It was exhilarating and terrifying all at the same time. Something was happening to her, she didn't know what it was yet, but she hoped it was something good.

Chapter Four

In February, they hired a new girl named Elise at the office, and neither Winnie nor Barb liked her. She was spectacular-looking, with a sensual body, and wore low-cut, tight clothes and miniskirts that showed off her legs. She was twenty-one. She had been hired for one of their lowest positions, as a girl Friday and assistant to everyone, before they assigned her to any one department. They needed to know her strengths first. Winnie could always use a spare pair of hands in her overworked production department, and Barb was working on layouts. The office manager started Elise off with taking orders for business cards, and the men who came in to order them were nearly rendered speechless by her looks. Hamm had her in his office constantly, giving her projects. She had spent a year in Detroit as a trade model, but said she didn't like it, and had come home. This was the first office job she'd ever had, and she mixed up the orders she took several times.

"Hamm looks like he's going to have a stroke every time he talks to her. He gets all red in the face," Winnie commented, and Barb laughed.

"Bad luck for him, the blood is rushing to his face instead of somewhere else," Barb said in an acid tone. The girl was getting on their nerves. Whatever she did wrong, Hamm was willing to forgive, while he was merciless with everyone else. He was clearly dazzled by Elise's youth and beauty.

A month later, whenever the new girl talked to Hamm, she practically pressed her body up against him, and Winnie noticed his hand resting on her shapely bottom and that Elise didn't move away. She knew who had the power and was milking it for all it was worth.

"I think she's sleeping with him," Winnie whispered to Barb one day, after watching her with Hamm again. There was something different about the way they talked to each other, and Hamm looked possessive whenever any man came too close to her.

"Don't be ridiculous. She's twenty-one years old, he's fifty-eight. And his wife would kill him if you're right."

"I'm sure she doesn't know. How's the wedding coming, by the way?" They were supposed to go to Flint to look for bridesmaids' dresses, but neither of them had had time yet, and the weather had been terrible since Christmas.

Things had been limping along with Rob since New Year's, but they hadn't had any major show-downs since then. He had finally backed down and stopped pushing her to watch porn with him, which was a relief. Whenever Winnie had time to herself, she watched the subsequent seasons of **Beauchamp Hall.** It just got better year by year, and the sixth season was the best one yet when she got it. She'd offered to lend them to Marje but she wasn't inter-ested. She still preferred her reality shows. Rob had stopped bugging her about that too. They were no closer than they'd been before, but things were peaceful again, and he worked late several nights a week. When he did, he usually got to her house ex-hausted and went right to sleep. He said he was in line for a promotion and was working hard to get it, so their sex life no longer took precedence. At least until he got the promotion, Winnie assumed. He had a strong sex drive and needed sex constantly.

In April, there was an opening at the printing company. One of the senior women, in a techni-cal position doing their digital artwork and graphic design, decided to retire, which created a vacancy that only a few people in the office could fill. The position was filled internally within a week, which left a managerial position open that Winnie was qualified for. It would have officially made her their production director, with a higher salary, a title, and an office. She was in direct competition with two of the men in the office for the job, but Barb was sure Winnie was going to get it. She'd been there longer, she had ten years' experience, and was so good at her job. She could have run the whole place if she had to. Neither of the men who wanted the position had been there for as long as she had. Thinking about it was exciting for Winnie, and the higher salary would be nice to have. She had saved a fair amount of money over the years, but the promotion would make a real difference to her. She talked to Marje and Erik, who were sure she'd get it too. She had even started dreaming that if she got the job, she'd make enough money to do some traveling.

The position sat open for three weeks, while Hamm said he was moving some people around in key positions, and an announcement would be made soon.

He finally broke the news to them on a Monday morning. Hamm gathered everyone around in the main room where they all sat. Winnie was disappointed because Barb was out sick with the flu, and she would have liked to be with her to hear the news. Barb had sent her a few texts that morning about how sick she was. Winnie tried to stay calm while Hamm made a short speech, and she noticed both of her male competitors looking smug. A minute later, he announced that each of the men had been made head of a department, which had taken some reorganizing. And he still hadn't announced who had gotten the position they'd all been angling for as production director. But the two men being given other jobs left only Winnie as a possibility for the position so the conclusion was obvious. With both men out of the running, only Winnie had the organizational skills to run production and finally get credit for it, which she never did, even if she was already doing the job and had been for years. She was starting to smile broadly when he made the announcement.

"And I'm very proud to share with you that Elise Borden is our new director of production. In the two months she's been with us, she has demonstrated her outstanding abilities." Winnie knew that Hamm thought the production department ran itself. Elise was beaming at Hamm, and Winnie's mouth nearly fell open as she stared at them both. What he had said just wasn't possible. Elise was twenty-one years old and a total airhead. What was Hamm thinking? But it certainly confirmed that he was sleeping with her. This made her Winnie's boss. Winnie would be reporting to her now. Hamm thought Winnie could do the job while Elise got credit for it.

Everyone went back to their desks a few minutes later, murmuring softly about Elise's miraculous promotion, and Winnie drifted back to hers with her ears ringing, as though an explosion had gone off in her head. After ten years, she had been passed over for a girl with no experience who had been there for less than two months. It was a massive slap in the face and humiliation. She sat stewing at her desk for the rest of the morning, and sent a slew of texts to Barb. Barb didn't answer, and then finally responded and said it was insane and she'd call Winnie later. She was feeling too shaken to want to talk about it anyway. Tears stung Winnie's eyes, and by lunchtime, she was so agitated that she walked into Hamm's office. Elise was moving her boxes and papers into her new office at the same time.

"What is it?" Hamm snapped at her the minute he saw Winnie come through the doorway. She thought he looked embarrassed but wasn't sure.

"Can I talk to you for a minute?" It was a question he dreaded and never good news, especially now. He knew that Winnie's request could only be about Elise's new job. The whole office was buzzing with it.

"I'm leaving for a lunch meeting in five minutes, you'll have to make it quick," Hamm said vaguely. She was sure that the lunch was with Elise to celebrate her new position. Hamm beamed every time he laid eyes on her, he was ridiculously obvious.

"I'll be quick," Winnie promised as she closed the door behind her. She didn't want anyone else to hear what she had to say, least of all Elise. She knew that if Barb had been there, she'd have kept her from walking into his office, but she wasn't, and nothing was going to stop her now. "What exactly just happened out there? Elise has been here for five minutes, I've been here for ten years. Is this some kind of joke? Or do you have to sleep with the boss to get ahead?" His face blushed purple, and he looked like he wanted to strangle Winnie on the spot. "If that's the way it works now, I never got that memo. It would have been nice to know, although the whole office has figured it out."

"She's had training in production," he said in a choked voice, lying about it shamelessly. "And if you had gotten the memo, Winnie, what would you have done about it?" He challenged her. He had never liked her and it showed.

"Actually, nothing. I don't give blow jobs under the boss's desk. But if that's the way it is now, I wouldn't have bothered to stick around for ten years or wait for a promotion you weren't going to give me. I just got screwed royally."

"Maybe if you were a little more 'cooperative,'" he said, with emphasis on the last word and a wicked look in his eye, "if you get my drift, maybe you would have gotten promoted before she did. She's a hell of a bright girl, and she knows what she has to do to get ahead." Winnie couldn't believe he'd said that to her, and made it quite so clear.

"What happens when your wife finds out?"

"I don't know what you're talking about. But in today's world, some women know what they have to do to get promoted and some don't." She had made him so furious because she had flushed him out.

"Damn, how could I have been so confused for all these years? I thought this was a printing business. I must have read the sign wrong. It turns out it's a prostitution ring." He looked like he was going to have a heart attack when she said it, and there was a vein throbbing on the side of his head. "I don't turn tricks with my boss, Hamm, even for a promotion I deserve. I don't need the job that badly. I guess she does. She's young. Someone else will offer her a bigger job for doing the same thing, and you'll look like an idiot. And by the way, I quit." With that, she pulled the door open and walked out. She went straight to her desk, put a few things she had on it in her purse, didn't bother to open or empty the drawers, got her coat, and walked out. She saw Hamm scurry into Elise's office before she left. He closed the door to talk to her with a worried look, and Winnie knew he must have been scared stiff she would file a discrimination suit, but she wasn't going to stoop to that. He was a pig, he always had been, just a bigger one than she'd thought. She felt sorry for Barb having to go back to work there, but she was going to quit and go to work for Pete anyway, after they were married.

Winnie wondered how long it would take Hamm to figure out what he'd just lost. Production would slow down to a halt without her, and no matter what her title, or his claims, Elise had no idea how to do the job. And there was no one to take over Winnie's job and make Elise look good in her new position.

Winnie couldn't remember ever being so angry in her life. She had gotten passed over for the girl he was sleeping with. It was so pathetic she couldn't believe he'd done that to her. She was going to text Barb and tell her she'd quit, but she wanted to go home first. She needed to cool off. She didn't even think about what she was going to do next when she quit. She was incredibly well organized, great at what she did, but there weren't many options for her talents in Beecher, Michigan. It was almost as if fate had forced her out of a job she shouldn't have stayed in anyway. But now what? She had no idea.

She parked her car in the driveway, and almost forgot to turn the ignition off. She was surprised when she noticed Rob's truck parked in the street. She figured he'd forgotten something and had come to pick it up, or maybe he was sick. She unlocked the door and walked in. The house was quiet, and she wondered if he was in bed asleep. She wanted to tell him all about what had happened, and ran up the stairs to check the bedroom and stopped dead in the doorway when she saw him. She almost choked when she took in the whole scene. Barb was tied to the bed by her hands with ropes, while Rob was performing oral sex on her, and one of his favorite porn movies was playing on the TV. Barb screamed when she saw Winnie, and struggled against the ropes, Rob thought she was writhing in ecstasy, doubled his energies, and Winnie was behind him so he couldn't see her and she didn't make a sound. She was too stunned to speak. Barb couldn't stop screaming, and Winnie felt as though someone had just ripped out her guts. It was the perfect follow-up to one of the worst days of her life.

"Are you two fucking kidding me? What the hell is going on here?" she said when she caught her breath. Rob's whole body went rigid when he heard her voice. He turned to look at her and groaned, as Barb burst into tears and continued to struggle against the ropes around her wrists. He untied her with shaking hands, and stood up to face Winnie, with his penis in full erection, as Barb jumped off the bed and ran past them to lock herself in the bathroom, sobbing hysterically.

"Winnie, please, this isn't what it looks like." It was the oldest lie in the world.

"I can't believe you just said that," she said, pointing at his penis. "What are you doing? Giving her CPR? Of course it's what it looks like. How long have you been sleeping with my best friend?" She was shaking from head to foot.

"It just happened a few times, I swear, it doesn't mean anything to either of us. We were just having fun. Pete's a dud in bed."

"Apparently I don't mean anything to either of

you. Get out of my house." Barb was out of the bathroom by then with her clothes on, still crying, and Winnie was trembling as she looked at them. She couldn't believe she was still standing and could talk. She was in shock. And she realized that they had probably used her house because his apartment was such a dump and Barb lived with Pete. If they'd gone to a hotel someone might have seen them and squealed. Winnie's house was so much nicer, and familiar to both of them. It had proved to be a disastrous choice.

"For God's sake, please don't tell Pete," Barb begged her. "He'll cancel the wedding. He won't understand." She was sobbing, pleading for mercy as Winnie looked at her in disbelief.

"Are you serious? You're planning to marry him anyway? After this? The two of you are really pigs," she said, looking at Rob.

"I love Pete," she cried miserably, as Rob pulled his jeans on.

"And you're doing this to him? You both make me sick. Now get out, and take your video with you. I don't ever want to lay eyes on either of you again."

Rob didn't try to stay to argue with Winnie. He knew better. She looked as though she was ready to kill someone. And Barb was so hysterical he wanted to get her out of the house before anything else happened. The scene had been bad enough. Barb had sworn to Rob that Winnie would never come home for lunch. They had done this before, several times, and pulled it off. This time they didn't. He wanted to give Winnie time to cool off.

Winnie's legs were shaking so badly after they left that she had to sit down for a minute, and then leapt to her feet at the sight of the ropes still tied to her bed. She went over and pulled them off, grabbed her sheets and blanket off the bed, and ran downstairs to put them in the washing machine. She didn't care if she ruined the blanket. She wanted to throw it all away. She was so upset she didn't know what to do. She turned on the washing machine, and a minute later she left the house and drove to her sister's, sobbing all the way. The floodgates had been opened and she couldn't stop crying as she jumped out of her car at Marje's and ran through the front door. Marje was sitting in her living room, watching one of her reality shows on TV. It was all she did every day until the kids came home from school.

"My God, what happened to you?" She got to her feet as soon as she saw Winnie, who was crying so hard she couldn't speak coherently. Marje tried to calm her down, but it was a full five minutes before Winnie could say anything.

"I've had a terrible day," Winnie said, sounding like a little kid again, and it reminded Marje of when Winnie was five and she was fifteen.

"I figured that much out. Tell me what happened," Marje said soothingly.

"I quit my job," she said, hiccupping through sobs. She told her about the promotion she didn't get and what she'd said to Hamm Winslow in his office when she quit. Marje smiled as she listened.

"Well, he won't forget you in a hurry, and the place will probably fall apart without you. I'd probably have done the same thing. What an asshole."

"Then I went home," she started to cry again. "Rob's truck was outside." Marje got a bad feeling as she said it, and suspected the story was about to get a lot worse. "I went upstairs to look for him." She described the scene in her bedroom when she walked in, and her sister winced.

"Oh, Jesus." She told her about the ropes and all of it. "What a couple of idiots. That was a rotten thing to do. I'm sorry, Winnie." She put her arms around her while Winnie cried.

"I don't think I'm even in love with him. I've been trying to figure it out. But we're still together and she's been my best friend since we were kids. I can't believe she'd do that to me." The memory of what she'd seen made her feel sick. She'd never been betrayed by a woman friend. It cut her to the quick, even more than Rob doing it.

"They're both shits," Marje said with a look of fury, and then looked more seriously at her sister. "This isn't your fault, Win, but maybe because neither of you ever made a real commitment to each other after all this time, he thought he was a free agent."

"He never wanted to get married either. It didn't feel right to me. I couldn't see myself with him for the rest of my life, but it was never bad enough to leave. I just thought we'd hang out together for a while, and then suddenly eleven years had gone by, and we never made a decision. We talked about it after Christmas. I think it's all about sex with him." Marje nodded. It sounded that way.

"I thought he was better than that."

"He isn't," Winnie said sadly. "And I've been so stupid to spend all these years with him. Now I'm too old to find someone, and I'll be alone for the rest of my life." It felt like a tragedy, and Marje smiled as she listened to her.

"Thirty-eight is not exactly the end of the road. You need some time to get over this." They walked to the kitchen together, and Marje poured a glass of water and handed it to her. Winnie's hand was shaking when she took it. She needed a job now too, but what Rob and Barb had done had over-shadowed her quitting. "Why don't you stay here tonight?" Winnie thought about it and shook her head.

"I want to go home. I put the sheets in the washing machine before I left. I never want to see either of them again." Marje nodded. "I never thought Barb would do something so low. Our friendship means nothing to her. And she still wants to marry Pete." She already had a dozen text messages from Barb by then and opened none of them.

Winnie stayed until the boys came home from school. They were surprised to see her there.

"What are you doing here, Aunt Win?" her younger nephew Adam asked her.

"Visiting your mom," she said vaguely and left a few minutes later to go back to the scene of Rob and Barb's crime and stupidity. Barb had kept sending her texts every few minutes that afternoon, begging for forgiveness, and pleading with her not to tell Pete. She'd finally read a few of them and erased the rest, unread. Rob had left her a long, rambling message about how it didn't mean anything, it was just fun and games, how sorry he was, and could he come to see her that night. She didn't answer either of them, and she took the clothes Rob had left in her closet and threw them in the garbage can outside.

She made her bed with clean sheets and an old blanket of her mother's and lay down and felt like she couldn't breathe, remembering what had gone on there hours before. She hated even being in the room. Then she noticed one of her **Beauchamp** DVDs sitting next to the TV where Rob must have put it. He had taken his porn video with him. She got up and put **Beauchamp Hall** in the DVD player, and hit Play on the remote control. It was comforting just hearing the familiar voices, like friends in the room. She didn't try to follow the story, she just stared at the TV and started crying again. It had been a clean sweep, her job, her boyfriend, and her best friend, all gone in one day. It was Barb who mattered to her most. There was no one left now in her life except her sister. She had no idea what to do next or where to start. Her whole life had come down around her. Ten years at her job, the promotion she should have gotten given to the girl who was sleeping with the boss, eleven years with Rob up in smoke, and her childhood friend's ultimate betrayal. She lay staring at the TV screen and cried herself to sleep.

Chapter Five

For the next two weeks, Winnie drifted between her house and her sister's, feeling dazed and numb. Most of the time, she was at her own house, and put one of the **Beauchamp Hall** DVDs in the machine, as a sort of background music for her fallen life. She had called the library and taken a leave from her volunteer job as "The Story Lady" and told them she was sick. She didn't want to do anything and couldn't face the children either, not for now anyway, until she regained her balance. She was nowhere near that yet.

She had no idea what to do next. She knew there was a position at the front desk of the hotel. She'd seen in the newspaper that an insurance broker needed a new assistant, and the local mortuary needed a hostess to greet the mourners. It was all so depressing, although working at a printing company hadn't been a dream job either. There weren't many opportunities in Beecher, and she didn't want to commute two hours each way to Detroit and back, nor move there. And she felt too old now to move to Chicago or New York to try to start over. It seemed as though her life had come to a full stop.

Rob was still sending her text messages saying he wanted to see her. He had even shown up at the house late one night. She'd had the locks changed the day after she'd found him in bed with Barb, and when he came by, Winnie didn't answer the door. She responded to nothing he sent. She was finished with him, mourning the lost years more than the man. He wasn't a loving person and hadn't treated her well, with kindness or respect. She saw that now, more clearly every day.

Barb had written her a long letter, trying to explain everything. She said that she thought Winnie didn't really care about Rob, so it didn't matter. They got together just for sex, and some fun. Winnie thought it was pathetic, and even more so because she was about to marry another man, who in fact bored her and didn't excite her in bed, but could pay the bills and drove a Porsche. Barb liked the idea of being a dentist's wife, but she was much more attracted to Rob, who only wanted to have sex with her. They were partners in porn. Winnie didn't bother to answer her. The bond between them had been severed and Winnie never wanted to see her again. She was grateful to Barb for introducing her to **Beauchamp Hall,** but that was it. After what had happened, it was clear that their nearly thirty-year friendship was over. Winnie had nothing to say to Barb and didn't respond.

Winnie kept trying to figure out what she was really feeling. In quiet moments, she realized that she wasn't heartbroken over Rob, but her trust was shattered by all of them. Her boss, her boyfriend, and her best friend had betrayed her, and she felt as though she'd hit a wall. She had enough money saved so that she wouldn't have to work for several months, and some money her mother had left her, which she had never touched. She wasn't financially desperate but she felt as though someone had pulled the plug on her life. She could barely get out of bed.

"You can't sit brooding in your house with the TV on forever," Marje told her. Erik had offered her a job as an assistant office manager at his plumbing company, but he didn't need her and was doing it as a favor, and she didn't want that either. There was a bookstore in town that didn't do a lot of business, several restaurants, some motels, a computer store, a realtor, and a smaller printing firm than Winslow's, which would have been happy to have her, and she was well trained for the job. But that didn't interest her either. None of it did.

"I feel like I'm having some kind of out-of-body experience," she tried to explain to her sister, "where I'm looking down at myself. It's like I'm swimming underwater. Everything is happening in slow motion. I think I'm drowning, and most of the time I don't even care."

"You're entitled to feel sorry for yourself," Marje said gently, "but at some point you have to come up for air." Winnie nodded, went home after that, flipped on the DVD player again, and hit the remote, without looking at the screen. She was surprised when she glanced at the TV and saw the same familiar faces, with the actors not in their costumes, and some of their accents slightly different and not quite so upper crust as on the show. She had accidentally clicked on the icon for "Extra Scenes" and "The Making of **Beauchamp Hall**."

She was about to turn it off, and go back to the episodes she knew almost by heart now, and then stopped when she saw one of the actors walking through the town where the show was shot, with the castle in the background. It was quaint, with little cottages and old-fashioned storefronts, with smiling people walking along and waving to the actor who was explaining how much he had come to love the village, his fellow actors, and the show. "This is home to me now," he said, "we've all been here for six years. We go home for a while during the hiatus between seasons, but most of us can't wait to come back. We love this place, and they love us." The camera showed the smiling villagers again, looking warmly at the actor who played one of the main heroes on the show. Winnie smiled. It gave her a warm feeling, just looking at the village and the castle that felt like home to her now too. The show had given her a rich fantasy life that kept her from getting even more depressed about her own. And as the segment ended, she sat staring at the dark screen and suddenly knew what she wanted to do. She had the time, enough money to drift for a while, and no reason to stay in Beecher right now, except to find another job that she'd probably hate. And she didn't want to run into Barb or Rob, which was so easy to do in a small town. She was afraid to see them whenever she left her house, even to buy food, so she went to the store at odd hours to avoid them.

With trembling hands, she called the airline and made a list of things she had to do, then went to the bank, and withdrew money. She didn't need too much cash, she had credit cards and no debt on them or unpaid bills. She checked her savings, and if she was careful she'd be able to coast for several months. She had never done anything crazy in her life, and she knew she was about to. But she had no husband, no children, no job now, no man, nothing to tie her down. She was as free as the wind, and as she thought about it, she could feel herself moving quickly toward the surface. She wasn't drowning anymore. She was swimming with long, clean strokes toward where she wanted to go.

She drove to the passport office in Detroit, and with her ticket booked, they promised her a passport the next day. She had to come back for it, but she was determined to get everything done.

She went to Marje's when she got back, and burst through the front door. The boys were doing home-work and Marje was getting dinner started. She looked up in surprise when she saw Winnie smil-ing at her. She looked like a different woman from the one who had left, deeply dejected, hours before.

"You look like you won the lottery." Marje smiled at her.

"I think I did. I know what I'm going to do."

"Does it involve a gun and any of the people who screwed you over?"

"Better than that. I'm going to England."

"England?" Marje looked startled. "What for?"

"To have some fun. I'm going to North Nor-folk, to a village called Burnham Market. It's a three-hour drive north of London, or two hours by train. It's supposed to be a lovely place, full of history, and I want to look around. It's where they film **Beauchamp Hall.** I have the time right now, and I'll never get to do it again. I just want to see it, and breathe the air there. There are supposed to be beautiful beaches too." Marje looked a little puzzled. Winnie looked as if she might be high on something, and Marje wondered if her sister was drunk.

"Have you been drinking?"

Winnie shook her head. "I know it sounds crazy, but I love that show. If you could meet the housewives on your Las Vegas reality show, would you do it?"

"Maybe. If they came here. I can't see myself going to hang out in Las Vegas, or stalk them," she said, worried about her sister. Winnie was euphoric.

"You have a husband and kids, I don't. I have nothing here right now." Marje stared at her. "Except you, of course," she added. "But you have a life here, I don't."

"And after you've seen it, then what?"

"I don't know. I'll figure it out. I don't need to work for a few months. I have to do it, Marje. I feel it in my gut. It's one of those things I have to get out of my system."

"It's just a TV series, you know," Marje reminded her. "Sooner or later you have to come back here to reality." But she was going nowhere for the moment, moving from her bed to the couch in her living room, living like a shut-in, and crying all the time. For the first time in two weeks, she was smiling and looked excited and alive again. Marje wondered if maybe it would do her good. "When do you want to go?"

Winnie took a breath. "Day after tomorrow. I got a good rate on a flight to London. I'm going to stay there for two days. I've never been there before, and then I'll head to Burnham Market. It looks like a really charming place. There's a house called Holkham Hall nearby, it was built in the eighteenth century, and is one of the grandest homes in England. I want to take a tour there. And Haversham Castle, where they film **Beauchamp Hall,** is even more fabulous. I want to visit them both. There's a lot of interesting history in the area, and they let the locals watch the outdoor filming of the show." She had seen it on the DVDs, and everyone looked happy to be part of it. She wanted to be there too. She'd been reading descriptions of the village and couldn't wait to see it, with quaint shops and antique stores, and a thirteenth-century church. The year-round population of the village was less than a thousand people. It was a small and very appealing place. "I know it sounds crazy, but it's what I want to do." She sounded like a kid, not a thirty-eight-year-old woman whose life had been hanging in limbo for years, and had totally fallen apart two weeks before. Marje wondered if it was what she needed to get her going again and to find someone decent to settle down with this time when she came home.

"It does sound crazy," Marje agreed with her, smiling at the unbridled joy in her sister's eyes. "You don't need my permission. If you can afford it, go. Then come back and get serious about finding a job and a new guy. Just don't stay in England, please. I'd miss you too much."

"I won't stay. I just want to see where they do the show. I dream about it at night."

Marje nodded. "Do you want to stay for dinner?"

"I have to go home and pack. Will you check on

the house for me?" Marje nodded. It had all happened so suddenly, it didn't seem real to her yet. But Winnie's life had fallen apart just as quickly, in the space of an hour, and that didn't seem real to her yet either. Now she was leaving, and starting to feel in charge again. "I'll come back and see you tomorrow after I pick up my passport. I have a lot to do before I go."

By the next day, in her usual competent way, she had everything organized. Her bags were packed, her passport in her purse, her bills were paid, and everything was put away neatly. She felt like herself again, or on the way to it. She had put her **Beauchamp** DVDs in her suitcase, although she wasn't sure why, and took a copy of **Pride and Prejudice** to read on the plane. She was taking mostly jeans and a couple of skirts and casual clothes, hiking boots, a pair of sneakers, one nice dress she was sure she'd never use, just in case, comfortable flat shoes, and a pair of high heels. She was going to wear a coat, since the weather in England was still chilly. She had everything she needed, and she felt ready to go. In her mind, she had already left when she went to Marje's for dinner that night, and afterwards said goodbye to her, Erik, and Adam and Jimmy.

"Maybe you'll bring back an English guy!" her brother-in-law teased her. "And don't forget you have a job with me if you want it when you come home." Working as an assistant office manager at a plumbing company wasn't her dream job, but she was grateful for the kindness of his sympathy offer and thanked him.

"Take care of yourself, don't do anything stupid or crazy," Marje told her as they hugged for a last time. She felt as though she were sending a child off to school, but Winnie would always be her baby sister, no matter how old she was.

"I promise, I'll text you. We can FaceTime or Skype."

"Let me know if you see any big stars on the set," Marje said, smiling at her. "Take care of yourself, Win. I love you." Winnie nodded, with tears in her eyes, and then made a dash for her car, sitting in their driveway. She knew that if she stayed a minute longer, she'd be sobbing in her sister's arms, and she didn't want anything to stop her from going. Marje was still waving with the brightly lit house behind her, as Winnie drove away. She was back at her own house five minutes later, and saw on her message machine at home that Rob had called again, since she'd blocked him on her cellphone. She erased his message without listening to it, looked around her house, and went upstairs to bed. She had to get up at 5:00 A.M.

Winnie woke up before the alarm went off. It was still dark outside, and there were light snow flurries in the air, although it was May. They often had late

snows at that time of year. She had left her bags in
the front hall the night before. She had one suitcase, a rolling bag, and a backpack. She was too excited to have breakfast, and called for a taxi to take
her to the bus depot, to go to Detroit. She was due
to arrive in Detroit at eight-thirty, and would then
take another bus to the airport. She had a short hop
to Chicago, a brief layover at O'Hare, and then a
direct flight to London leaving at 2:00 P.M. That
would take eight hours and land her in London at
3:00 A.M. local time. She had booked two nights
at a hotel in London she'd found on the Internet,
the Westminster Hotel. She was going to spend
two days exploring the London sights she had read
about for years and never seen. The Tower of London, Buckingham Palace for the Changing of the
Guard, the Victoria and Albert Museum, the Tate
galleries, Hyde Park, Madame Tussauds wax museum. She wanted to at least have a drink at Rules,
the oldest restaurant in London. She had seen it
on the show. She wanted to visit everything, and
drink it all in, although she hadn't given herself
much time. She was eager to get to Burnham Market, and she could always come back to London if
she wanted to, or cover more of the tourist sights on
her way home. She had an open ticket for the trip
back since she didn't want to limit her stay in England. She wanted to be there for as long as she was
happy, or until her money ran out, but that wasn't
likely to happen for quite a while. She didn't travel

extravagantly, and she had the luxury of time, to go where she pleased and do whatever she wished.

Marje texted her while she was on the runway, as she was about to turn off her phone before they took off on the flight to London. "Have a ball, little sis. Make every minute count. I love you, Marje." There were tears in Winnie's eyes when she read it, and she shot back, "I love you too. Be back soon. All my love, Win." And then she had to turn off her phone. It felt crazy to think that she was thirty-eight years old and had never done anything like this before. The years had sped by her, and suddenly she felt young and free again. She was almost glad that Rob had caused their relationship to end. She would never have had the guts to do it otherwise and their relationship would have dragged on for years. Instead he had shot her out of a cannon with Barb's help, into the chance to follow her dreams. It wasn't all bad after all, although it had been a shocking way to get where she wanted to be. But all of that was behind her now. And there were good times ahead, she told herself, as the plane took off.

She slept on the flight and woke up when they announced that they were about to land at Heathrow. There was a light mist when they touched the ground. And she went through customs and immigration easily, managed her own bags, and treated herself to a taxi to her hotel. She texted Marje from the taxi to say she had arrived safely.

They arrived at 4:00 A.M., as she had warned the

hotel she would. She had a small plain room over-looking a narrow ugly street in a seemingly safe commercial district, with a lot of shops and res-taurants around. It was in the Bayswater section of London, and the price was right. It wouldn't strain her budget to stay there, and she would be out of her room most of the time anyway. She fell into bed shortly after she got there, and woke up at nine-thirty local time with sunlight streaming through the window. And an hour later, she was outside, with a map she'd gotten at the hotel in her hand, and started on her blitz tour of London. She took double-decker buses, and the Underground, which got her very efficiently to everywhere she wanted to go.

She started at the Tower of London, visiting the dungeons, and saw an amazing exhibit of the queen's jewels. From there she went to Westminster Abbey to see where kings and queens had been crowned for centuries, and stood at the gates of Buckingham Palace, fascinated by the idea that the Queen of En-gland was somewhere inside. She walked around the Tate Modern for several hours, took a walk in Hyde Park, and got to Rules for a drink as she'd promised herself. And by the time she got back to her hotel, she was exhausted but thrilled by every-thing she'd seen, and happy she had managed to do so much, moving quickly from place to place. She'd bought some fish and chips on the way back to the hotel, and ate it in her room. Afterwards, she took a bath, went to bed, and passed out almost the minute her head hit the pillow.

The next morning at ten o'clock, she started all over again, and had an equally successful day. She saw Parliament and Trafalgar Square, went to the British Museum, and rode on more double-decker buses. By that night, she had covered all the high points on her list. And she loved watching the people bustling everywhere. She had gone to New York a few times when she was in college, and the electricity and energy of London seemed similar to her, but with a lot more history at hand. People were busy, rushing, and she was mesmerized by all of it. She felt alive just being there. But she was looking forward to the peaceful atmosphere of the country village she was going to, the quaint surroundings, the elegance of the castle, and the excitement of the show. She could hardly wait.

She was up at six o'clock on her third morning in London. She got a cab to King's Cross Station at seven, and had breakfast. It didn't bother her at all to be traveling alone. The whole experience was an adventure, and she had managed London without a problem, despite noise, people rushing around her, cars on the wrong side of the road, and an unfamiliar city.

Burnham Market was going to be a great deal easier. The train left at eight-thirty, and the trip would take two hours through the British countryside to the town of King's Lynn. It looked beautiful and peaceful as she watched it drift by, and once they were well out of London, she saw cows and sheep, farms, rolling hills, and the brilliant green of new grass. Her heart pounded for a minute as they entered the station. Winnie had been told that the original King's Lynn station had been closed since the 1950s and housed an antique store now and some other shops. It was used in the series, and she wanted to visit it while she was there.

For an instant, she had an odd feeling that she had been here before and she was coming home. She was smiling when she got off the train, and the stationmaster touched his hat and smiled back.

There was an elderly man in a tweed cap standing next to a battered taxi, and Winnie walked over to him with her bags. She had taken a chance on her accommodations and wanted to check out the options when she arrived. She had read on the Internet that the best hotel in town was The Hoste, a fairly fancy inn on the green, but for the sake of her budget and local charm, she wanted to stay at a simple B and B. The cab driver agreed to take her to Burnham Market, which he said was thirty minutes away. Once in the car with him, she asked him politely, as they drove past farms and the lush green countryside, "Could you suggest a good B and B where I could stay, close to the center of town?"

"So you can see them film the show?" He smiled.

He'd had lots of requests like this in the last six years, and he'd even driven many of the actors from time to time.

"Yes, I guess that's right," she admitted, looking a little sheepish. She felt like a combination groupie/tourist, and in fact she was both, although she hadn't thought of it that way before.

"I know just the place. Prudence Flannagan, you'll love it." Half an hour later, after seeing cows and pigs and horses along their route on a narrow country road, she saw the village up ahead. There were charming cottages and stone houses, with rose gardens in front and picket fences. And in the distance, but not too far away, she saw Haversham Castle in all its dignified nobility, and she recognized it immediately. "You know what that is, of course." The driver smiled at her in the rearview mirror and she smiled and nodded. "The Marquess of Haversham and his sister, Lady Beatrice, still live there. They're nice people, a little odd like all of their kind, but the show saved them. They were about to lose the castle, couldn't afford to keep it, but the show changed all that. They must be rolling in money now, for what they get paid to let it to the show. The Havershams are good to the people of the village, though. My grandfather was one of their great-grandfather's tenant farmers. He always spoke well of the family. Everything's changed, of course, since then. But the show reminds everyone of how it used to be. We like that around here, and the show gives lots of jobs to the locals. It's been good for all of us. It brings people like you here, aside from summer visitors." He smiled broadly as he stopped the car in front of a neat stone cottage that looked like something in a fairy tale, with crisp white curtains in the windows. "There's Prudence now," he said, as a small round woman stepped out into the road, and wiped her hands on her apron. She looked like the fairy godmother in Cinderella, and she smiled at the driver who had brought Winnie to her.

"Morning, Josiah. Fine weather."

"Indeed it is." He turned to indicate Winnie as she got out of the cab. "I brought you a guest from America. She's here to watch the show." Prudence Flannagan smiled at the mention of it, and looked warmly at Winnie.

"Welcome, come in and take a look around and see if it suits you." Winnie stepped into the cottage as Josiah unloaded her bags and left them standing outside, as he waited to be paid. There was a delicious smell of fresh bread in the oven, and something bubbling on the stove that looked like stew as she walked through the kitchen. There was a cozy front parlor, a small dining room, and a back garden. The ceilings were low, and the staircase old-fashioned, she noticed as she went upstairs to view the three bedrooms reserved for guests, in addition to Prudence's. All three bedrooms were small and cheery, with flowered chintzes at the windows and on the beds that Prudence had made herself. Two of the rooms shared a bath, and one had its own, and all three were vacant at the moment.

"You can have your pick," she said cheerfully, as Winnie went from room to room. "I imagine you'll want your own bath. Americans always do." Winnie nodded agreement, and was delighted with the accommodations. "You can do whatever you like, except smoke in the rooms. But you can smoke in the garden. Breakfast is included in the price of the room, and I serve dinner every night if you want it, for a small extra fee. I can give you a better rate week by week or month by month, if you decide to stay. Most people do if they can, once they get here. I'll do laundry for you if you like, at no extra charge. It's no trouble. I have to do it for the house anyway."

It was an ideal situation, and Winnie asked for the room with its own bath. She could see the town square and Haversham Castle from her window, and the price was ridiculously low. A week's rent was barely more than the price of a good dinner at home. Prudence Flannagan wasn't taking advantage of the tourists brought in by the show. She said she got plenty of business, and the house was full most of the time. All three guests had just left the day before, and she had three more arriving that week, one from Italy and two from Germany. The show was aired all over Europe, and popular in every country where it was shown.

Josiah brought Winnie's bags upstairs for her, and she tipped him handsomely for his kindness and for bringing her to Mrs. Flannagan's B and B. She felt as though she were visiting an aunt, or someone's grandmother. And it occurred to her that her mother would have loved this. It was so perfectly English, and old-fashioned and cozy. She couldn't imagine being lonely here.

She unpacked in her room, and came down a short time later, as Mrs. Flannagan took her freshly baked bread out of the oven, and there was a plate of scones with clotted cream and strawberry jam sitting on the table.

"Help yourself, dear," she said with a wink at Winnie. "You'll be doing me a favor if you do. If you don't eat them, I will." She patted her hips as she said it. Winnie put a scone on a plate with the clotted cream and jam and the first bite melted in her mouth.

"Oh, that's delicious," Winnie said, smiling.

"Thank you. If you want to watch them filming, they shoot outdoors most mornings, and at the end of the day. They do the studio shots indoors in the middle of the day and at night."

"I'd like to watch them film outside," Winnie said hopefully.

"Of course. They're very friendly and congenial about it. They don't seem to mind at all, you have to stand behind barriers they set up, but they let people get very close. You have to stay quiet, though."

"I'm addicted to the show," Winnie confessed, as she finished the scone and helped herself to another.

"We all are, the whole world is. People come from all over to see it. No one knew we were here until the show came on. You should take a tour of Haversham Castle too. There are parts they don't use for the show, and they'll take you through them. And then there are the family quarters. There are only two of them now. His Lordship the Marquess, and his sister. Their parents died quite a long time ago. The marquess inherited his title and the estate when he was barely twenty, and his sister is a year or two younger. That was more than twenty years ago now." Listening to her was like watching the show, and Winnie loved it. "They haven't changed much in the castle. They couldn't afford to. They have titles and a beautiful castle, but had no money to maintain it. The show changed all that, and now the producers don't want them to modernize anything. It works for the show as it is."

She seemed to know all about it, and Winnie set out on foot a few minutes later, to explore the village. She walked around the village green, soaking up the sunshine, and walked into the little shops. There were several pubs that she didn't venture into, and the restaurants in town were supposed to be excellent. She was on her way back to the cottage several hours later, when she saw cameras on rolling platforms appear, barriers set up, a cluster of people in period costumes, makeup artists and hairdressers and a flock of assistants, and she realized they were going to start filming. She stood under a tree, behind the barrier, and watched them for two hours. This was what she had come for, and as they put tape on the ground to mark where the actors would stand, she saw the two stars walking toward her, talking seriously, and then repeating it again and again. The actress was wearing a beautiful hat and an embroidered Chinese coat of the period, and the actor looked dashing. Winnie's heart pounded as she watched them, and there was silence all around. Then the whole group walked back to the castle after the scene was shot, and the two stars were talking and laughing and looked like they were teasing each other. She swatted him with her elegant hat, and they waved at their fans as they walked by, while the locals cheered them. They were gone in a minute and Winnie looked awestruck as she walked into Mrs. Flannagan's kitchen.

"I just saw them shoot a scene!" she said, still amazed by it, and Mrs. Flannagan laughed. They did it almost every day, and the townspeople were used to it.

"Welcome to **Beauchamp Hall,** my dear," she said warmly, and Winnie ran up the stairs to her room, feeling as though she had died and gone to Heaven. This was just what she had wanted when she decided to come, and what she had dreamed of. It was perfect.

Chapter Six

Winnie watched another scene being shot early the next morning when she went for a walk before breakfast. The actors were different this time, some of the younger stars, and the father on the show was with them. She recognized them all and stood rapt until they finished shooting. She couldn't imagine getting tired of it or becoming blasé about it. It was magical watching them.

After breakfast, she walked up to the castle, and waited for a tour of the parts they showed visitors. The history of the place was fascinating. Its heyday of opulence and luxury had been in the nineteenth and earlier part of the twentieth century. The family had had serious reverses after the Crash of 1929. Changing times had continued to diminish their fortune after the Second World War, and by the 1960s they were in serious trouble, but had managed to hang on to the castle and estate by selling works of art, valuable objects like Fabergé boxes, or the occasional investment that did well. The days of armies of servants like on the show, grandeur, and unlimited funds had ended some ninety years before. And parts of the castle showed it and were in need of repair. The days of the castle's occupation by the Haversham family went almost all the way back to the Norman Conquest, and many of the crowned heads of Europe had stayed there. Queen Victoria and Prince Albert had visited the family frequently, so had King George VI, and Queen Elizabeth II was the godmother of Lady Beatrice, the current marquess's sister. There was no question of their noble birth or importance in the British aristocracy, and some of the rooms of the castle and their contents were magnificent. The tour guide explained that the parts of the castle being used to film the show were the most beautiful, and were not on the tour at the moment as they were in use for filming on a daily basis. Learning about it was fascinating and Winnie bought a book about the family and the castle on the way out.

She asked the guide if one could watch filming inside the castle and was told with a smile that you had to know someone in the cast or the producers to do that, but she said that the actors were frequently seen around the village, and the outdoor shots were easy to see happening, and all observers were welcome.

After the tour, Winnie looked around for a place to have a cup of tea and noticed a bright yellow food truck parked in a corner of the main square. She wandered over to it. A man about her own age was handing out tea and coffee, and selling sandwiches and pastries to visitors and locals. He smiled at her, and she asked for a cup of Earl Grey tea, and he handed it to her. As soon as she paid him and thanked him and he heard her speak, his smile grew wider.

"American?" She nodded. "Came to see the show being filmed?" She nodded again. "You know, they hire extras right off the street. We've all been in it at some point. You should get on the list, it's fun, and you probably don't need a work permit for a day of occasional labor. You don't have to do anything, just stand there looking like a villager in whatever costume they put you in. They pay you something for it, not much, but I do it for the amusement and to see the actors. You might enjoy it."

"I'm sure I would." She looked interested by what he was saying. "Where do I sign up?"

"Just watch where they're shooting at the end of the day. They often walk around asking for extras. They sign them up for the next day. One of the assistants will have the list, you'll see it."

"Thank you, I'll watch for it." She smiled at him.

"My name is Rupert, by the way." He reached out of his food truck and shook her hand.

"Winnie," she supplied, still smiling.

"Where are you from?" He was curious about her, and he thought she was a pretty woman.

"A small town, north of Detroit, Michigan. It's very cold there."

He grinned. "It's not tropical here either. How long are you staying?"

"I haven't decided. I'm free for a while." He nodded and then got busy with other customers, so she walked down one of the narrow streets she hadn't explored yet, and the truck was gone when she got back.

She didn't see anyone making lists of extras for the next two days, and then on the third day she saw a young man doing exactly what Rupert had described, asking for volunteers as extras and jotting down names as people put up their hands. Winnie approached and put up her hand so the assistant would see it.

"Name?" he asked her quickly.

"Winona Farmington."

"Great, thanks." And when he had as many as he needed, he told them to come to the main entrance of the castle at seven the next morning, and they'd be given costumes. He warned them all not to wear jewelry or modern watches, and he told them that they would receive a small token amount, paid in cash.

Winnie could hardly wait as she went back to

the cottage, and told Mrs. Flannagan as soon as she walked in.

"Good for you!" she congratulated her. "Maybe they'll discover you and you'll become famous like Marilyn Monroe." Winnie laughed at the comparison.

"I don't think so, but it sounds like fun."

"It is," she admitted. "I've done it myself. It takes a lot of time, though, they keep you standing around for hours while they shoot the scenes again and again. I'm too busy here to do it more than every now and then. I was an extra in Lady Charlotte's wedding scene as the carriage drove her and Lord Hamish away." Winnie had watched the wedding repeatedly and knew the scene she meant. "But you have the time, you'll enjoy it," Prudence added.

The German guests had arrived that morning, they were a young couple and avid fans of the show, as was a young Italian man, who said he was writing an article about it. The other guests were quiet and kept to themselves, and spent as much time exploring the town as she did, so she didn't see them often. The B and B was very well run, and immaculately clean. All the guests loved it.

The next morning, Winnie walked up to the main entrance of the castle, wearing no watch or jewelry, and lined up with about sixty or seventy people. They were going to be a crowd at a church fair, and Winnie loved the coat, hat, dress, and shoes they had for her. A makeup artist gave her a cursory once-over with blush and powder, and two hours later they were taken by bus to the local church where tents were set up, pens with live animals in them, and food stalls, and the crowd was to wander around enjoying themselves as the actors played out the scene in the foreground. Winnie saw three of her favorite actors appear and one of them smiled at her. She felt like a schoolgirl after he did, and she chatted with the other extras between scenes. They were all locals, except for her, and they were impressed that she had come from so far away. She had a great time with all of them. They were given lunch from a giant food truck, and sent home with a little cash for each at the end of the day. The pay was very little, but she didn't care.

"Did you have fun?" Mrs. Flannagan asked her when she got back, she could see that she had, Winnie's eyes were dancing. She had sent Marje a text that she'd been an extra on the show that day. And her sister had teased her that she would become famous.

"I had a ball," Winnie said and went up to her room, smiling. It was the most fun she'd had in years. She went for a walk that night after dinner, and saw two of the major actors taking a stroll and talking earnestly. She would have loved to say hello to them, but didn't dare.

And the next day, at the pharmacy, she saw a

beautiful woman with long blond hair speaking to the pharmacist. Winnie recognized her from a photograph in the book she'd bought. It was Lady Beatrice Haversham, the sister of the marquess who owned the castle. The book had explained the rights of primogeniture, which dictated that the current marquess had inherited everything, the castle and the entire estate, along with his title. But being a modern man, he had given the dower house and a portion of the estate, with some of the old tenant farms, to his sister, so she would have a home there forever, and was a part owner of the estate. In earlier times, she would have inherited nothing. Lady Beatrice turned and smiled at Winnie warmly, as though she knew her.

"Sorry to be taking so long," she apologized. "My brother always sends me with a ridiculous list, for vitamins, plasters, headache medicine, he's hopeless!" Winnie smiled at the British pronunciation of "vitamins," and had learned that "plasters" were bandages for small cuts.

"It's fine, I'm not in a hurry," she assured her, and then she couldn't help saying something about the book she was finding fascinating. "I'm really enjoying the book about your home and family," Winnie said cautiously, not sure how she'd take it, and the beautiful aristocrat smiled broadly at her, since she'd written the book.

"How nice of you. That sort of thing is so embarrassing, and of course there are all sorts of idiotic stories in it that make one's relatives look ridiculous, but it helps sell the book, and one has to do something to make money," she said with a smile. "Are you here to watch the series being filmed?"

Winnie nodded. "I am. I love the show, it was sort of a dream to come here. I just decided to do it." There was something so genuine about the way she said it that it touched Lady Beatrice.

"Well, thank God for people like you, you keep a roof over our heads. I do love the show myself. I sit and watch it for hours, and my brother tells me how stupid I am. But the writer is brilliant and quite creative, and it's not all based on us. In fact, most of it isn't. He just used the house and a bit of our family history for inspiration. The **Beauchamp Hall** family are far more interesting than we are. Our parents were quite dull actually, and I don't think my grandfather spoke more than once or twice in his lifetime. Although my grandmother was a bit naughty, quite a few indiscretions, I'm afraid, but she was very beautiful and my grandfather was very boring. And all my brother ever does is play with his cars, he's more or less a mechanic. It's his only activity, other than shooting, riding, and playing with his dogs. And I have no talents whatsoever." She was modest and funny, and Winnie thought she was utterly enchanting. There was nothing pretentious about her, and she had no trouble laughing at herself.

"I have no talents either," Winnie said simply.

"I wish I could write something like **Beauchamp Hall.**"

"So do I!" Lady Beatrice said enthusiastically. "Think of the pots of money we'd make." The two women were laughing like old friends when the pharmacist handed Lady Beatrice an enormous bag across the counter. "See what I mean?" She turned to Winnie. "All for my brother. He's a dreadful hypochondriac. He needs to marry a nurse really. Or a doctor." She smiled at Winnie again as she walked past her. "Enjoy your stay here. And thank you for buying the book! We need it to fix the roof, it leaks dreadfully!" She waved and then hurried out of the shop, and Winnie turned to the pharmacist, a bit stunned by the encounter.

"What a nice person," she commented and the pharmacist agreed with her.

"She's a good woman. Her brother is very pleasant too, very handsome, but a bit eccentric, I think. Neither of them has ever been married," she volunteered, then took care of what Winnie requested and handed it to her. When she left the pharmacy, she saw Lady Beatrice being driven away by a good-looking man with dark hair in an old Jaguar. He took off at full speed. They were both about Winnie's age. And they were laughing as he drove back toward the castle.

Winnie spent the rest of the day exploring the village again. She had a nice lunch on her own in a little tea room, and went back to the cottage late in the day. Mrs. Flannagan said she'd had a message from the casting department of the show. They needed extras again and wanted to know if she was available. She called the number back, and told them she'd love to do it. She had to be at the set this time at 6:00 A.M., for a hospital scene. She was going to be one of the nurses rushing up and down a hallway. It sounded like fun to Winnie.

By six-thirty the next morning, she was wearing a nurse's uniform of the period, her hair was crimped in neat waves beneath her cap, and tied up in a little bun. She was fascinated to notice a prim little man watching every scene. Someone explained to her that he was their "manners coach," the person who corrected them about how women sat and walked and spoke at the time, and on what men could and couldn't do. He gave the look of the show accurate historical authenticity, in terms of the mores of the era, along with a historical consultant. The two men conferred constantly, and advised the cast.

In the scene Winnie was in, she brought a lunch tray in for one of the main actors, and when she set it down in front of him for the fourth time, and murmured, "Your lunch, Your Lordship," he whispered to her.

"Can I have you for lunch?" he asked sotto voce with a look of innocence, his lips barely moving. She burst out laughing, and they had to shoot the scene again. Afterwards he apologized to her.

"Sorry, I couldn't resist. You look gorgeous in that uniform."

"Thank you," she said and could feel herself blushing. He didn't pursue it any further, but it was a nice compliment, and the next day she saw Rupert and his food truck in the square and went over to talk to him.

"Thank you for telling me about signing up as an extra, I've done it twice since I saw you. It's so much fun." He laughed and handed her the tea she had ordered.

"We've all done it. So how are you settling in?" He acted as though she'd moved there, and she almost felt that way too. She had no desire to leave anytime soon. Everyone had been so welcoming. She had Skyped with Marje several times and told her all about it. She'd told her that now she had to watch the show so she could see her baby sister on TV in the church fair scene and in a nurse's uniform at the hospital. "You ought to apply for a job on the set," Rupert suggested.

"I don't think I can work here," Winnie said, looking pensive. "I'm sure I'd need a work visa."

"They can get you one if they want to. If you're going to stay here long enough, it might be good to work there, unless you're a lady of leisure," he said hesitantly. Winnie smiled at him.

"I'm definitely not that. I'm between jobs at the moment. But I wasn't planning to work for a while."

"They might not have anything. You could put yourself on a list and if something comes up, they'll call you." He was very helpful once again, and the idea appealed to her enormously. She thought about it for a few days. She'd been in Burnham Market for a week by then, and it was starting to feel like home. The Italian and German guests had left the cottage, and been replaced by two French couples who were traveling together. The town had definitely become a destination for people who loved the show, and wanted to see where it was made and get a closer look at the cast. She had caught another look at Lady Beatrice too, but didn't speak to her this time. She was driving down the high street in a banged-up old Fiat 500.

After Winnie had been there for two weeks, she screwed up her courage and walked up to the castle, asked for the HR office on the set, gave them her details and how to contact her, and handed them her CV. They explained that with no experience working on the set of a TV show, and no work permit, only the most menial jobs would be open to her. They could hire people like her for the lowest possible salary, sometimes on a part-time basis. For a better job, she'd need a work permit and the union would get involved.

"I don't mind what I do," she said easily, and meant it. For the thrill of working on the set, she would have done almost anything. She really had become a groupie, she told herself, and said as much when she wrote to Marje again. She deleted two more emails from Barb without opening them. Rob had finally stopped calling and texting her. He had obviously moved on. She felt relieved, mostly.

She got a chance to be an extra again, and a week later she was shocked when she got a call to come in and interview for a job. They didn't say what it was on the phone, and she knew it could only be a minor job, but any opportunity to hang around on the set was a thrill to her. She could watch them film the indoor scenes that way.

She wore a short navy skirt and white blouse with sandals when she went for the interview, and she saw a different HR person than she had the first time, and had to explain her job experience again. The woman hesitated, and then finally said that they needed an errand girl on the set. They'd had one and just lost her. She said the position was very poorly paid and was such a minor job that they paid for it out of their petty cash budget rather than payroll, which would have been more compli-cated. It was perfect for Winnie, because she didn't need a work permit that way. The HR woman warned her that she was not to be overly personal with the stars of the show, nor intrusive, she was not to ask anyone on the set for autographs and she was basically expected to do whatever they asked her for, within reason, as long as it wasn't illegal or dangerous. She was there to make everyone's life easier and spare them from doing menial tasks themselves. She was what was commonly called a gofer in the States. It was a job she would have been offended by at home, and was delighted to have on the set of **Beauchamp Hall.** She was told which production assistant to report to and that her work hours would be decided on, as well as what days they needed her. The woman warned Winnie that the hours could be long if they had night shoots, or a shooting day went to overtime. Winnie had nothing else to do and she couldn't wait to start.

She wandered around the various sets they used after the meeting, some of them were replicas of rooms in the house, and she finally found the assistant she was looking for in the library, setting up a shot and piling books on the floor. She looked up when Winnie walked in, and Winnie thought her new boss looked about fourteen years old.

"Hi, I'm Winnie Farmington, I'm your new gofer," she said without ceremony, and the young red-haired girl looked surprised. She had a face full of freckles and her hair was in braids, which made her look even younger. She was wearing overalls and clogs.

"Aren't you kind of old to be a gofer?" the girl said bluntly. Her name was Zoe. Winnie smiled at what she'd said.

"I probably am, but I'm here for a while and I wanted a job, and this is about all I can do here, so here I am."

"What are you in real life?"

"I worked at a printing company in the U.S. for ten years. Not very exciting, but I'm very good at being organized and getting things done." It seemed like a small skill to show for ten years of work and was hard to explain.

"How are you with putting books all over the floor so it looks like someone had a fit and threw them? Our set dresser is sick today, so I got stuck with it," Zoe asked hopefully, wanting to reassign the task.

"No problem." Winnie started pulling books off shelves and placing them in haphazard piles. It took her five minutes to do it, and Zoe had her get everyone's lunch orders, and then bring them back from the commissary truck. There were dozens of assistants of varying kinds, as well as hairdressers, makeup artists, stylists, costumers, seamstresses, four people just to deal with the hats, five who worked on the wigs for the entire cast. And all kinds of technical people, for sound and light, mixers for the music. It was interesting to learn what everyone did. Bringing back lunch on a rolling cart was a good way to see all their faces, and write down their names, although she knew she'd never remember them all. In the end, she had brought lunch back for forty people, and only a few stuck out. The stars were served lunch in their trailers, or they could go to the commissary truck. The people she'd gotten lunch for preferred to eat on the set, and a particu-larly tall young man thanked her, and asked if he could have a second sandwich, so she went back and got him another one. He was a sound technician, and his name was Nigel. He thanked her when she handed him the second sandwich and she saw him staring at her as she walked away.

The day flew by doing small assignments for everyone whenever she was asked. She got to watch a scene being shot, but most of the time she was too busy, looking for some object that was lost, or tracking down another one, or satisfying someone's whim for candy, or a sweater, or a pair of socks, or softer towels, better tissue, their favorite mineral water, or the kind of toilet paper they liked. She was a combination requisition officer/magician, and she managed to find everything they asked for, and even walked the dog of one of the stars. It was a Jack Russell that tried to bite her the minute she was out of her mistress's sight. But Winnie didn't mention it when she brought her back. Zoe let her leave at seven-thirty when all the actors were off the set, and Winnie was surprised by how tired she was when she walked back to the cottage. She'd been on her feet, and running, for eleven hours. The day had been kind of a treasure hunt, without a map.

"How was your day?" Mrs. Flannagan asked her when she walked in.

"Fun. I don't think I sat down all day. They all want special stuff, and expect me to find it, or invent it out of thin air. But actually, it's kind of challenging in a menial way." She'd also had to find an unusual kind of hypoallergenic lip balm, and a special kind of surgical glue for one of the makeup artists, who was pulling up one of the older actresses' face with elastics under her wig. She had learned some of the tricks of the trade, just watching what they did all day. There was a lot of artifice involved. This was show biz!

Winnie sat down in the kitchen, and was almost too tired to eat Mrs. Flannagan's shepherd's pie, but she made the effort to please her. And then she went to bed right after dinner, and woke up with a start at 6:00 A.M. She had to be back on the set at seven, and this time she put a little kit together, with needles, thread, safety pins, two kinds of tape, super glue, several colored rubber bands. They were the things everyone seemed to ask for most. She even took a spot remover from her own travel kit. And this time she wore jeans and running shoes, which seemed more appropriate to the job, and a T-shirt and sweater. It was a sunny day, but there was still a chill in the air.

She dealt with most of the same people and a few new faces and the same sound technician asked her for two sandwiches again, and he smiled broadly when he saw her.

"We haven't run you off yet?"

"No, I'm enjoying it," she said honestly, as she

sank down on a stool to rest for two minutes before they asked her for something else. They just looked at her and thought of things they needed or had to have.

"How'd you end up here?" Nigel was curious about her. "You're from the States, right?"

She nodded. "Michigan. Beecher, Michigan, home of record-breaking tornadoes, and not much else."

"I'm from Leighton Buzzard," he supplied, although she had no idea where it was. "It's near London.

"You didn't answer my question," he prodded her. "Why here?"

"Because I love the show. I quit my job and I had nothing else to do, so I thought I'd check it out. And now I have a job. It's worked out pretty well, so far."

"Lucky for us," he said with a smile and went back to work. He was doing a sound check of the mikes before the next scene. A minute later, Zoe called her away, and asked her to walk the Jack Russell again. It was the only part of the job she didn't like. She was a nasty little thing and she barked the minute she saw Winnie coming, and snarled when Winnie reached down to pet her.

The time flew by and each day was different. Everyone seemed to like her. Some more than others. Nigel was constantly finding excuses to talk to her.

They all had the weekend off, and as she was getting ready to leave, he wandered over. "Can I interest you in dinner tonight or tomorrow?" He looked nervous as he asked her. He was sure she'd turn him down. She was a pretty woman, and he figured she probably had a dozen men pounding on her door, or maybe one she already lived with. He had noticed that she didn't wear a wedding band, which he took as a hopeful sign. Winnie hesitated when he asked her. She hadn't thought about dating anyone so soon after Rob. But Nigel didn't seem like a serious threat, and she thought they could just be pals.

"Sure," she responded, and thanked him. "How about tonight?" She was thinking about renting a car and exploring the countryside on Saturday.

"Sounds great. Where do you live? I'll pick you up." She told him, and he said he knew where it was, and said he would fetch her in his chariot at eight o'clock, which was only an hour away. She barely had time to change. But she put on a skirt instead of jeans, and nicer shoes with little heels.

Nigel arrived promptly in a battered Jeep, and she hopped in next to him. He took her to a Vietnamese restaurant he had discovered, where he said the food was very good.

"All right. So tell me everything. Husbands, kids, why you came here, brothers, sisters," he asked her at dinner.

She smiled at the question. "That's easy, no husbands, no kids, no brothers, one sister. I quit a job and broke up with my boyfriend of eleven years, all on the same day, and now here I am." She made it sound easy, but it wasn't. She didn't mention Barb. It still hurt too much. And she still missed Rob at times. He was familiar, but she didn't want to think about him after what he'd done.

"That is simple. I've got four siblings, no wife, no girlfriend, and a black Lab named Jocko my brother takes care of when I'm away. I'm the only one in my family not married, so they think I'm weird. And I'm not gay."

"Then why aren't you married?" she asked him.

"I'm a nomad, always working on a show or a movie. No time for girls." He grinned. "And it's a temporary life. Working on shows is like being in the merchant marine. I'm always shipping out somewhere. And I always seem to get shows that go on location a lot. This one's pretty tame. But you never know how long it will last."

"Six years sounds pretty good to me," she said, after they ordered dinner.

"They can cancel a show anytime. The show gets stale, or they want to leave on a high note. Or three of the stars want to leave and it falls apart. You never know what's going to happen." She had never thought of that, and hoped that **Beauchamp** never fell apart. She'd be crushed. "You move around a lot in this business."

"Sounds good to me," she said, thinking about it. She liked Nigel. He seemed like a nice guy. He was easy to talk to and wasn't full of himself. "I've been sitting at the same desk for ten years. That gets pretty old."

"Is that why you quit? So you could come here?"

"No, I got passed over for a promotion I should have gotten, and I got pissed."

"And the boyfriend?" He wanted to know all about her. There was something about her that he liked. She had spirit, but just enough. She didn't seem like one of those pushy women who wanted to compete with a man all the time, or that was the impression she gave him. There was a gentleness to her, but she had her own ideas. She hesitated before she answered his question, and then decided to be honest. It was simpler.

"I walked in on him having sex with my best friend. In my bed."

"Ah, a true gentleman. Classic. So you came here?" She nodded.

"It was a spur-of-the-moment decision, and a dream come true. I always wanted to get out of my hometown. And I did, for college, but then my mother got sick, so I went back. I nursed her for seven years, and after she died, it seemed too late to leave, so I stayed."

"And you're thirty-two? . . . four . . . five?"

"Thank you! Thirty-eight." She smiled.

"I beat you. I'm thirty-nine. I had one of those

walk-in-on-them experiences too, about ten years ago. Also with my best friend. I think it's a pretty standard gig. I was very upset. They got married, and have a house full of kids now. I never forgave them for it, though." A pained and still-angry look flitted across his eyes, and then disappeared.

"I don't think I will forgive them either. It's an unforgettable experience. She was tied to my bed."

"Exotic." She didn't tell him about the porn.

Their dinner came then and it was delicious. The conversation was easy and light, and he drove her back to Mrs. Flannagan's afterwards. They talked about a lot of the movies he had worked on, there were some big ones, with big-name stars.

"I had a really lovely time, Nigel, thank you," she said as she got out.

"What are you doing tomorrow? We may not get another day off for a long time." She told him about her plan to rent a car, and explore the surrounding area. "Why don't you let me drive you? I've been here for four years and know it pretty well." He looked hopeful and she liked the idea.

"That would be great."

"I'll pick you up at ten. Bring a bathing suit. There are some nice beaches around here." She had thrown a bathing suit into her suitcase at the last minute, in case she stayed at a hotel with a pool. She nodded, and waved as she went inside and walked upstairs to her room, thinking about him. She hadn't thought she wanted to date yet, and didn't think it would come up while she was here. But she had enjoyed the evening with Nigel. And he seemed like just what she needed right now. A friendly, pleasant person with no strings attached, no agenda, and no complications. He seemed like an easygoing guy.

Chapter Seven

Nigel and Winnie spent Saturday cruising around in his Jeep. They drove to a monastery he knew, which was a spectacular building he wanted to show her, and from there they went to a beach, and went swimming. They lay on the sand afterwards talking, watching children wade into the water and picnic with their parents. They had lunch at a nearby inn, and ate sausages called "bangers," then drove around some more. They talked a lot about their childhoods, their families, and their dreams. She loved his openness and kindness and how different he was from Rob.

Nigel wanted to have his own sound business one day, and Winnie said how much she had wanted to move to New York, before her mother got sick. He had her back to Burnham by 6:00 P.M. Her reason for leaving him early wasn't glamorous but honest, she had laundry to do that night. She was too busy to do it when she was working, and she didn't want to take advantage of Mrs. Flannagan, although she was a good sport about it, and was always offering to help.

They were both in good spirits and had enjoyed each other's company and the relaxing day, and they both reluctantly turned their phones back on, as they approached the cottage. They had agreed to turn them off all day, so no one could intrude on them. As soon as Nigel turned his on, he had a slew of messages, texts, and voice mails. He listened to a few of them, and looked at Winnie in shocked dismay.

"Something wrong?" she asked, and he nodded.

"Very much so. It's Tom White." He turned to her with a stricken look and tears in his eyes. "He went riding today with some of the cast." Winnie knew he was an avid rider from what she'd read about him. He even rode in a fancy hunt regularly. "He had an accident, and was killed an hour ago. He broke his neck." Nigel said he knew Tom had a daughter in London. She had visited him on the set. Tom White was one of the more important members of the cast, with a dedicated following. But aside from that, he was a nice human being, and only forty-six years old. Winnie stared at Nigel for a moment, trying to absorb what he'd just said. They'd been driving around having a good time all day, and Tom White was dead. "I'll call the producer after I drop you off. This is going to throw them into a tizzy," Nigel said, looking distracted and anxious.

"What'll they do about the show?" Winnie asked him. It seemed unimportant in the scheme of life, but would matter to the producer.

"They have to write him out, but there's no way to prepare the viewers in a case like this. There will be a reaction from his fans to whatever scenario they come up with, and the ratings will suffer." But his daughter would suffer more. They were both somber when they left each other, and Mrs. Flannagan had just learned of it too. She'd heard it on the radio. And someone had told her that reporters were already gathering at the hospital and the castle to interview members of the cast and production team, and photograph grieving people who knew him.

"That's really so sad," Mrs. Flannagan commented to Winnie before she went upstairs. He was one of the actors she liked best on the show. He was also one of the most likable members of the fictional Beauchamp family.

The atmosphere was funereal on the set the next day. An announcement was made to the entire crew, management, and all the stars. Matthew Stevens, the originator and writer of the show, went into seclusion, to try to write Tom out and find a solution for the storyline. It wasn't easy and there were other scenes they'd have to reshoot without him.

Tom's body was being sent to his family in Hertfordshire, and there was to be a memorial service for the cast and crew organized by Michael Waterman, the executive producer, in two days. Tom's death was bound to sink everyone's spirits for a while. He had been on the show since the beginning and it was a huge loss, personally and for the show. He was a lovely person and added a strong element to the show.

By the end of the day, Matthew was still struggling to make the changes he had to, when the executive producer walked into the office he used in the castle, and sat down heavily across from him.

"Not good news," Michael said as Matthew dreaded what would come next. "Miranda Charles wants to leave the show. Apparently, she's been waiting to tell us, and she thought she should do it now, with Tom gone, while you're working on new storylines." He rolled his eyes as he said it. Her timing was atrocious. It was always all about her. "She's had an offer to do a play." It was what they both hated about their jobs, the unpredictability of actors. They'd had losses before, but never as big as this, and not two at a time. It could kill the show. The viewers needed to be weaned gently from characters they loved, not brutally like this. Both men knew the ratings would drop as a result. It couldn't be helped about Tom White, but Miranda was pure self-indulgence. She was a total narcissist.

"Oh shit," Matthew said grimly. "Should we let

her go or fight her on it?" They could hold her to her contract, but she'd punish them for it.

"I hate hostages," Michael Waterman said. "They make one's life miserable every way they can. Do you think the show would survive our losing both of them at once?" He looked seriously worried.

"I'll do my best with the writing. But it's hard to predict how attached the viewers are to them." It was going to affect every script for a long time. Matthew took his computer home with him that night, and worked intensely for several days, considering the options for new plot lines, and new characters to complete the cast without Tom, and now Miranda. Everyone else went to the memorial service and Matthew slipped in at the last minute. The press was there en masse. Winnie saw Lady Beatrice and her brother, but Winnie was too far away in a rear pew for the owner of the castle to notice her. It was particularly moving with Tom's daughter there, sobbing in his ex-wife's arms. It brought things into sharp focus for everyone how short life was, and how everything could change in the blink of an eye.

The set was very quiet after that, and all the actors and crew subdued.

They let Miranda out of her contract, after some heavy pressure from her agent, and intense negotiation. Someone leaked it to the press who predicted that without two of its strongest actors and biggest stars, the show would flounder in six months and not survive. But nothing they had said had convinced Miranda to stay, and she didn't want to work without Tom. She was desperate to do the play, which everyone thought was poor judgment on her part, and a bad career move.

Michael and Matthew had tried to tell her that, historically, actors who had big roles in successful series and left to do other projects, seeking greater stardom, had never done as well, and often faded from sight. The show had taken Miranda to another level of fame in the past two years, and she refused to believe that she might vanish without a trace without it, and insisted they were wrong.

It took Matthew two weeks to come up with some storylines and scripts that were plausible, exciting, worked to replace them both, and created new characters to fill the void. Miranda was leaving the show in July, which wasn't far away.

"I told you everything can change overnight," Nigel reminded Winnie when they had dinner again. They'd had no time together since Tom's death. Too much was going on.

"Do you think it will hurt the show too badly to lose both of them?" She was worried about it, she didn't want anything to damage the show irreparably or get it canceled.

"It won't help it, but Matthew is clever. It happened three years ago, if you recall. He had to kill two characters. Their contracts were up. They wanted too much money, and it turned into a standoff. The show was actually better after they left, which no one expected." It was always hard to predict how the public would react to characters leaving the show.

It had been a stressful two weeks for everyone, and Tom's death had cast a pall over the set.

A few days later when they had a Sunday off, and she was out walking around town, Winnie stumbled onto a surprise. It was a tiny cottage not far from Mrs. Flannagan's, with a FOR RENT sign out front. It looked like a dollhouse and Winnie fell in love with it on sight. She told Nigel about it the next day.

"Are you thinking of getting your own place here?" He looked pleased and surprised. He hadn't expected her to do that and stick around.

"I wasn't, but I love it here. I have nothing to go back to now, and hopefully **Beauchamp** will run for a long time. And if it doesn't, I can always sublet the cottage or try to get out of the lease. If I do stay, HR said they can try to get me a special work visa. The authorities have been very sympathetic to the show. I guess I'll do that if I rent a house here." He loved the idea, and so did she. Nothing had gone forward with them, despite the pleasant time they spent together. She was still feeling gun-shy after Rob, and Nigel sensed that and didn't want to rush her, but her wanting to rent a cottage seemed like a good sign, and if she got a work visa, better yet.

Their producers had powerful connections, and were willing to use them for the show.

"Why don't we look at the cottage together after work?" he suggested, and she agreed. She called the number on the sign and made an appointment to see it. And Nigel drove her there after work. He had to duck his head to get through the doorway, but the little jewel box of a cottage was as pretty inside as out. It had been freshly painted and was furnished with just enough furniture to live comfortably. She would only need a few things she could find in town to make it homey and really attractive. It was big enough for one person or a couple, and the rent was very modest. She could easily afford it. She was making a minimal salary now, so she had some money coming in, along with her savings at home. She told the realtor she would think about it that night. And just as she had when she decided to come to England, everything about it felt right. She called back in the morning and said she'd take it. She told Nigel when she got to work, and he looked thrilled. She told Mrs. Flannagan that night. And she had asked HR to try for the special visa. She wanted to stay with the show. They promised to do all they could to help her.

"I'm going to miss you," Mrs. Flannagan said sadly. Winnie was good company and she loved talking to her when Winnie came home at night.

"I will miss you too," Winnie said gently, "but I'll

come to visit. We can have dinner together, just like we do now."

Winnie moved into the little jewel box the following weekend with Nigel's help, and afterwards, they went shopping for what she was missing.

She was washing a new set of glasses and a set of plates when he came up behind her and put his arms around her, and he felt her hesitate. He turned her around to face him, set down the glass she had in her hand, and looked her in the eye, with a serious, loving look.

"Is it too soon, Winnie?" he asked gently. She wasn't sure if it was. She just didn't know if she was ready to have a man in her life again, or when she'd ever want one. She didn't know how long she'd be staying, and the years with Rob seemed like such a waste. She didn't want to do that again with a relationship that went nowhere. But she had just rented a house, so she obviously wasn't going anywhere soon.

"I don't know what I'm doing, Nigel. I don't want anyone to get hurt," she said in a voice raw with emotion, and held him tightly. He bent to kiss her and she didn't resist. She wanted him, but she was scared, and she didn't know what the future held for either of them.

"We don't have to make any big decisions," he said softly. "We're just two people who care about each other. We don't have to know what the future holds. You never know that in the beginning. Look at Tom White."

"That's how I got to be thirty-eight years old with the wrong man," she said sadly. But Nigel didn't feel wrong to her, any more than coming to England had been, or renting the cottage. He wasn't Rob, he was a good man, and she could tell that he cared about her. And as he kissed her again, she could feel the passion mount in both of them, and they couldn't stop kissing and fondling each other. She unzipped his jeans ever so slowly, and he pulled off her blouse. And suddenly they were wrapped around each other, and she could barely breathe she wanted him so much, as he led her toward the bedroom, and they fell onto the bed she had just made with new sheets.

Their clothes were off seconds later, and he was making love to her, and it felt clean and right and honest, and just what they both needed. He had wanted her since the first moment he'd seen her. She forgot everything else while he made love to her, and she used everything she'd learned with Rob to please him. But it felt different this time, and right. It wasn't just sex. They genuinely had feelings for each other, even though the future was uncertain.

They lay breathless on the bed afterwards, as he ran gentle fingers down her spine and gave her shivers.

"You're an amazing lover," he whispered to her,

"I'm falling in love with you . . . no, that's not true. I've already fallen." She kissed him, and wouldn't let him leave her, and a few minutes later they were making love again.

He stayed with her that night, and she had no regrets. He was part of the dream she had followed to England, and a new life had begun for both of them. For Winnie, it was long overdue.

They went to work together the next day, and she felt shy and mildly embarrassed, and wondered if their coworkers would notice something different about them. You could always tell when people were intimate. There was no hiding it. But they walked into the building separately and went about their jobs, and didn't see each other until noon. He melted when he saw her and smiled immediately.

"I want you," he whispered to her longingly, as she handed him the sandwich she had gotten him. "I wish we had time to go home for lunch."

"Me too. We'll make up for it tonight," she whispered to him and went back to work.

As she went about her job that afternoon, Winnie was thinking about her sister. She had given her the change of address when she left Mrs. Flannagan's B and B, but hadn't told Marje she had rented a house, and was applying for a special visa. She knew it would panic her, and make her think Winnie was never coming home. And she hadn't decided that. She just liked having a house of her own here, and being able to stay as long as she wanted.

When Winnie gave her the new address, Marje had texted her. "You changed B and Bs? I thought you liked the other one so much?" To which Winnie had responded, "This is better. I found it by accident while taking a walk." She hadn't told her about Nigel either. For the first time, she had people and places in her life that no one knew about. She didn't want to upset her family, but being here was something she knew she needed to do for herself. She had lived her life for others for so long, her mother, Marje, Rob, Hamm Winslow. It was her turn now.

She was still thinking about it, when one of the production assistants asked her to take a manila envelope to Elizabeth Cornette, the most important actress in the show, and biggest star. The production assistant whispered to her discreetly that it was a piece of jewelry that Cartier was lending her. It was valuable and the instructions were to place the package directly into her hands. Winnie had every intention of following the PA's directions, and knocked firmly on the door of the actress's trailer when she got there. She could hear voices inside, but no one answered. Clutching the package to her, she knocked louder until she heard the actress's voice.

"Who is it?" Winnie could hear a man's voice inside too.

"Winnie Farmington, Miss Cornette. I have an important package for you," she said clearly through the door. She didn't want to shout as loudly what it was or from where. She had never spoken to the actress directly before because she had had no reason to.

"Can you come back later?" Winnie knew she couldn't and had to be persistent. They couldn't have a valuable piece of jewelry floating around when the directions were to put it in the hands of the star herself. It had to be in her possession, on her body or in a safe, for insurance purposes, as the PA had explained. There was a safe in her trailer for the jewels she wore on the show.

"I'm sorry, no, I can't come back," Winnie said firmly, and she heard a male voice raised.

The door opened a moment later, and Elizabeth Cornette was wearing a white satin bathrobe, with her makeup smeared and running down her face. She had obviously been crying. Beyond her, Winnie could see Bill Anders, the equally important male star of the show. He looked angry at Elizabeth, and annoyed when he saw Winnie. She was obviously interrupting something unpleasant and it gave credence to the rumors that the two famous actors were having an affair. Both of them were married to other people, but according to gossip on the set, their romance had been going on for months, ever since he'd joined the show. He was a recent addition.

"It's from Cartier," Winnie said as she handed it to her.

"Why the hell are you bothering us?" Bill Anders shouted angrily at Winnie.

"It's a four-hundred-thousand-pound bracelet," Elizabeth said, turning to him. "She can't just slip it under the door. They're lending it to me for the shoot tomorrow, when we go to the queen's ball." She was trying to reason with him, with a tone of exasperation in her voice. He was usually difficult on the set too. He had been famous for many years and was used to people kowtowing to him, and he was known to have affairs on every show.

"Fuck the queen's ball, Elizabeth. My wife is threatening to divorce me. Do you have any idea what that will cost me? I think she's having me followed," he said, ignoring Winnie, as he paced in the small trailer, while Elizabeth looked at Winnie in despair. And Winnie didn't know whether to leave or not. It was an awkward moment, and Elizabeth told her to come in. She had something to return to Cartier too, the forty-carat emerald ring she'd worn the day before. "Why the hell did you let her in here?" Anders complained when he saw Winnie walk into the trailer and wait for Elizabeth to get the box with the ring out of the safe. It was twice as valuable as the bracelet, and Elizabeth wasn't supposed to keep them. Winnie hadn't been told about the emerald ring. And Bill Anders stood glaring at her. "Who've you been talking to?" he shouted to Elizabeth, as she nervously pulled the ring box out and was about to hand it to Winnie, but hadn't yet. "I told you to keep your mouth shut." He was wearing a satin bathrobe too. Winnie felt as though she had walked into their bedroom, and wished Elizabeth would just give her the box and let her go.

"I didn't tell anyone a damn thing!" Elizabeth shouted back at him, still clutching the box that Winnie was waiting for. "You're not exactly discreet yourself. I told you this would wind up all over the press." A scandal of that nature would be good for both their careers, and add spice to the show, but Anders obviously had a lot at stake, and his wife was going to make him pay. Winnie knew from reading about him that he'd had numerous affairs before, always with big stars.

"This is your fault if she nails me for it. I don't know about you, but I'm not willing to give up what we're making this season for the privilege of sleeping with you." His tone was disrespectful and his words were cruel. Elizabeth was crying again, and she opened the door wider and looked straight at him over her shoulder.

"You'd better go," she said clearly, and he looked like he was going to hit her. For a minute, Winnie was afraid for her.

"I'll go when I goddamn want to," he said angrily and strode to the door. He stopped where Elizabeth was standing. "Let's not forget that you seduced me, this was your idea," he added viciously. "We both know you're a whore, and now my wife knows it too." And with that, he pushed past both of them, hurried down the steps of the trailer in his dressing gown, and went back to his own. Elizabeth collapsed in a chair then, sobbing, still clutching both the package with the bracelet and the ring box, and Winnie gently closed the door, so no one could see what was going on. She went to get Elizabeth a drink of water and handed it to her without saying a word.

"Thank you." Elizabeth took a sip, set the glass down, and blew her nose on a tissue she had in her pocket. "I'm sorry you had to hear all that. Please don't tell anyone." She looked humiliated and deeply upset.

"Of course not," Winnie said, feeling desperately sorry for her. She had a reputation for sleeping with her leading men, but she didn't deserve to be berated and abused. He was just as guilty as she was, and Winnie hated the way he treated her. She couldn't stop herself from saying what she thought. She'd been through it herself with Rob. "He shouldn't talk to you like that. You can't let him. And if his wife is angry at him, it's his own fault." Elizabeth nodded and looked gratefully at Winnie. She handed her the ring box, and put the envelope with the bracelet in the small safe. "What he's doing to you is abuse," Winnie said in a small voice, sure that she'd be fired for saying anything at all. "I've been there myself."

"And did he stop eventually?" Elizabeth asked hopefully. "I'm in love with him. He's not always like this. He's just worried about what his wife is going to do and what it will cost him."

"That's no reason to talk to you that way. And no, he didn't stop," Winnie said honestly. "He cheated on me. I caught him, and I walked out."

"You're a brave woman. Men have cheated on me for years, and I've never walked out." She looked sad as she said it. It was as bad as if he'd beaten her with his fists. She was a spectacular-looking woman. She didn't have to put up with this. Nobody should, star or not. "Please don't tell anyone about what you heard just now." She looked imploringly at Winnie.

"I promise I never will. Just try to walk away from it the next time. You'll feel a lot better when you do." Elizabeth wiped the tears from her face again. And they were both thinking about Bill's harsh words and insults, which had hit the actress with full force. She looked badly shaken and depressed.

Winnie left her trailer a few minutes later, and tried not to think about it as she went to find the production assistant to return the emerald ring. She looked horrified when Winnie found her.

"Oh my God, I forgot to get that back from her last night. Thank you." And then in an undertone, "Please don't tell anyone, I'd get fired."

"Of course not," Winnie assured her. She was

suddenly keeping everyone's secrets, but the scene in Elizabeth Cornette's trailer haunted her all afternoon.

It was still on her mind when she left work. Nigel had told her that he'd meet her at her place. She had barely had time to make the bed, and put her breakfast dishes in the dishwasher, when he rang her doorbell and she let him in. She just had time to say hello to him, when he gently pulled off her clothes and wanted to make love with her. She'd been looking forward to it all day too.

They almost didn't make it to the bedroom, and he carried her the last few steps, kissing her, and then he laid her on the bed, and she reached up to him, and he entered her as they both gasped. Their lovemaking went on for hours, until they finally fell away from each other, and she smiled at him as they lay on their sides facing each other. "That was very nice," she whispered to him.

"Yes, it was," he whispered back, "very, very nice indeed." And with a peaceful smile, he fell asleep.

Chapter Eight

Despite Elizabeth Cornette's insistence that she hadn't told anyone about her affair with Bill Anders, it was all over the papers two days later. They were both just too famous for anything about their love lives to stay quiet for long. Someone inevitably talked and usually got paid by the press to do so. Winnie saw Bill Anders slip into Elizabeth's trailer several times after that. Nothing about their affair had slowed down, no matter what he was risking with his wife. The paparazzi were pursuing both of them, on and off the set, and it was bothering all the other actors. The paparazzi crawled all over them like ants.

And to complicate matters further, one of the other principal actresses had a stalker. She was young and beautiful, and played an ingénue on the show. The stalker was an obsessed fan who claimed he was madly in love with her, and constantly left her letters on the set, or on the steps of her trailer. It became so extreme and intrusive, they had to get a security guard to accompany her everywhere she went. The fan seemed relatively harmless, but you never knew with someone like that if he could suddenly turn and become violent when he realized that his sentiments weren't returned.

A few days later, Elizabeth Cornette's assistant gave notice. She had worked for Elizabeth since the beginning of the show, but her boyfriend was moving to Paris and she wanted to go with him. After six years with Elizabeth, she gave her a week's notice, and Elizabeth was frantic to have them find her someone else **now.** People were away for the summer and on the day the girl left, the PA still hadn't found a replacement, Elizabeth was having a tantrum over it, and the PA turned to Winnie in desperation.

"You do it," she said, looking desperate.

"Me?" Winnie looked horrified. "I can't be her assistant. I don't know what the job is. She's the biggest star on the show. I'll screw it up and she'll kill me." Winnie was panicked.

"All you have to do is help her get dressed, put on her jewelry for her, answer her phone if she wants you to. Call hair and makeup when she's ready for them and keep the paparazzi out of her trailer. It's not very complicated. What you're doing now as an errand girl for the cast and crew is harder. And when she's on the set, you get to read a magazine. Working for one person is easier, and she's not crazy like a lot of actresses. She probably won't even want you around most of the time, so she can sneak around with Bill Anders. You've got to do it for me, Winnie." The production assistant was near tears. "I don't have anyone for her. I'm going to get fired over this. Just do it till I find someone. I'll owe you my life if you'll do it." Winnie hesitated and felt sorry for her. She was a nice girl, about ten years younger than Winnie, with a lot of pressure on her and constant demands. She was always jumping through hoops of fire for someone.

"Okay, but only until you find a real one. I guess I can fake it until then." She wasn't enthusiastic about it. She was doing it as a favor to save the PA's neck.

"You might get to like it. Assistant to the star of the show is a cushy job, and a lot of perks come with it. People will be giving you presents all the time to get to her."

"I like the job I have. I don't have to deal with any personal issues or divas. All I have to do is run around the set, and do everyone's errands. What you're describing sounds like being a lady-in-waiting in the court of Marie Antoinette. That's too complicated for me." It actually sounded like being a lady's maid on the show too, which didn't appeal to Winnie either. But she thought she could do it for a short time.

She showed up at the star's trailer half an hour later, knocked, and stepped in when Elizabeth answered. She looked surprised when she saw Winnie, and remembered her immediately from when she'd had the big fight with Bill about his wife. But things had calmed down since.

"Hello, reporting for duty, Miss Cornette. I'm your new assistant." Winnie felt awkward when she said it, because she could see that the star remembered her from an unpleasant moment.

"You're my new assistant? Aren't you the errand girl on set?"

"I am." Winnie didn't try to deny it. "It was the only job they had open when I applied here."

"Have you ever been a personal assistant before?" She looked skeptical.

"No, I haven't. I'll do my best until they find you a real one. I'll try not to screw up too badly," she said humbly, and Elizabeth Cornette smiled.

"Don't worry about it. I forget my lines every day. We'll manage till they find somebody." Winnie nodded, and hoped it would be soon. This was more of a job than she wanted, with a high-strung actress and an abusive boyfriend, it sounded stressful to her.

"What can I do for you?" Winnie said, feeling like the lady's maid she didn't want to be. She felt faintly obsolete, or anachronistic, and could almost see herself wearing a black maid's uniform and lace cap and apron.

"I'm going out to dinner with Bill tonight. Will you help me get dressed? Call Angelica in hair, and Ivan to do my makeup." She had already taken her stage makeup off. "If there's press out there, I don't want them to see me like this." Winnie didn't dare ask her how things were going with Bill's wife. "There's a white silk dress with a pleated skirt and beading around the neck in my closet. Why don't you grab that? You may need to press it. I'll wear the high-heeled silver sandals," she said and then started sending text messages, while Winnie went to look for the dress and shoes. She found them easily, and mercifully the dress didn't need ironing. She would have been terrified to do it and ruin what was obviously a very expensive dress. She called Angelica and Ivan in hair and makeup, and they showed up five minutes later. As they got started, Winnie asked Elizabeth if she wanted something to drink.

"I'll have a glass of water," she said easily, and chatted with her hairdresser, which left Winnie with nothing to do.

An hour later, Elizabeth was dressed and ready. She looked very glamorous, and thanked Winnie for her help. She left as soon as Bill showed up, looking equally dashing, and Winnie tidied up the trailer and left a few minutes later, feeling as though she had climbed Everest. It was stressful being there, tending to someone's every need. Nigel was waiting for her outside in the Jeep.

"Where were you? I haven't seen you all day." He had missed her.

"I'm not sure if I got a promotion or a demotion. They haven't been able to find an assistant for Elizabeth Cornette. Hers quit. So they asked me to fill in until they find one. I'm kind of a lady's maid, waiting to cater to her every whim. It scares the hell out of me. What if I screw up? I'll get fired and they'll send me away, after she kills me, but I guess by then it won't matter."

"She's usually pretty decent, or that's what I've heard. She's nice to the tech guys on the set. Was she tough on you?"

"No, she was fine. I was just scared to death. I hope they find someone for her soon."

"Listen," he said to her seriously, "that's a big deal. Assistant to the star is a plum job around here. And I'm sure you'll be fine at it. It's way more money and half the universe will be kissing your ass trying to get to her."

"That's what the PA told me today. I don't need to have my ass kissed. I just want to do my work."

"Maybe you need to be more of a diva yourself," Nigel said, glancing at her. "You're so easygoing and helpful, you never demand anything for yourself." It was how she had gotten through eleven years with Rob, expecting nothing, which was pretty much what she got. Nigel was right. "There's nothing wrong with your making some demands too. Everyone will respect you more if you do."

"My old boss at the printing company was always rude to me. He was rude to everyone, so I figured it wasn't personal. Except of course, he was charming the girl he was sleeping with, who got the promotion I was supposed to get. He acted like the rest of us were cockroaches, and I was no different."

"You know, Matthew Stevens is smart about these things. It shows in what he writes. The people he writes about demand respect, they have boundaries, most of the characters don't take crap from anyone. The ones who do always take it on the chin and have to learn the lesson. It's something to think about."

"I never thought about it that way, but I think it's why I love the show so much. The good guys are very clearly that, and you know who the bad guys are, and they usually get their just deserts. And the weak ones learn to be strong. It's the way we all want to be. Funnily enough, I think it's why I quit my job when I didn't get my promotion. It happened right after an episode where Annabelle finally put her foot down and stood up for herself. So I quit, and threw Rob out when I found him in bed with my best friend. I think the show gives me courage." He smiled at what she said. "I've been feeling guilty about it, but lately I've been thinking about when I dropped out of college to take care of my mother. I never insisted on going back. I loved her dearly, and I had some precious moments with her, but I sacrificed seven years of my life, and all my dreams.

And after she died, it seemed too late, so I just gave up. But my sister never helped or offered to pitch in. She was having babies by then, and she just assumed I would do everything since I wasn't married and didn't have kids. She should have helped. It's water under the bridge now, but looking back, after that it didn't matter to me that I had a job I hated, and a boss who treated me like shit. The pay was good so I put up with it. And I didn't expect Rob to treat me any differently. I kept telling myself it was just temporary, but one day temporary becomes your whole life. You wake up, and you're not twenty or twenty-seven anymore, you're thirty-eight and you've given up all your dreams. I don't want to do that again. That's why I came here. From now on, I want things to be different, and this was the first step. I want to make decisions, not just float along letting life happen to me. I want more than that." He was touched, listening to her.

"I want that too," he said gently, "as long as it lasts."

"What does that mean?" she asked, frowning at him. It sounded like he expected them to fail. She was disappointed to hear it, now that she had decided to take a chance on him. He was an improvement over Rob, but he had his own issues, since he was still single at thirty-nine.

"We're in a business where everything is temporary, Winnie. It's all stage sets and illusions. Nothing is built to last. The show feels like it's forever, but it isn't. One day we'll get canceled, or Matthew will want to stop writing it, take what he made and go live in the South of France, or start another project, and then the coach turns into a pumpkin, and we all turn into white mice and scurry off in separate directions. It's hard to have a relationship living like that."

"Is that what you see happening to us?" She looked sad as she said it. She was hoping for better from him. He seemed to be so willing to be defeated. He was already preparing for it, which Winnie found discouraging.

"I've been on a lot of shows and that's how it happens," he said, convinced that he was right, and they would lose in the end. "No matter how much people like each other while they work together, when the show is over, they scatter. **Beauchamp Hall** looks solid, but nothing ever is. And it's damn hard for two people to get jobs on the same show. When the time comes, we'll have to figure something out if we're still together. I told you, it's a nomadic life. That's why a lot of people in this business are single. Or eventually, you give it up, and find a different way to use what you know. That's why I want my own sound business one day, maybe in London, working on commercial videos and films, either for industry or advertising. I've thought about it a lot. It's the only way I'll be able to settle down, get married, and have kids. It's in my plans," he said, smiling at her, as they got out of the car. She hadn't thought as far ahead as he had. She had just arrived and was new to the business, but she was impressed that he was making plans for the future. She suspected that a lot of the people in the business didn't. They just moved on, and created new relationships wherever they went. Nigel was smarter and more thoughtful than that, and at least he wanted a more stable life. It was why she was falling in love with him. Maybe she could help him start his business one day. For the first time, she was starting to think about her future. For Winnie, it was a big change. She had drifted from year to year till then. And woke up at thirty-eight.

They cooked dinner that night in her tiny kitchen, and went to bed right afterwards. They made love until after midnight and fell asleep in each other's arms.

Working as Elizabeth's assistant was less frightening than Winnie had feared it would be. It was even fun at times, and interesting. She was learning a lot. They did research together in books and magazines on her costumes and hair styles, which Winnie then transmitted to the costumer. And Elizabeth took Winnie's advice seriously. Winnie was intelligent and had good taste, and was supremely efficient. The rest of the time she was a combination social secretary, psychiatrist, and maid.

Elizabeth's affair with her male costar was turbulent. Winnie discovered that he drank a lot, and most of the time when he was abusive to Elizabeth it was because he'd been drinking, but he was also a fierce narcissist, and felt that the world should revolve around him. His wife was still threatening to divorce him, not just over Elizabeth, but because of the dozens of women before her, and every time his wife upped the ante and wanted a bigger settlement from him, he blamed Elizabeth. He even suggested that she should contribute to what his wife wanted. She asked Winnie what she thought about it, and Winnie told her it was outrageous. He had to take responsibility for his own behavior, and bear the weight of it himself. Winnie saying it gave Elizabeth the courage to stand up to Bill. He didn't like it, but he had new respect for her after she did. He didn't ask her to contribute again, which was a victory for Elizabeth that she attributed to Winnie. The two women were becoming friends. Elizabeth was two years younger, although she looked older than Winnie, who had more natural looks. The artifice of Elizabeth's makeup, hair, expensive clothes, and jewels subtly aged her, but it was part of her identity and essential to her career.

After two weeks, they hadn't found her a "real"

assistant yet, and Winnie was surprised by how comfortable she was in the job, and startled when she got the wrong pay envelope. She opened it by mistake, and was mildly envious of the salary the other person made, whoever it was. She took it to the production assistant and ruefully handed it back.

"I got someone else's salary by mistake," she said, smiling. "I'd love to know what they do. I could use some of that." The PA looked inside the envelope, checked some notes in a stack on her desk, and glanced back at Winnie.

"That's not a mistake. It's your salary, as personal assistant to the star. We're still paying you in cash." She was still part of the budget for "miscellaneous expenses on set," since she didn't have her visa yet.

"That's what I make as an assistant?" She looked shocked and grinned. "But I'm just temporary."

"Yeah, but it's what you're doing right now. She's crazy about you, by the way. She says she's never had such an efficient assistant. I haven't found anyone for her yet. Are you sure you don't want the job?" The salary was five times what she'd been making as the errand girl on the set. Winnie hesitated for a moment, thinking about it. It was tempting and she was enjoying the work. She liked Elizabeth more than she'd expected to. The one she didn't like was Bill Anders, he was pompous, pretentious, and the most self-centered human on the planet in Winnie's opinion. And Elizabeth was madly in love with him. She and her husband had just separated officially, so she was free now, but Bill was hanging on to his marriage, and didn't want to give half of what he owned to his wife. "Let me know if you decide you want the job. HR tells me we can get the work permit to go with it," which they couldn't do for her as an errand girl so they paid her in cash.

The next morning, she had made her decision, she wanted the job. Elizabeth was thrilled and so was she. They celebrated with champagne at lunch.

"Now you're really my assistant," she said, looking pleased. Winnie had talked it over with Nigel the night before, and he agreed. She discussed all her decisions with him now, he wanted to be involved in every part of her life.

Everything was going smoothly until an actor came on the show who'd been signed on for three episodes, as a brief romance for one of the younger female members of the Beauchamp family. He was sexy, handsome, and thirty-two years old. He looked like a player, and two days after he arrived, he was trying to seduce every woman on the set, and had slept with one of the hairdressers on his first day. His name was Gillian Hemmings, he was one of the hot new young talents, and had just made a movie in the States. He was expected to become a big star, and it was a coup to get him on the series for three episodes. They were considering making him long-term, but he hadn't agreed so far. He was more interested in feature films in Hollywood than a British TV series.

He had Winnie go out and buy his new under-wear, he said he'd run out. Then he needed T-shirts, a bathing suit, a prescription filled for a sore throat. He wanted a bottle of very expensive malt whiskey in his dressing room. And then asked Winnie to pick up a box of condoms for him, the largest box available, for an extra-large penis, he explained to her, with ribbed sides. He asked for it as though he was ordering a ham sandwich and she did it equally straight faced, although she reminded him it wasn't her job.

"I'm Elizabeth Cornette's assistant, Gill. I don't have time to do your errands." She had done it to be nice, but he was stretching her boundaries with the box of condoms, and his precise instructions supposedly to show off his size.

"They told me you were the errand girl on the set," he said, looking boyish and apologetic. "Besides"—he lowered his voice conspiratorially— "I thought maybe you'd like to try out the condoms with me, and let me know how you like them. I'm staying at the Hoste." He had come down from London, driving a new Rolls, and was starting to ruffle feathers on the set. Bill Anders particularly didn't like him, and said that he would object strenuously if they kept him around for more than three episodes. None of the men liked him, but most of the women adored him, and were flattered by his attentions, which were indiscriminate. He had already hit on most of the younger women, and considered Winnie a challenge since she paid no attention to him. She thought he was ridiculous and she was happy with Nigel, sexually and otherwise. Their relationship was growing like a flowering plant.

"I think you'd better get the condoms yourself. I don't have time," Winnie said brusquely. She didn't want to flirt with him, or give him the mistaken impression that she was interested. She wasn't.

"Sorry, darling, I'll pick them up myself. See you tonight at my hotel?"

"No, thanks, Gill. I'm busy. I've got a boyfriend."

"That's fine. A little variety never hurt anyone. I'm only in for three episodes."

"Try someone else," she said coldly and walked away. She checked in with Elizabeth to see if there was anything she needed, brought her an iced latte, and went to find Nigel just to say hello. She couldn't find him on the set. He sent her a text at the end of the day, to say that he had to go to a production meeting and couldn't drive her home. She didn't mind, since the weather was warm and she liked the walk. But she found it strange when he didn't call her or show up that night. It wasn't like him, and had never happened before.

She texted him in the morning. "What's up? I missed you last night."

"Sorry. Busy," he responded, and she walked to work wondering what was going on with him. She didn't see him until she went to the commissary truck to get some fruit for Elizabeth and saw Nigel eating lunch alone. She walked over to him with a smile, and he looked at her icily.

"Did you have a nice night?" he asked in a glacial tone.

"Very exciting. I did laundry." She could see that he was furious with her, but she had no idea why. "Would you like to tell me what's going on? I don't like mysteries. What are you pissed about?"

"I hear you've been testing condoms with the Boy Wonder," he said, glaring at her.

"Are you kidding? Do you think I'd sleep with that little jerk? He asked me, and I told him to find someone else, and that I have a boyfriend. Was I wrong? I thought I did. It doesn't sound like it right now."

"How do I know you didn't sleep with him?" He still glared at her suspiciously.

"Hopefully because you trust me. I wouldn't lie to you. He's ridiculous. Do you actually believe I'd sleep with someone like him, or that I'd cheat on you?"

"I don't know. Maybe you would." It was the first ugly side she'd seen of him. He was insanely jealous. Gillian Hemmings was undeniably handsome, but she thought he was a total horse's ass, and another narcissist. She was starting to discover that they were rampant in the business, men and women who made their living because of how beautiful they were, not how intelligent or talented. Although a few had both looks and brains, they were rare. Many of the pretty ones had slept their way to where they were. It had been said about Gillian, and that he was equally willing to sleep with women or men to get ahead.

"If that's what you think of me, Nigel, I have nothing else to say to you," Winnie said, looking as angry as he was, and she took the fruit for Elizabeth and left.

He came looking for her on the set an hour later, while they were watching Gillian do a scene with their ingénue. Elizabeth was due to enter the shot in a few minutes, and Winnie was putting her jewelry on, carefully checking the list of what she was supposed to be wearing for continuity from the day before.

"Can I talk to you for a minute?" Nigel asked, ignoring Elizabeth, and Winnie didn't look up at him.

"No, you can't. I'm busy." He looked embarrassed and skulked off a minute later, and Elizabeth smiled up at her.

"Pissed at him?" she whispered.

"Very," Winnie said emphatically, and the two women exchanged a smile.

Winnie didn't see Nigel again until she left work that night. He was waiting for her outside.

"I'm sorry. I shouldn't have said those things to you. I get jealous, and he's such a good-looking guy."

"He thinks so too," she said coolly. "I think he's a jerk. And you're much better-looking." He fell into step beside her as she walked home.

"I just thought . . . One of the guys I work with overheard what he said to you."

"Then he should have heard what I said back." She stopped walking and turned to look at him. "I'm not going to cheat on you, Nigel. If I wanted to be with someone else, I'd leave you. I don't play those games."

"I'm sorry . . . I've just been played so often, sometimes I assume all women do it."

"I'm not one of them," she said and started walking again.

"I'm a jealous guy," he confessed, looking sheepish. "I just didn't see how I could compete with someone like him."

"You have everything to offer, he doesn't, except his looks. And you're a good person. I'd have to be crazy to want him." They walked on in silence then, back to her cottage, but she had seen a side of him she didn't like. She didn't like that he had been so angry and assumed the worst from her. But at their age, they each had their scars from the people they had been with. And she had hers from Rob.

They had a quiet dinner that night, and went to bed afterwards, and when they made love, quietly and gently, she forgave him for what he had assumed so wrongly about her, but she didn't forget it. He had a strike against him now.

Chapter Nine

The following weekend Nigel surprised her. He'd been trying to make it up to her for his jealous fury over Gillian Hemmings. Gillian finished up his three episodes that Friday, and left the set. Winnie and Elizabeth amused themselves by trying to figure out how many women he had slept with while he was there. They guessed that in ten days, he had slept with thirteen members of the cast and staff, and Winnie suspected he had slept with one of the grips as well. He drove off in his Rolls and no one was sorry to see him leave. He was a walking sex machine but not much else.

But Nigel surprised her by asking her to spend the weekend at his home in Leighton Buzzard. He said it wouldn't be exciting, but he wanted to introduce her to his parents and one of his sisters who lived nearby. She was married and had three children. And Winnie was touched by the invitation.

They drove for three hours to get there in his battered Jeep, and Winnie was looking forward to it.
She had just told Marje about him, and that she
was going to meet his parents for the weekend,
which made Marje nervous. She didn't want Winnie putting down roots in England, but Winnie said
he was a great guy.

Marje talked to Erik about it afterwards, and he
told her not to worry. Winnie had gone away for an
extended vacation to get over a breakup and the loss
of her job, she hadn't run away from home. Marje
wasn't so sure, and she missed her. It made her even
lonelier for Winnie when she saw her on Skype.
But Winnie seemed happy, had a job she was having fun with and experiences she would never have
had at home. Working on the set of a hit TV series
was an incredible opportunity Winnie was grateful
for every day. It was a dream come true for her.

They got to Leighton Buzzard before dinnertime,
and his parents were having tea when they walked
in. His mother looked thrilled to see him, and his
father smiled to see his youngest son. Nigel hadn't
been home in several months, and they were intrigued to meet the American woman he said he
was bringing with him. She would be sharing his
childhood bedroom with him.

His parents were retired, his father had been an
electrician, which was what had gotten Nigel interested in sound equipment when he was young. He
had a brother who was an accountant in London,

a sister in New Zealand, and the sister who lived nearby was a nurse. His youngest brother worked at a resort hotel in Spain. His mother had worked for the post office. They were solid middle-class people and loved their son. The house was small, but tidy and well kept. His parents looked older than their age, and had worked hard all their lives to provide for their five children. And Nigel was grateful for all they'd done for him and was happy to see them.

They were very polite to Winnie, and asked her about her life in Michigan. She showed them pictures of Marje and Erik and her nephews. And after tea, they went to visit Nigel's sister Julia, who was just coming back from work. She was a surgical nurse in orthopedics and had three young children who were running wild in the house while they chatted. Her husband was a policeman, and had recently been promoted to detective.

She asked about the show, and she and Winnie discovered that they were both addicted to it. Winnie told her that was why she had come to England, and now, through a series of coincidences, she was working as a personal assistant to the lead actress.

"Well, aren't you the lucky one?" Julia said, ignoring the screams of glee from her children and the pandemonium around them. "It all sounds very glam to me. And very brave of you to come to England just to watch the show from close range. I'd love to do something like that." She looked envious as she said it. "Do you think you'll stay here?" she asked, curious.

"I haven't figured that out yet." Winnie smiled easily. "I'm just letting things unfold for now." She glanced at Nigel and he smiled at her. His sister could see that he was very taken with Winnie, although none of his relationships had lasted so far and were usually short-term, which she said to Winnie. Nigel looked annoyed, and gave his sister an angry look to stop her from saying more.

Nigel and Winnie stayed for dinner that night. Patrick, Julia's husband, was Irish, and the four of them had a good time at dinner, and the children entertained themselves while the adults finished the meal.

The following day, he took Winnie to see where he'd gone to school, and they had dinner with his parents. His father was a history buff, and an expert on World War I. He had made a model of the **Lusitania,** which was displayed in their living room.

And on Sunday, they drove back to Burnham Market, with a tin of cookies his mother had made for them. It had been a relaxing, cozy weekend, which helped Winnie to get to know him better. She liked his family a lot, particularly his sister Julia. She was a smart, sensible woman, and very down to earth.

On Monday, they both went back to work, and Winnie was happy to see Elizabeth and hear about her weekend. She had flown to Nice, and met Bill in Saint Tropez, where the paparazzi had besieged them, which was to be expected there. He could hardly complain about being in the press after that, or blame Elizabeth for it, as Winnie pointed out. They were going to Spain together later that summer. He had rented a house in Ibiza, and a yacht to go with it. It was a far cry from Winnie's weekend in Leighton Buzzard, but they each had their own lives, and liked each other despite the differences between them.

Winnie made a decision after her weekend away with Nigel, and she called Marje on Monday, told her about the cottage she'd rented and that she wanted Marje to rent out the house in Beecher for her.

"Does this mean you're never coming back?" Marje asked in a choked voice, and Winnie felt sorry for her. She didn't want her to feel abandoned. But she wasn't willing to give up her dreams this time either.

"I haven't made that decision," she said honestly. "I want to stay here for a while. It's all working out so far. And it seems stupid to let the house just sit there. I might as well make some money on it. I'll split it with you," she offered, since they both owned the house. "Why don't you rent it for six months? You can put my clothes in boxes, so the renters can use the closets." It made Marje sad to think about it, but it sounded sensible to her too.

"Why don't you try to come home for Christmas?" Marje suggested, and Winnie nodded and said she didn't know yet. She'd been gone for three months, and Christmas was four months away.

"That would be nice, though," Winnie said, thinking about it. They both knew a lot could happen in the next four months, good and bad. Things might be really established with Nigel by then, or over, it could go either way, although things seemed to be getting more serious between them. They were talking about going away in September, during the hiatus before they started shooting the next season. But they hadn't figured out where to go yet. They had time to decide.

Marje promised to list Winnie's house with the realtor in town as a six-month furnished rental. She wouldn't get a lot for it, but it never hurt to make some money. Both sisters were sad when they hung up: Marje because she felt as though Winnie was slowly severing her ties with Beecher, and Winnie because she felt guilty for leaving her sister. But Marje had her own life, and now Winnie had to try and figure out what to do with hers.

"I wish she'd gotten something else in that damn white elephant game at her office last Christmas, instead of the DVDs of the show she's so crazy about. Another set of coasters maybe," she said with tears in her eyes, and Erik smiled at her.

"Don't worry, she'll be back," he said, sounding certain. "She's just spreading her wings a little. She'll be happy to come home eventually."

He didn't doubt it for a minute, but as Marje cleared away the dinner dishes, she wasn't nearly as sure. She sounded much too happy in England, and she was leading a fantasy life, watching the series she loved being made, working for a big TV star, and now she had a boyfriend on the wrong side of the Atlantic. It was fun for Winnie, but it did not sound good to her.

Elizabeth was strangely quiet for the next week or so, and Winnie was worried she had said or done something to offend her. Their joking and friendly exchanges had suddenly stopped. She wondered if Elizabeth felt ill at first, but she claimed she was fine whenever Winnie asked her. And after a few days, Winnie didn't want to bother her. It was obvious she didn't want to talk. She spent a lot of time conferring with Bill Anders in private, and frequently asked Winnie to leave them alone, which she hadn't done till then either. Winnie didn't want to pry but she began to believe she was going to be fired, and talked to Nigel. She asked if he'd heard any gossip. The rumor mill was very active on the set. But he said he'd heard nothing about it.

"It probably has to do with his divorce. They can't go on having a flagrant affair like that forever. Everyone loves a love story, but sooner or later, the viewers will just think they're cheaters and the sponsors won't like it." Winnie hadn't thought of that.

"I guess so. But they clam up every time I walk into the trailer. Before, she wasn't afraid to say anything in front of me. Now she barely talks to me. I think I must have done something to offend her."

"Don't be so paranoid," Nigel teased her, but Winnie had a weird feeling in the pit of her stomach that wouldn't go away.

The following Monday, she and Elizabeth were picking which wig to wear in the next shot. Elizabeth had tried several and didn't like any of them, and they'd just asked the wigmaker on the set to bring over more, when Michael Waterman, the executive producer, burst into her trailer without knocking. His face was purple and he was waving several sheets of paper in his hand.

"When did you cook this up?" he shouted at Elizabeth, as she lowered her eyes and didn't look at him. He waved the papers in her face and tears sprang to her eyes. "You couldn't have the guts to talk to me about it? You had to send me a goddamn **letter**? We work together for six fucking years and you tell me four weeks before we go on hiatus? Do you know what this is going to do to us? You just torpedoed the ship. The **Titanic** is going down. Is that what you wanted? Well, I've got some news for you. I'm not going to let it sink. We've all worked too hard and love this show too much to let you destroy us. I thought you had a heart, Liz. We can sue you, you know."

"No, you can't," she said, speaking for the first

time, as she raised her head to look at him. She was deathly pale, in contrast to his face, which was scarlet and looked like it was going to explode. "My agent checked the contract, and I have three escape clauses that apply. I can't help it. I have a right to take a better offer. That show is going to make my career. I can't turn it down." She looked deeply regretful, but he couldn't sway her. And Winnie suddenly realized that she had been so silent because she was making a major decision. It had nothing to do with her.

"Make your career, and destroy mine and everyone else's on this show. Does that seem right to you?" They both completely ignored Winnie, who shrank into the background in the small trailer, and when the wigmaker showed up, they sent her away.

"I can't turn down an opportunity like that. I love this show, but they're offering me three times the money, and an incredible opportunity. I can pick my own cast. They're giving me everything I ever wanted. And one of these days you're going to shut down **Beauchamp Hall,** or Matthew will get tired of writing it, and I'll have passed this up."

He ignored what she said, which wasn't entirely unreasonable, from what Nigel had explained to Winnie. "And who are you picking for your cast?" He took a step closer to her, and glared at her ominously.

"I'm only taking Bill with me," she said in barely more than a whisper.

"Oh my God, you bitch. He hasn't even told me yet." If it were possible, Michael's face went from red to purple.

"I asked him to let me tell you first."

"How could you do this to us? And why didn't you tell me sooner and give us a chance to negotiate with you?"

"Because you'd never give me that much money. And the deal just finally came together a week ago. I thought they were just bullshitting before that, but they're not."

"I don't know what to say to you. I like you, Liz. You've been great on the show. But you have no heart. You're just like everyone in this business. It's all about you, and you don't care whose lives you destroy to get ahead. Well, I'm sorry to disappoint you. We'll make it without you. **Beauchamp Hall** has a lot more going for it than you and Bill Anders."

"This is just business," she said limply, which was the phrase everyone used to stab someone in the back. Even Winnie already knew that, and she felt sorry for the producer.

She fully understood what had just happened. Elizabeth was leaving the show, and taking Bill Anders with her, to star on another show. They were the two biggest stars on **Beauchamp Hall.** They had lost Tom White when he was killed earlier in the season they were shooting. And Miranda Charles had left shortly after. Matthew had compensated for it admirably, with new storylines and several new actors. But Elizabeth and Bill leaving would be an even bigger blow, and would be much harder to make up for, to keep the show interesting to their loyal viewers who were emotionally attached to every one of the players, as Winnie had been when she got there. It had changed subtly for her now, because she was part of the behind-the-scenes making of it, which made it seem less real to her, though even more fascinating. And she knew what went into making it convincing. She saw the artifice now, not just the plot.

He stormed out of the trailer then, and there was dead silence after he left. Elizabeth stole a careful glance at her assistant, and Winnie looked at her.

"I'm sorry you had to hear all that."

"I thought you were mad at me for the last week."

"Of course not. I was just stressed out trying to make the decision, and I wanted Bill to come with me. He wasn't sure at first. He's made the decision now. I'm leaving when we finish shooting the season in four weeks."

"Matthew will have to work hard to make up for it. Do you think he can do it?" Winnie asked, looking worried. It hadn't even occurred to her she was about to lose her job too. She was the assistant to someone who was about to leave. But her job was minimal compared to everyone else's. And she cared deeply about the show.

"I hope Matthew can do it," Elizabeth said seriously. "I love this show. I don't want to hurt it. But I have to think of my career too. Shows like this rarely go past six or seven seasons. Viewers either get tired of them, the cast wants to do other things, or the writer runs out of gas, or wants to quit before it all falls apart. The handwriting was on the wall before I did this. Michael just doesn't want to see it, but he knows it too." Winnie nodded, trying to absorb it. "And I'm sorry, Winnie. You've been the best assistant I've ever had. Do you want to come with me? We'll be shooting in London, with location shoots in Monte Carlo, Dubai, Las Vegas, and Macao. It's about a professional female gambler, who's basically crooked, an embezzler and a thief, so we'll be on location in the gambling capitals of the world. The scripts are great. Bill is going to play the sexy, handsome James Bond–style detective who's always trying to catch me, but never does. But I sleep with him occasionally." She smiled.

"It sounds like a great show," Winnie said sincerely. But not a family show with strong values like **Beauchamp Hall.**

"I think it will be. Want to come on board?"

She thought about it for a minute and shook her head. "I didn't come here for a career in show business. I came here because I love this show, and everything it represents. It won't be the same without you, but I think I'll stick with the **Titanic,** if that's what happens. I'm not ready to get in the lifeboat yet." Elizabeth nodded and respected her for it. She admired Winnie's integrity.

"Loyal to the end. I think Matthew will be able to keep it going for another season or two, if he wants to. But I don't think he could have done it for longer than that anyway. Almost no show has ever made it to ten years. What'll you do?" she asked Winnie, worried about her for a minute.

"Go back to being an errand girl on the set," she said philosophically. "I had a lot of fun working for you. Thank you for giving me the chance to do it. As long as I don't have to buy super-sized condoms for Gillian Hemmings and test them with him, I'll be fine." They both laughed at that, and Winnie asked the wigmaker to come back. Elizabeth picked two she wanted to wear that day, and her performance was brilliant. Winnie knew she would be sorely missed. She was a pro and a terrific actress, one of the best, even if she wasn't loyal. She had her eye on her own career, which came first for her.

The news was out by the end of the week, and there was mass panic on the set. At first, everyone thought it was just a rumor and didn't believe it, but management confirmed it. A brief announcement was issued, with the assurance that they would be shooting another season after this one, as planned, but the more experienced players and technicians were dubious that the show would survive Elizabeth and Bill leaving, and that Matthew would want to

write it without them. They all felt the sands shift-
ing under their feet. The more optimistic members
of the cast and crew wanted to believe it would
go on. Others didn't. Fear was rampant and tan-
gible on the set.

Nigel took the news badly, and said it wasn't
handwriting on the wall, it was a neon sign that the
show would be canceled.

"I was there when she told Michael. He said he's
not going to let the ship go down." Winnie tried to
reassure him.

"It's not up to him, it's up to the network, the
viewers, and the sponsors. If the ratings blow, it'll
be over in five minutes. Why didn't you tell me if
you knew?" He looked angry about that too.

"I only heard it a few days ago. I wasn't supposed to be in the room, and I was told to keep it
confidential."

"And that includes me?" he asked and she nodded. "I'm about to lose my job, and you couldn't
warn me?" He wanted to blame her for what was
happening.

"You're not about to lose your job. They say
they're going to do another season."

"Don't count on it. You don't know this business.
I do. I guarantee you we'll be out of work by the
end of the year. I'm going to start putting out feel-
ers," he said, with a grim look. He went to stay at
his own place that night, and left for London for
the weekend to see some producers he knew. He

acted as though the show had already been canceled and he was in a black mood. They had all
signed confidentiality agreements about Elizabeth
and Bill leaving, so Winnie couldn't talk to Marje
about it. She spent a quiet weekend watching re-
runs of **Beauchamp Hall,** which always calmed her,
and reading her dog-eared copy of **Jane Eyre.** She
wondered what Matthew was going to do to bring
the show back to life without Elizabeth and Bill. It
made her realize how difficult his job was. She used
to fantasize about writing a show like this, and now
she realized what it took to do it. She didn't envy
him the task ahead.

Nigel was in no better spirits when he came back
from London. He couldn't tell anyone he'd met
with why he was looking. He'd just said he was getting restless and thinking about moving on, but no
one had had any hopeful suggestions for him.

"What about starting the sound business you've
been talking about if they cancel the show?" Winnie was trying to be helpful and he looked annoyed
when they talked about it over dinner.

"I'm not ready to do that yet. I don't have the
money. It'll cost a fortune in equipment. That's
probably ten years away. If the show goes down, I
need another job, Winnie. I can't do what you've
done, and come over here and hang out for six
months and play around."

"I didn't come over here with a fortune. I did it with my savings."

"Yeah, and if you run out of money, you can sell a house in Michigan."

"Half a house," she reminded him. "My sister owns the other half. You make me sound like an heiress. I saved most of what I have, and the money my mom left me eleven years ago, which wasn't much."

"Well, I haven't saved my money like you did, I don't own half a house, and my parents barely have enough to live on now that they're retired. I'll have to go to work on another show if **Beauchamp** dies, or when it does, since it's not an 'if' anymore, it's a 'when.' Sometime in the next year or two, if it takes that long, I'll be out of work."

"So will I," she said quietly.

"And then what? You'll go back to Michigan?"

"Let's figure that out when it happens."

"I told you, Win, everything in this business is temporary, that's why I never married and don't have kids. Because all you do when you work on shows like this is go from one to the next, if you're lucky and get another job." She had come to understand that. It wasn't like working for a bank or a business that would be there forever. It appeared, it had its moment of glory, and one day it disappeared. It made her sad to think about it. She didn't want **Beauchamp Hall** to end either. Coming here had been her dream. But for Nigel, it was a matter of earning his livelihood. This was his career.

A few days later, she got a note addressed to her that was dropped off at Elizabeth's trailer. Elizabeth was out when she found it, and she sat down to read it. It was from Edward Smith, one of the actors on the set, who asked her to give him a call. She had hardly ever spoken to him. He played the oldest son in the Beauchamp family. He was in his early forties and played a married man with four children, with a wife he had married out of duty and didn't love. He'd had an affair with his true love for years, and had a second family with her, living in secret in a home he'd built for her a few miles away. The actor who played the part was Australian, from a fancy family. He had gone to the best British boarding schools, and had no trace of an Australian accent, only an aristocratic British one. He was good-looking, and a wonderful actor, and Winnie had no idea why he wanted her to call him. She thought about it, and finally called him that night from home.

"It's good of you to call me," he said as soon as she said who it was. "I would have talked to you on the set, but it seemed awkward. There's so much angst these days with Liz and Bill leaving." Winnie couldn't figure out if he was asking her for a date or something else, but he came to the point quickly. "I've been envious of Liz ever since you went to work for her. I saw how efficient you were, even when you were the errand girl on the set. I don't know what your plans are now that she's leaving. But my assistant is having a baby and wants to stop working for good. Her husband has a good job and she can afford to. She wants to leave as soon as I replace her, so she can stay home and eat ice cream and relax. I wondered if you'd come to work for me. It's less glamorous than working for Liz, but I gather that we both have a need, possibly you for a job, and me for a new assistant. I thought I'd put it out there before someone else snaps you up." He made it sound straightforward and clean, and she was flattered by everything he'd said. "You'll have fewer wigs to deal with, and more hunting weekends to arrange," he said and they both laughed.

"Wow, that's amazing. It certainly solves the problem for me. They're going to shoot all Elizabeth's shots now, and Bill's, so they can leave before the hiatus. To be honest, the producers are pretty upset so I think they want her off the set. So I'll be available as soon as she leaves."

"That works perfectly for me, Rebecca would love that. They hadn't found anyone for me yet, and then I thought of you. It sounds like it could be a good thing for us both."

"Yes, it would. Thank you, Mr. Smith," she said respectfully.

"Edward, please. Well, I'm very glad I dropped you the note, and you called. I'll let them know that we're all set. It's a pretty simple switch."

She was pleased with the new arrangement, and relieved to know she'd still have a job when Elizabeth left. She told Nigel with a big smile as soon as he got home. He didn't say anything at first, and then came to discuss it with her while she was making dinner, and she could see from the look on his face that he was upset.

"So now you're going to be the assistant to a man? What's that all about? Why isn't he hiring a guy? Is he after you for sex?"

"Not everyone sees me as an opportunity for hot sex," she said smiling at him. "I'm thirty-eight, not nineteen. His assistant is leaving, and he needs a new one. And she's a woman too. So he wants me to work for him when Elizabeth leaves. It's pretty simple, and works for both of us."

"I'm not so sure it works for me," Nigel said, picking at his food at dinner. He was too disturbed to eat. It reminded her of when he'd had a fit over Gillian Hemmings. But Gillian had been a creep, and had propositioned her. Edward Smith was a stand-up guy, and a gentleman. Nothing about his offer had been lascivious, and she'd never heard of his having affairs on the set, which was unusual. From the rumor mill, she thought he had a girlfriend, who had a title and lived in London.

"I need a job, Nigel, and he seems like he'd be

nice to work for. If he's not, and he puts the make on me, I'll quit and go back to being an errand girl. But if it's okay with you, I'd like to make a decent salary too. This is about your being jealous, not about who he is."

"I don't like him. He's too good-looking. And what happens when he struts around his trailer in his underwear, or bare-ass naked. Then what will you do?"

"If he's a decent guy, he won't. If he does, I'll quit. You have to trust me on this."

"I don't trust him."

"Well, I do."

They argued about it all evening, and Nigel went to bed mad. He was still angry when he woke up in the morning, and roared off to work in his Jeep without breakfast or saying goodbye to her, and she didn't see him all day. He didn't come for dinner that night.

They argued about it until she started work for Edward. She had decided to work for both him and Elizabeth for Elizabeth's last week on the set, so she could get used to him before the hiatus. And Nigel never relented for the entire time. He got angrier and angrier, convinced that Winnie would have an affair with her new boss.

"Nigel, you have to stop," she said finally. "I'm not going to give up a job just because you're jealous. He's done nothing inappropriate."

"He will." Nigel was convinced of it and didn't trust either of them.

"This is ridiculous!" She wasn't going to give in on principle. "I make five times the money as an assistant than I do as an errand girl, and I get a work permit with it. The salary pays my rent. Be reasonable, for God's sake."

"He's a TV star. How do you expect me to feel?"

"You're a handsome guy and I love you. You have nothing to worry about." Winnie finally gave up and stopped discussing it with him. She kept the job, Nigel would have to learn to live with it, and grow up, as far as she was concerned. His jealousy was one of the things she liked least about him, and she wasn't going to indulge him. But his jealousy and paranoia were beginning to erode the good times and the relationship they'd had. He was worried and angry now all the time.

She told Elizabeth about it before she left, and Elizabeth said she'd had a boyfriend like that once.

"How did you deal with it?" Winnie wanted all the advice she could get, and she was closer to Elizabeth than anyone else.

"I started cheating on him because he thought I was anyway. Eventually he was right, so we broke up." Winnie laughed at her solution, which was typical of her. She had confessed to Winnie that she had never been faithful to any man. "But Edward Smith is so serious and straightlaced. I doubt he'll even make a pass at you. I tried with him once," she said with a laugh, "and he turned me down. I thought maybe he was gay, but he's definitely not. He's a one-woman man and I hear he's been with the same girl for years. I think you're perfectly safe with him."

"So do I. But I can't convince Nigel of that. He's been furious ever since I told him."

"I hate jealous men, they're such a bore," Elizabeth said with a sigh, and Winnie agreed. The first time she thought it was flattering, and a little childish. This time it was just upsetting. She had thought he was better than that, but he wasn't. It was his worst flaw, and a serious one if it was going to interfere with her job. And she couldn't only work for women to please him. This time a man had offered her a job, and a very good job she liked. He was an excellent, considerate employer.

Winnie was sad the day Elizabeth left the set. She gave Winnie a gold bracelet to thank her and told her to come and visit her new show, and Winnie promised to do so if she came to London. Winnie waved as she drove away, gathered up her things, and walked down the road to Edward's trailer, where he was waiting for her with a stack of work and calls to make. She liked working for him. He was more businesslike than Elizabeth and treated her more like a secretary, and he was unfailingly respectful and appropriate. She never even saw him in a dressing gown when he got his hair and makeup done. He was entirely proper. Nigel had been totally wrong. But he still spent a lot of their time together complaining about him, to the point of being bitter about it, and she was beginning to understand why none of his relationships had worked out. His jealousy and rages were hard to overcome. Her new boss was a perfect gentleman, which Nigel refused to believe. Day by day he got worse, and Winnie loved him less and less, until she could barely remember what it was she loved about him. His jealousy burned white hot and consumed everything she'd liked about him until there was nothing left.

Chapter Ten

Despite Nigel's constant unpleasant comments, Winnie enjoyed working for Edward Smith. He was professional, intelligent, had a good sense of humor. He studied his lines diligently so he was always prepared on the set, and followed direction easily. He was well liked by the cast, and Winnie couldn't imagine having such an easy boss. It turned her workdays into a pleasure.

And one day, while they were trying to guess how Matthew was going to rewrite the next season without Elizabeth and Bill, Winnie admitted that she had done some writing in college, and had dreamed of working in publishing in New York, and being an editor.

"I wanted to be a commercial fisherman, or a big-game hunter when I was growing up. That didn't happen either." They both laughed at the fallen dreams of their youth. "Do you ever do any writing now?" She shook her head. "You should. Who knows, maybe one day you'll write a screenplay, or a bible for a show like this. Stranger things have happened. I know plenty of actors who've given it up to become screenwriters and been very successful. And you're around the show enough to get an idea of how it works, and it sounds like you know all the episodes verbatim," he teased her. She had long since confessed her addiction to the show, and said that was why she had come here. "You should study the scripts." He gave her a stack of old ones to take home with her, and she started reading them at night, to see how they were constructed, and how they moved from one scene to the next. She found it fascinating. But her doing it annoyed Nigel intensely. He had started spending the night with her less and less often, and would show up without calling her, acting as though he expected to find her in bed with someone, presumably Edward. Instead, he would find her at the kitchen table, making notes on a script.

He annoyed her particularly one night, when she opened the door for him in her pajamas. Nigel looked like he'd been drinking, and he staggered slightly as he said, "No Edward?"

"I locked him in a closet when I heard you coming," she said tartly. She found his jealousy childish and a waste of energy and time and refused to take it seriously. He was basically a decent guy, but he was obsessed by his concern about her with other men.

"Why are you always fooling around with the scripts?" he asked her, as he sat down across the table from her.

"Edward thinks I should try and write a script one day," she said innocently, thinking Nigel would be intrigued by the idea, and pleased for her.

"Oh, Saint Edward, of course. Are you going to try and save the show?" he said bitterly.

"I wish I could. I think Matthew can do that without my help," she said quietly. "At least I hope so."

"We'll be lucky if we get another year out of it," Nigel said, "and then we'll all be out on our asses, and looking for jobs again." It was a possibility she couldn't deny, and Edward was worried about it too. They all were, but their attitudes were more positive than Nigel's. His fear of the future and jealousy over Winnie were slowly poisoning him, and making him toxic to be around. His mood was very dark.

"Well, let's enjoy it while it lasts," she said calmly.

"This is just a hobby for you, Winnie," he accused her, and there was truth to it. But she was learning a lot from reading the scripts, and her dream of writing was coming to life again. It had been dormant for nearly twenty years, but she could feel it stirring.

"This is a job for me, my livelihood. If they cancel the show, I'm liable to wind up on some show I hate. Like one of those sick reality shows, with a family of drug addicts who all go in and out of rehab." His comment made her think of Marje and her Las Vegas housewives.

"My sister loves those shows, but not about drug addicts. About housewives who look like hookers." She smiled as she said it and he relaxed a little. She could still see glimpses of the Nigel she knew and loved from time to time, but anxiety had him in its clutches and he was tense and different than he had been when she met him. His bitterness was toxic.

He spent the night with her that night, but the beer he'd been drinking caught up with him and he passed out the minute his head hit the pillow. It reminded her of Rob and the nights they spent together when they didn't even talk to each other. She didn't want to face it, but she could sense that what she had shared with Nigel was slipping away. She wasn't heartbroken over it, but disappointed. He wasn't a bad person, and he had a kind side to him, but he had become hard to live with. Impossible in fact.

Edward said something about it one morning. "I've seen you with one of the sound men a few times, away from the set. Is that your boyfriend?" She nodded.

"He has been, it's a bit on and off at the moment. We've only been dating for a few months, since I got here." She didn't tell him that Nigel was consumed with jealousy of him. He didn't need to know, and Nigel wasn't dangerous, just neurotic about it, which made him unattractive. She didn't find it charming, in fact less and less so.

"Relationships are like that," he said, thinking about it. "We all make compromises about something. It's never perfect. I've been dating the same woman for thirteen years. We get along brilliantly, although we're not together all the time, or maybe because of it. Her father is in the House of Lords, and he doesn't want her to marry an actor. I don't want to give up acting. I've put too much into it, and I don't know what else I'd do, and she doesn't want to defy her father. So we've never married. I'm forty-two, and she's thirty-seven. It's not a drama for me, but she's getting anxious about having children, so we'll have to figure it out one of these days. It's awful to say, but he's quite old, and I think she's been waiting for him to die before we get married. But he's made of sturdy stuff and quite a tyrant. I'm sure he'll outlive us both." He smiled as he said it. "And she's not the sort to have babies without being married. I wouldn't mind it. Things seem to change as you get older. The things one used to think were so important turn out not to be. And the things you thought didn't matter actually become very important one day. What matters to me about Grace is being with her. I don't care if we marry or have children. She's the only woman I've ever loved. That's worth hanging on to. And you never know what's going to happen."

"I think I'm getting there too. I spent eleven years with the wrong man before I came here. I realize now that I don't really care if I get married or have children. I want to be with the right person. Being with the wrong one is pretty miserable." She smiled and he nodded agreement.

"You don't know what surprises life has in store for you."

"Coming here was the best surprise I've ever given myself," she said happily. And she wasn't going to let Nigel spoil it for her.

"How are you doing with the scripts, by the way?" he asked her.

"I've been studying them every night. Writing a screenplay seems easier than writing a book. The construction is simpler and more economical."

"Precisely. And it's all visual. It's all in the actor's face, if he's any good." He gave her a list of calls to make for him then, to his banker, his lawyer, a dinner reservation. He was planning to go to London in the morning for his days off. He and Grace had separate apartments, but she stayed with him when he went to London. Listening to him talk about her made it even clearer how absurd it was that Nigel was jealous of him. He was madly in love with his girlfriend, and Winnie loved the way he talked about her. She would have liked to have a man say things like that about her.

She tried telling Nigel about it that night, and he didn't want to hear it. He left shortly after, to meet up with friends at one of the pubs he'd been frequenting recently. He was drinking more than he used to, she suspected out of anxiety about his job and his future. The atmosphere on the set was tense these days, and Bill and Elizabeth's departure had made everyone's anxiety that much more real.

The phone rang a few minutes after he left, and she assumed he was calling to apologize or ask if he could come back later, which wasn't as much fun as it used to be. He was fine if he was sober, but having him stagger in drunk and pass out in her bed next to her was a déjà vu of Rob for her, and she didn't enjoy it or want to relive it.

But it wasn't Nigel on the phone, it was her sister. Marje sounded hysterical and she was crying. Winnie couldn't understand her at first, but it was obvious that something terrible had happened. The first thing that came to Winnie's mind was Erik. He had just turned fifty and sometimes bad things happened to men his age with no previous history.

"Calm down . . . take a breath . . . try to tell me what happened . . ."

She managed to get out one word. "Jimmy." Her seventeen-year-old son. Winnie froze as she tried to guess what might be wrong.

"He was swimming in our neighbor's pool. They were having a pool party," which made no sense to Winnie either. The people they knew in Michigan didn't have pools, they hardly ever got to use them. But Marje's neighbor was a contractor and had built it himself for his kids. "The kids were horsing around, and he slipped and hit his head."

"Oh my God, is he okay?" Obviously not, with Marje sobbing, and Winnie was starting to panic too.

"He's in a coma. He fractured his skull and has a severe concussion. I've been with him since last night and my cellphone doesn't work at the hospital. Erik is with him now. I came home to see Adam. Win, they said if he doesn't regain consciousness soon, he'll be brain damaged."

"That's not going to happen," Winnie said automatically, rejecting the thought as soon as her sister said it.

"He's got swelling of the brain, and they want to see if it goes down. If it doesn't they'll have to operate. They might have to take out part of his brain." She collapsed in sobs and Winnie looked at her watch, wondering how fast she could get to London, and on a plane. It was nine o'clock at night. She had no idea what time the last train left, but if there was one around eleven o'clock or midnight, she could be on it, which would get her to London at one or two in the morning. With luck, she could catch a morning flight to Chicago, and from there to Detroit. The time difference was in her favor, and even with all the stops she had to make, she could be in Beecher by early afternoon.

"Marje, hang in. I'll get home as fast as I can. I'm going to get off now so I can get organized. I'll call you as soon as I know what time I'll be there."

"You can't, you're working. . . ."

"Never mind. I love you. It'll be okay." She had no idea if it would, but she didn't know what else to say. Her mind was racing as she hung up, and the first thing she had to do was call Edward, and tell him what she was doing. He was going to London for four days, and she didn't want him to think she'd disappeared. She glanced at her watch again, it was still early enough to call him at just after 9:00 P.M. He picked up, and was in good spirits. He was excited to be going to see Grace.

She told him what had happened to her nephew, and he sounded shocked.

"How awful, Winnie, I'm sorry."

"I hate to do this to you, but I've got to go home for a few days. I'll try not to be gone too long, depending on what happens."

"For Heaven's sake, don't be ridiculous. Stay as long as you have to. I can manage on my own. I won't even be back on set for five days. When are you flying out?" He sounded deeply concerned.

"I don't know yet. I called you first. I'm going to try to get on the first morning flight to Chicago, or New York if I have to. I need to get to Detroit after that. My hometown is two hours out of Detroit. I'll see if I can get on a train to London tonight."

"No, you're not. I'm all packed. Grace is having dinner with her father tonight, so I was going to drive up in the morning. Call the airline. I'll pick you up in an hour. I can get you to London in three hours, or less. You can stay with us until your flight if you need to."

"Are you sure?"

"Of course. Grace never lets me drive the way I want. I'll enjoy it," he said, trying to make it seem lighthearted. He was very sorry for her. He had a nephew the same age.

Winnie didn't waste time arguing with him. She called the airline, and they had a 7:00 A.M. flight to New York, which connected to a direct flight to Detroit. The flight to Detroit was due to land at 12:30 P.M. local time. With luck and no delays, she could rent a car at the airport, and be in Beecher at 3:00 P.M. She threw jeans and a stack of clean shirts into her small rolling bag, got the toiletries she needed, a nightgown, some sandals, and some papers she thought she might need. An hour later, she was ready when Edward arrived in his Aston Martin. She turned off the lights, locked her front door, ran out to the car, and hopped in.

"I can't thank you enough for doing this for me," she said gratefully, and as soon as they cleared the village, he put his foot on the gas, and never picked it up. They were on the freeway in no time, and they talked from time to time, but mostly he kept his mind and eyes on the road.

They reached the outskirts of London at 1:00 A.M., and they agreed that it made the most sense to take her directly to the airport, since she had to check in by 5:00 A.M. for the 7:00 A.M. flight.

He called Grace from the road and told her that he was coming in that night and why, and just listening to him talk to her made Winnie realize that what she wanted was a man who spoke to her like that. The tone of his voice told the woman at the other end how much he loved her, and couldn't wait to see her that night.

Edward dropped Winnie off at the international terminal at Heathrow at 1:30 A.M. and wished her luck. She had three and a half hours to spare before she had to check in, and could doze in a chair in the airport, and then get something to eat. She thanked Edward profusely again and he hugged her and told her to text him and let him know what was happening. He was worried about her and her nephew. She waved as he drove away, and walked into the terminal.

She couldn't call Marje because she was back at the hospital by then, so Winnie texted her to see how Jimmy was doing, and Marje texted back "No change," and Winnie responded with "Yet." She texted Nigel after that, and said that her nephew had had an accident, and she was flying home on a 7:00 A.M. flight, and would be back as soon as she could. She was sure he was sound asleep by then after a night at the pub, but at least he wouldn't worry when he didn't see her at work in the morning, or think something had happened to her.

She sat thinking about Marje and Jimmy until she boarded her flight. He'd been so sweet as a baby, and was so grown up now. This couldn't be happening to him. He had to wake up. She wanted to will him into opening his eyes and looking at his mother.

The flight took off on time, and she fell asleep almost as soon as it did, exhausted from being up all night, and before it took off, she texted Edward to thank him again. He had turned out to be even nicer than she'd expected, and she loved working for him. He was intelligent and down-to-earth, talented and disciplined, and modest, which was rare in his business. And thanks to the show, he was a rising star and his career had taken off. She was thinking about him when she fell asleep, and how lucky he and Grace were to have found each other thirteen years before. She hoped she met someone like him one day, minus the Aston Martin. She didn't need all the trappings of success and riches, just a good man to spend her life with.

The plane landed in New York at 9:00 A.M. local time, after a seven-hour flight. And she had an hour and a half before her flight to Detroit. She called Nigel then, and hoped he wasn't on the set. He couldn't answer if he was, and would have his phone on vibrate, but he was outside taking a break, and he picked up immediately, and sounded angry when he did.

"Where are you?"

"I'm in New York. On my way to Michigan. I'm between flights. My nephew had an accident. I sent you a text last night. Didn't you get it?"

"Yes, I got it. I went by your place last night. It was dark. Where are you, Winnie? Really. In London with Edward? I saw the call sheet. He's off for five days."

"He's with his girlfriend," Winnie said, shocked. "You think I'm lying to you? Do you want to call the hospital and check on my nephew? He's in a coma." Nigel sounded mollified for a minute, but uncertain as to whether to believe her or not.

"I'm sorry, if it's true."

"You know what, Nigel," she said, suddenly furious, "you're pathetic. Edward is madly in love with a woman he's been with for thirteen years. He treats me with respect, I don't think he even notices that I'm a woman, and you're so busy trying to catch me cheating on you that you can't even think straight and think I'm lying to you about my nephew being in a coma. This is sick."

"How did you get to London?" Nigel asked suspiciously.

"Edward drove me, so I could make a seven A.M. flight. Is that considered cheating too? We both had our clothes on, and he dropped me at the airport at one-thirty this morning and then he went home to his girlfriend. I'm sorry if that doesn't work for you, but with my nephew in a coma with a fractured skull, I was damn glad to get a lift."

"Why didn't you call me?"

"Because I'm sure you were drunk out of your mind by then, and you would have killed us both. Besides, you had to be at work this morning. He was going to London today anyway. It all made sense."

"How bad is your nephew?" he said, returning to the human race.

"It sounds bad. They might have to do brain surgery. I couldn't let my sister go through that without being there with her. I'll come back as soon as I can. But I don't want to hear about Edward anymore. It's gotten old, Nigel, it's just too much."

"I'm sorry. I just keep thinking that . . ."

"I know what you keep thinking, but you're wrong. I'll let you know when I'm coming back." She hung up then and texted Marje again. Marje wrote back that there was still no major change. Jimmy was still in a coma, but the swelling of his brain had decreased a little. At least that was a hopeful sign, but nothing else was encouraging. Her neighbor was taking care of Adam.

The flight to Detroit left only a few minutes late, and landed shortly before noon. She went straight to the rental car desk, picked up a car, and was on the road fifteen minutes later. She was going to go right to the hospital to meet her sister. She saw Erik crying in the parking lot when she got there and nearly had a heart attack. She parked the car at an angle in the nearest parking spot, jumped out of the car and ran over to him.

"What happened?"

"Nothing. I was just calling my office. Thank you for coming home, Win." He put his arms around her and hugged her and they both cried, and then went upstairs to the ICU together. Erik said they had picked Jimmy up by police rescue helicopter right from the neighbor's front lawn.

Marje saw her and came out and hugged her. She looked ravaged and pale and frightened, and Winnie wasn't prepared for the sight of her nephew, with tubes and monitors attached all over his body. His heart was beating steadily, and Marje said he had brain waves but he hadn't regained consciousness since the accident. But the swelling of his brain was coming down, so they had postponed surgery for now.

"I just want him to stay alive. I don't care if he's a vegetable," Marje said, sobbing, and Winnie turned to talk to Jimmy, and told him she had come to visit him all the way from England and she had a lot to tell him, so she expected him to wake up. She talked to him for about half an hour and then went out to the hall with Marje while Erik stayed with him.

They walked up and down the corridor for a

while, and then went back, the trauma team was checking Jimmy, and left after a few minutes. And at six o'clock Erik went to take Adam to dinner, who was worried sick about his brother too. When Erik left, Winnie went down to the cafeteria and brought back sandwiches for her and her sister, and the nurses brought them each a cup of coffee. It was one in the morning in England by then, and the time difference and travel were starting to catch up with Winnie. She needed the coffee. They took another walk around the floor, after they ate the sandwiches while sitting in the hall outside ICU, and when they went back, Winnie saw that a whole team of doctors were with Jimmy. Winnie couldn't see past them, with their backs turned, and both women were terrified of what they'd see when they entered the cubicle, but when they got there, one of the doctors turned and smiled at them. Jimmy opened his eyes, and looked straight at his mother. They had taken the tube out of his mouth, and his voice was a hoarse croak when he spoke to her.

"Hi, Mom," he said, and then he looked at his aunt. "Why are you here?"

"I missed you," she said as tears filled her eyes and spilled over onto her cheeks. "Actually, I came to beat you up for scaring the hell out of your mother," she added, and he smiled.

"Sorry, Mom." Marje was smiling through her tears and hiccupping on sobs.

"I love you. Thank you for waking up," she said to her son and touched his leg.

"Yeah, you've been pretty boring. I drove to London in an Aston Martin. I wanted to tell you about that," Winnie said to him.

"Cool," he said, and closed his eyes, tired from the effort he'd made, and he drifted back to sleep for a few minutes as the chief neurologist ushered them out of the room, walked out to the hallway with them, and gave them the rundown on his condition.

"He's not out of the woods yet. He's still at risk for seizures and complications from the brain injury. But I'm guardedly optimistic. We're heading in the right direction. And it's a great sign that he's regained consciousness." Marje was still crying in relief, and Winnie's legs felt like Jell-O. She had been terrified that they had lost him when they walked back in from the hall. "We should see ongoing progress from now on," the doctor told them. "Pool accidents can be ugly. Boys his age usually get cervical injuries from them, and wind up quadriplegic."

"I'm cementing over the neighbor's pool myself when we get home," she whispered to Winnie after the doctors left, and they walked back into Jimmy's room in the ICU. Erik returned from dinner ten minutes later, and Marje had saved the surprise for him. Jimmy said, "Hi, Dad," when Erik walked in, and Erik burst into tears like Marje and Winnie. He kissed Jimmy's cheek and told him how worried they'd been about him. And then Jimmy turned to Winnie.

"Where'd you get the Aston Martin?" he asked her, and they all laughed.

"Now we know you're not brain damaged. It belongs to my boss. He drove me to the airport."

"I want one, one day," he said dreamily.

"You must have fallen on your head," Winnie joked with him. It was a very different scene than it had been when she'd arrived five hours earlier. "Tell you what, I'll buy you one someday, if you promise never to scare us like this again." They talked to him for a while, then the nurses wanted him to go to sleep and get some rest. Marje had been planning to spend the night with him, but they told her she didn't need to, and they'd call if there were any problems. The three of them left Jimmy a few minutes later, and walked out to the parking lot together. The two sisters hugged each other in relief, and then Marje kissed her husband, and said she wanted to pick up Adam on the way home. They wanted to tell him the good news too.

Winnie followed them back to the house in her rented car, and when they got there, Marje turned to her sister.

"Do you want to stay here tonight?" Winnie nodded. She didn't want to go back to her place just yet. She wanted to be with them. They'd all been through a lot worrying about Jimmy. Marje pulled out the convertible couch in the playroom for her, and they made the bed together, and then Winnie put on her nightgown while she talked to her sister. She had been terrified of a very different outcome when she caught the plane at Heathrow that morning. And from everything the doctor had said, Jimmy had been very lucky.

"You're happy over there, aren't you?" Marje asked her sadly.

"I like my job, and I love the show. I'm glad I went. I don't know how I got the guts to do it, but I'm glad I did."

"And Nigel?"

Winnie shrugged in answer. "It's kind of up and down. They've had some problems on the show, and he's worried about his job. That doesn't bring out the best in anyone. And he's insanely jealous of my boss, and afraid I'm going to sleep with him." She looked tired as she said it.

"And are you?" Marje looked interested and Winnie shook her head.

"No, he's a great guy, in love with a terrific woman. They've been together for thirteen years, and I actually think he's faithful to her. But Nigel doesn't believe it. I'm not sure we're going anywhere, or that we should. His jealousy has really turned me off." Marje was disappointed to hear it. There was no point going all the way to England to wind up in another dead-end situation. And Winnie thought that herself, she just hadn't dealt with it yet.

"I ran into Rob and Barb the other day," Marje said cautiously, not sure if she should tell her.

"Separately or together?" Winnie asked her.

"Together. I gather from her mother that the dentist found out about Rob and canceled the wedding, so she and Rob have been dating since you left."

"They deserve each other," Winnie said without regret and lay down on the bed. Marje bent down to kiss her and the two sisters smiled at each other. "I'm glad you got your boy back. I think telling him about the Aston Martin did it." They both laughed and Marje walked up the stairs from the playroom, feeling a hundred years old. They had been the worst days of her life, and she was grateful to Winnie for coming home. Erik was waiting for her in their bedroom, and Adam was already in bed.

Marje was so tired she could hardly brush her teeth and put her nightgown on, and Erik put an arm around her as she got into bed.

"Thank God he woke up," Erik said with deep emotion in his voice.

"I don't think I could have survived it if he didn't," she said, exhausted.

"We'd have had to for Adam. We don't have to think about that now."

"The doctor said he may have headaches for a

while. And he's not going back to that pool again."
Erik smiled at what she said.

"How long is your sister here for?"

"I didn't ask her. I'm just glad she came." He nodded and turned off the light. They lay in bed, holding each other, slowly returning from the terror they'd lived through. Winnie was already sound asleep in the playroom. It had been the longest, most terrifying day of her life.

Chapter Eleven

Winnie texted Edward and Nigel when she woke up the next morning to tell them that her nephew was out of the coma, though still under observation and in the ICU. Edward texted her back immediately to tell her he was relieved, and to stay as long as she needed to. Nigel sent a message a few minutes later, telling her he was happy for her and wanting to know when she was coming back. She answered him that she didn't know, but would let him know when she did.

They stopped at Winnie's house on the way to the hospital. Everything looked clean and in good order. It hadn't rented yet. Marje said the realtor had shown it to a doctor who had just come from Detroit to work at the hospital, and liked the idea of renting a furnished house until he got situated and found something to buy, but he hadn't made a decision yet.

"How long do you think you'll stay over there?" Marje asked when they were back in the car, on their way to see Jimmy.

"I just don't know. I have a job I love, and I have nothing to rush back for here except you and the kids. And I won't find a job here I like as much."

"Not working for a TV star," Marje said regretfully. And as they drove down the street, everything looked familiar to Winnie, but she suddenly realized she had no attachment to it. It didn't feel like home anymore. It felt like someone else's town, her mother's, her sister's, but no longer hers. Something inside her had come unhooked, but she didn't mention it to Marje. It would panic her sister if she thought Winnie wasn't coming back. Winnie didn't know if she would or not. But it was interesting being here, and being aware of how little she felt. It was good seeing Marje, Erik, and the kids, but not much else.

"Thanks for telling me about Rob and Barb last night. I'd have been pissed if I'd seen them walking down the street together and you hadn't told me."

"That's what I thought. Do you care?"

"Not a bit," Winnie said honestly. "They're both dead as far as I'm concerned." Marje nodded and didn't comment. She didn't think she could have recovered from it herself.

Jimmy was sitting up in bed when they got to the hospital. He said he had a headache, but the nurses weren't surprised. They got him out of bed and had him walk a few steps, but he got dizzy very quickly and had to sit down, which they said was to be expected. He wanted to hear about the Aston Martin again and how fast they'd gone. And when the doctor saw him, he said they wanted him in the hospital for a week for observation, to make sure he had no complications before he went home. Jimmy was upset about it, but all the adults thought it made perfect sense. Adam came to see him that afternoon and brought him a pizza, and they shared it for dinner. Jimmy's appetite hadn't come back yet. Adam was beaming and peaceful after he saw him. Winnie drove him home after the visit.

"I thought he was going to die, Aunt Win," Adam said in a small voice.

"I think that occurred to all of us, but he's going to be fine now. He's very lucky, and so are we." Adam nodded again and looked subdued when he got out of the car. Almost losing his brother had been terrifying for him, and for all of them.

When Marje came home from the hospital, the adults had dinner together, and Winnie told them about her work on the set and how interesting and rewarding it was, and how huge a crew it took to film the show. She told them about Alexander Nichols, their historical consultant, and the manners coach, who advised them about every aspect of appropriate behaviors and manners of the time, how the women should sit and stand, what they could and couldn't say, and he was just as rigorous about the men in the cast. He would stop them from filming the instant anyone made a faux pas about the customs of the period.

"I thought he was a pill at first," Winnie said to them, "but he's brilliant. He knows everything about the era. He goes around with a ruler measuring how far apart people should sit. He's what keeps the show historically accurate and so believable. It's fascinating to listen to him," she said, her eyes shining brightly in admiration of how the show was made. "And the castle they use is beautiful. I took a tour when I got there. The descendants of the original family that built it still live there. Having the show use their castle as the location helped them to keep from selling it. They were dead broke before the show. There's a book about them I can send you if you want." She loved everything she had learned and what she was doing there and they could see it.

"I'd rather watch a reality show about them," Marje said and all three of them laughed.

The day after, Winnie made a reservation to leave the next day. There was nothing more for her to do, and Jimmy was out of danger. She had to get back to work. She wanted to get back and be on the set the same day that Edward returned, which seemed only fair. She'd come to Michigan for an emergency, not a vacation. Her stay had been action-packed and had a happy ending. And more than ever, she felt as though she didn't belong there, although she never said it to Marje. She had found greener pastures in a bigger world, not where she'd expected to find them, but in a place that suited her. She was eager to get back to her cottage and daily routine.

She said goodbye to Jimmy at the hospital that night, and to Adam and Erik the next morning at breakfast. She had another half hour of sisterly gossip with Marje and then she had to leave for the drive back to Detroit. She was following the same route that she'd come by.

"I get the feeling you don't feel like you belong here anymore," Marje said cautiously as they shared a last cup of coffee.

"In some ways I don't," Winnie said honestly, "in other ways I always will. I like living in England for now."

"Mom always said you don't belong here, and would end up somewhere more sophisticated." It was odd how different the two sisters were. Winnie couldn't imagine Marje anywhere else and neither could she.

She hugged Marje close before she left for the drive to Detroit, and realized how much she had missed her. "I'll call you when I get back," she promised. Nigel had been driving her crazy with texts every day, asking when she was coming back. But she was getting in too late to see him, and would meet up with him at work the next day. It seemed soon enough. She wasn't in the mood for his jealousy and accusations, and crazy assumptions about her boss.

She turned the car in, in Detroit, and caught the

flight to New York. She texted Marje that she'd landed safely, and walked around the airport before the next flight. She felt as though she were going home. She watched two movies and had a meal on the flight to London, and slept for an hour before they landed. And although she'd only been at Heathrow twice before, it really did feel like home when she got there. She took a train back to King's Lynn, a taxi from there to the village, and smiled when she walked into her cottage. She didn't even want to call Nigel, or miss him. She was thrilled to be there in her bed alone.

In the morning, she got up, showered and dressed and made breakfast, and walked to work. She was happy to see all the familiar faces, and then she saw Nigel watching her. He walked over slowly and gave her a hug.

"You didn't call me last night when you got in," he said softly.

"I got in very late. I didn't want to wake you." He nodded and went back to work. She walked to Edward's trailer to report for work, and she saw Nigel watching her when she left the set.

"How did it go?" Edward asked as soon as he saw her. He looked fresh and happy and relaxed.

"He'll be fine. He came out of the coma the day I got there, and he's making steady progress. He has headaches, but it could have been a lot worse." It could have been a tragedy, and she was grateful it hadn't been. "How were your days off?"

"We went to Venice for the weekend, and I proposed," he said proudly. "We're going to get married next year. Grace is going to break the news to her father next week."

"Congratulations!" Winnie smiled at him. "Where are you going to get married?"

"Someplace gorgeous and romantic that we both love. The Caribbean, St. Bart's, Tahiti, the top of a mountain, or in our apartments. We haven't figured it out yet. Her father will probably want us to do it at his club. We want to avoid that at all cost. But wherever we do it, it's time. We've waited long enough." Thirteen years seemed like more than enough to Winnie. And she hoped Grace's father didn't give them a hard time. They didn't deserve it and Edward would be a wonderful husband.

He gave her some projects to do for him while he studied his lines and got ready for their shooting schedule that day. His costumes were lined up on a rack, and the hairdresser was coming to trim his hair. Winnie handed him his schedule a few minutes later and he smiled at her.

"It's nice to have you back." He loved how organized she was, and how efficiently she kept his life on track.

He was on the set on time for every shot, knew his lines flawlessly, as he always did. The day unrolled smoothly like a carpet, and they both left work on time at six o'clock. And when she left, Nigel was waiting for her outside.

"Want a ride home?"

"Sure." She smiled at him and got in the Jeep, and hoped he wouldn't mention Edward again. He didn't, and he came in while she made dinner for both of them, and they enjoyed a relaxed evening together and went up to bed. Their lovemaking was tender and sweet. When he was that way, she always hoped that things would work out between them. But when he played the jealous lover, all she wanted to do was get away from him. She was happy he hadn't done that tonight. It was a perfect home-coming, and just what she needed from him.

For the next week on the set everything went smoothly, and everyone seemed in a good mood, even Nigel. Winnie noticed Matthew sitting on the sidelines several times that week, and then conferring with Michael and nodding. She wondered if he had figured out a storyline yet to cover Bill and Elizabeth's absence the following season, and if they would be bringing in new actors. At the end of the day on Friday, before a weekend off, the production team called a general meeting, and when she got there, Winnie saw Matthew waiting to speak to all of them, and she got an odd feeling about it. He waited until everyone was there before he started.

Before saying anything else, he praised them for how exciting the season had been. They had a week left in their shooting schedule before the hiatus, and he said he thought it had been their best season. The most impressive and the most professional, and breathtaking in every way. He said what they'd been shooting would play in the coming months as their seventh season. They were due to return in October to shoot the following season, but he didn't mention it. Everyone knew it anyway. He said he'd been working frantically to come up with alternate plot lines to explain Elizabeth and Bill's absence from the series. And he had come to the conclusion that no matter how many new actors they added or plot turns he devised, they had already given the viewers their best work, and it would be a mistake to dilute it now or trivialize it in some way, and disappoint people. He said every show had its lifetime and he had realized that **Beauchamp Hall** had reached the end of its natural life, and trying to extend it artificially would be a grave mistake. So with gratitude to everyone involved and great regrets, they were canceling the show, and ending it when they finished shooting the remaining episodes. He had tears in his eyes when he said it, and added, "I will never be able to thank you enough for the life you have breathed into this series. We have pleased people all over the globe and given meaning to their lives, just as you have to mine. From the bottom of my heart, I thank you. I'll miss **Beauchamp** as much as you will, and much, much more," he said, and then walked quietly off the set with tears running down his cheeks. The entire cast and crew sat mesmerized, watching him go, as though they hadn't understood what he told them, and then burst into tears and hugged each other. It was over. They had pulled the plug. **Beauchamp Hall** would never have another season beyond the one they were shooting now. It would be over forever in a week, and all the joy it represented for the viewers and for those who made it. After almost seven years, it was finished.

There was chaos on the set for half an hour, and then people disbanded, to discuss it among themselves, digest it, mourn it, and celebrate it. Winnie made her way to where Edward was sitting and he looked like he was in shock.

"Are you okay?" she asked him and he nodded.

"I'm stunned. I didn't expect that, but maybe I should have when Liz and Bill left. I thought he'd pull a rabbit out of the hat one more time. But no more rabbit, no more hat. I'll be okay," he reassured her, and also himself. "I'd better call my agent tomorrow."

"You'll get another series," she said with conviction. He was one of the best actors on the show, and the most reliable, even if he didn't have top billing, which was the problem. The actors who had left them flat were their strongest and most marketable, and Matthew didn't think they had a viable series without them, no matter how talented the rest of the cast was. He didn't want to weaken the show now with inadequate support, and new stars who couldn't carry it.

When Edward left the set to call his agent and fiancée, she went to look for Nigel and couldn't find him at first, and then she saw him in a knot of sound technicians who looked thunderstruck. They had feared that the end was coming, but no one was sure until now. Now it was certain. The worst had happened. The end had come for all of them. Matthew had always pulled it off before, but this time he refused to. He didn't want people comparing the show to what it had been and not liking it as much, or sponsors abandoning them. It was a reasonable concern, and had been a wise decision, and surely a hard one, that would affect a multitude of people, all of whom had just lost their jobs.

"Are you okay?" she asked Nigel when she walked over to him. He looked both angry and sad at the same time.

"Do I have a choice?" he said with an ironic look.

"There's always a choice," Winnie said gently. "Especially in how you look at it."

"Don't give me that philosophical Pollyanna bullshit. I just lost my job, and God knows where I'll be working two months from now. Probably somewhere heinous on a shit show, or wherever the union sends me. There's something to look forward to. And they certainly didn't give us much notice. They never do when they cancel a show."

"So I've been told," she said, sympathetically. "I think they just made the decision. Bill and Elizabeth didn't give them much notice either. Do you want to come home with me?" she offered. This was a blow and a loss for her too.

"I'm going out with the guys," he said with a hard edge to his voice, as though their canceling the show was somehow her fault. She was sad about it, very sad, but it wasn't as devastating to her. She loved the show, but didn't need it to survive. He did. She had come here on a lark, taken a break from her life, and fallen in love with the people involved and the production. But she could still go back where she came from, in theory. Except she didn't want to, even now. She wanted it to go on forever, but destiny, and the writer, had decided otherwise. She had no idea what to do or where to go next.

She walked home alone, feeling sad about the show being canceled and almost like a symbol of closure, she saw Rupert with his food truck. She had seen him when she first arrived, and now here he was again. She hadn't noticed him in weeks.

She stopped to say hello, and he looked as devastated as the crew and cast when they left the set. "I just heard. That's terrible news for all of us. The town will never be the same without **Beauchamp Hall.** The show saved us. There won't be any jobs here again now. All the life will go out of the place."

"What about you, Rupert?" she asked him with concern. "Will you be okay?"

"I'll have to give up the truck. I'll sell it. No customers after you lot go. There may be a few tourists for a while, but not enough to live on. I feed the crew every day. They won't be here now. Another week and it's all over for me, and a lot of people around here. This is a hard blow for us. I guess I'll go back to what I was doing before. I'm a chimney sweep. I hate it, but there it is. My father was too. I sold the business when I bought the truck. I'd rather sell tea and orange juice than be crawling up everyone's chimneys with a black face for the rest of my life." His voice quavered as he said it, and her heart went out to him.

"I'm sorry," she said gently, listening to him for a few more minutes, and then they said goodbye and she went home. It was going to be a tough situation for the villagers, not just the cast and crew. Matthew Stevens had made a big decision that had hit them all hard, and as Winnie walked the rest of the way to the cottage, she was crying too.

Chapter Twelve

Winnie spent a quiet night watching old **Beauchamp** DVDs from previous seasons. There had been some incredibly wonderful episodes and twists and turns of events. Unforgettable moments, and spectacular performances from amazing actors who had brought their talents and well-honed skills to the show. Many who had grown from being on it. And a few who had gone, thinking they were forging ahead to greatness, and instead had disappeared, as often happened when actors left a successful series. Thinking about ending the show now made her sad. But losing two major players, shortly after losing two others, was a crippling blow Matthew Stevens didn't think the show could recover from, and possibly he was right. They couldn't afford to lose that much. The hole in the hull was too big now for the ship to sail on. And he was left to wrap up all the plots and subplots as elegantly as he could with the cast and material on hand. Winnie was sure it would be a challenging task.

When she got up in the morning, the day after the announcement, she realized that Nigel hadn't called her the night before. His concern about his future had given him a sharp edge recently, and that coupled with his unfounded jealousy of Edward had impacted their relationship considerably, and it wasn't likely to get better now. She hadn't come to any definite conclusions about it, but he wasn't seeking solace with her, instead he was at the bars with his coworkers. And she suspected he'd been too drunk to come over the previous night, so it was probably just as well that he hadn't.

She was thinking about him when she made a stop at the dry cleaner on her way to work. They had all gotten a text asking them to work through the weekend to shoot the final scenes until they wrapped. They had a lot of work to do with new scripts to conclude the show.

She dropped off her laundry too. She didn't have the convenience of Mrs. Flannagan's two big washing machines now that she had her own cottage. There was a tiny machine that didn't work very well.

She found herself standing behind a familiar blond figure ahead of her. When the woman turned around, Winnie could see that it was Lady Beatrice Haversham, and this time she didn't smile when she saw Winnie, although she recognized her.

"Bad news yesterday," Lady Beatrice said cryptically. She didn't know what Winnie's job was, but knew where she worked. "It'll be back to Poverty Flats for us, when the show goes. My brother and I will be selling scones and pencils on the street one of these days." Winnie hoped she didn't mean it, but clearly the castle was expensive to maintain, and the show had provided a big cushion for them, and been their primary source of income for the last seven years. "And not much notice on top of it. It'll be all over in a week. It's quite a shock." There was a sad look in her eyes.

"People will want to come and visit here for a long time," Winnie said, trying to sound encouraging, but the young noblewoman shook her head.

"Not for long. They'll forget. They'll fall in love with some other show, and we'll fade back into the mist like all the other great houses with owners who've run out of money. Faded curtains run out of charm rather quickly, when there's nothing else going on there. The show was a great blessing for us for a long time. I'm grateful for it, but the situation is going to be dire for all of us who depended on **Beauchamp Hall.** My brother is going to have to sell his horses, like it or not."

"Just so you don't sell the house," Winnie said, deeply moved by her admissions.

"It could come to that. That's where we were when they decided to set up the show here. We had just come to the conclusion that we'd have to sell. We've had a nearly seven-year reprieve. But half the businesses in town will be closed this time next year, and us along with them." It was in fact the situation the British aristocracy had been in for the last hundred years, their lifestyle dramatically changed, their homes in jeopardy, trying to squeeze out enough to live on however they could. There was a long list of houses in England, castles, manor homes, and great halls that the public could tour.

"Don't give up yet. You'll figure something out. The show must have come as a surprise when it happened. As they say, 'They're not the only show in town.'"

"They are in this town," Lady Beatrice said realistically. "No one will set up a show here again. It's been done. We'll have to get creative, but I haven't figured out how yet. My brother is more inclined to wait for a miracle to fall from the sky." Winnie remembered that it was Lady Beatrice who had written the book, and whom she saw from time to time on the set, conferring with the producers and consulting on the show. She knew everything there was to know about the history of the house, who had visited there and stayed there, and colorful anecdotes that turned up in the plot. Her brother never seemed to be around, although he lived at Haversham too. He looked more aloof the few times Winnie had glimpsed him. Lady Beatrice seemed more down-to-earth, and engaged with people around her, as she was with Winnie now. "I suppose I'll see you around for a while longer," she said almost wistfully and Winnie smiled.

"We'll all be sad to leave and I've only been here since May."

"We'll be equally sad to see you go." She smiled warmly and then left, and Winnie paid for the sheets they had laundered and the skirt she'd had cleaned. She thought about Lady Beatrice as she walked up to the castle, and what a blow this was for them. Winnie felt very sorry for her. Others weren't as interested in the family, and thought they were just a bunch of silly old snobs who were no longer relevant, but Winnie had been intrigued by them since the first time she'd seen the show. The history of the castle and the family gave credibility to the whole series, and the issues they had dealt with at the time. And what they were dealing with now wasn't much different. They were fighting to keep their heads above water and were the last survivors of a lost world.

Winnie went to look for Nigel as soon as she got to the set, and forgot about the Havershams. She was worried about him.

"How was last night?" She tried to sound light about it, but he looked rough.

"About the way you'd expect. Sorry I didn't make it over. At least I had the good sense not to knock on your door. You should be glad I didn't. I called the union yesterday. There are half a dozen new shows starting. The new ones are pretty well staffed by now, but something will turn up." He tried to sound optimistic, but didn't look it, and she knew pride had kicked in. He didn't want to look pathetic to her. She kissed his cheek lightly and headed for Edward's trailer. He was reading the London **Financial Times** when she walked in, and seemed surprisingly calm, when he looked up and smiled at her.

"Wow, everyone's in an uproar all over town. The food truck, the Havershams, the sound guys," she said to him.

"It's going to make a hell of a difference to the locals. The rest of us should be used to it. It's the nature of the business. I called my agent last night. He's not worried. We've turned down some good parts in new series recently. If they haven't filled the parts, I liked a couple of them very much. One in particular, and I hated to turn it down." He was the consummate professional, and Winnie was impressed by how calm and philosophical he was. "The ones who will probably take a hard hit are the small businesses who depend on us and have done well because of us for all these years. And the Havershams were probably hanging by a shoelace when we got here. Running a place like this costs a fortune. They won't be able to afford to without the show."

"I saw Lady Beatrice at the laundry this morning, and that's pretty much what she said. And I get the feeling they may not have been saving a lot of it, between upkeep and expenses." She had looked seriously worried.

"Her brother has some very fancy horses and cars. He gave me a tour of all of it one day."

"She said he'll have to sell his horses."

"I'm not surprised. That's the trouble with the aristos, they always put their money on the wrong stuff. They have no sense of commerce or investment, they're not equipped for the modern world. You'd think they'd have learned that much by now."

"She seems pretty practical," Winnie defended her.

"I'll wager you her brother isn't, not with a stable like that. And he has some fabulous antique cars in the barn. He has three or four Bugattis, he let me drive one of them. I'd have bought it from him, but I couldn't afford it, and he wouldn't sell it. Great car to own, just for the thrill of it." Edward loved cars, and had several of his own, including a Ferrari, a Lamborghini, and the Aston Martin he'd used to drive Winnie to the airport.

Other than Edward, who seemed remarkably stable, the whole cast seemed distracted, anxious, and off-kilter that day. Actors who normally learned their lines perfectly were stumbling and blowing them, with new scripts they had to learn rapidly. One of the producers had distributed new scripts to the entire cast. Matthew had reworked the storylines and outcomes leading up to the end, to conclude the show. It was a challenge to make it all go smoothly and tie up all the loose ends, so people who had studied the scripts and knew their lines had to learn an entirely new script for each remaining day. It would be that way now for the next week until the end. And they all expected to work overtime to finish it.

It was a long stressful day, and even Edward looked tired by the end of it, and Winnie felt drained. She was so worried about everyone that she was distracted too. She hadn't called Marje to tell her the news about the show being canceled. She didn't want to mislead her and give her the impression that she was coming home. Going back to Beecher after Jimmy's accident had convinced Winnie that she didn't belong there, at least not yet. She hadn't played out her hand in England, and Edward had said that day that he wanted to take her with him if he got a part on a new show. It was an appealing idea and she was flattered. But he didn't have a new show yet and they still had **Beauchamp Hall** to deal with, before she thought of anything else. For now, and for some time, Michigan was not in her plans.

Marje called her a few days later, and had heard a rumor that the show had been canceled. They'd said it on **Entertainment Tonight.**

"Is that true?" She sounded shocked.

"Unfortunately, yes. They announced it to the cast and crew a few days ago. They're not going to shoot a new season. After this one, we're done. They're wrapping up the conclusion now. Everyone is very upset about it, even the local townspeople." Marje could hear that she was sad as she said it.

"Does that mean you're coming home, Win?" She sounded hopeful, which was exactly what Winnie had wanted to avoid. "Should I take your house off the market to rent?"

"I don't think I'll come home for a while. I still want to rent it."

"What would you do there without the show?" Winnie could tell she was disappointed.

"I'm trying to figure it out, we all are. My boss offered me a job as his assistant, if he gets another series, and he probably will. He's hot right now. **Beauchamp** really put him on the map. I could do that. I like working for him. He's very business-like and matter-of-fact and polite, not like a lot of other actors." She hadn't been favorably impressed by many she'd seen, except him. She liked work-ing for him even more than she had for Elizabeth, who had been very flighty, although she was sweet and good to Winnie. But Elizabeth's personal life was a mess, with the affair with Bill Anders. They were still all over the press, even after she left the show. Edward kept his private life much more dis-creet. "I'll let you know what I'm doing, when I know." She asked about Jimmy then, and Marje said he was doing well, and the headaches had got-ten better.

Nigel came over that night and hadn't been there in three days, a long time for him. But he just hadn't been in the mood. He was quiet that night too. She didn't ask if the union had called about upcoming jobs. She didn't want to upset him more than he was.

"I may stay with my parents for a while after we wrap," he said quietly. "Or go to stay with my cousin in Ireland. Would you want to come, Winnie?"

"I might," she said vaguely. "I haven't figured out my plans yet either." And then she decided to tell him. "Edward offered me a job on his next show, when he gets one. I might do that. He's good to work for. Simple and direct, and no nonsense. He's a pro." Nigel looked depressed by what she said.

"Are you in love with him?"

"Not at all. He just got engaged, and he's crazy about her. They're getting married fairly soon. He's not a cheater. And neither am I." Nigel had heard it all before and didn't believe her, but this time he looked as though he might. He was so down and lethargic he was even less jealous.

"I don't know if that's true about him. But I think it is about you," he said fairly, for the first time. "What do I have to offer you anyway? You'd have a much better life with him. I'm just a broke sound guy, about to be out of a job."

"You'll have another job soon. And he's not offering me a 'better life,' he's offering that to his fiancée, some lord's daughter in London. I'm no fancier than you are. He's offering me a job, not marriage."

"You won't go home to Michigan?" He seemed surprised.

"I don't know yet. I haven't decided. It seemed pretty dreary when I went back. I've gotten spoiled here. I love it."

"Well, you can't stay here when the series ends. It'll be a ghost town, half the shops will be closed, and people will have to go to other towns for jobs. That's what England is like these days."

"Beecher isn't exactly a hot job market either. That's why I left. I didn't want to work at a motel, or the hardware store."

"You'd look cute in a set of overalls," he teased her. "Small towns are like that."

"I should have gone to New York fifteen years ago, but I didn't. I missed my chance. I can't start out there at my age. And I really love it here. I'll be sad to move on."

"Won't we all," he said wistfully.

They made love that night, but he didn't spend the night. Their relationship seemed more tenuous now, like a summer romance as the leaves begin to fall. They could both sense a reckoning time coming and needed to face if the relationship was viable or not. She wasn't looking forward to that either. And she didn't think their brief romance would survive.

She picked up the book about the Havershams from her night table after Nigel left, to help her sleep. She liked reading in bed. She fell asleep with the light on and the book in her hands. She slept fitfully, woke, dozed, and woke again, with strange people she didn't know in and out of her dreams. She was in a grand house surrounded by people and there was a woman in a wedding gown, and a director shouting at all of them that someone had been murdered and everybody laughed. It felt like a nightmare, but it wasn't, and she sat up in bed with a jolt at four in the morning, shaking, and everything about the dream came clear. She thought it was important, and wanted to remember all of it. She grabbed a yellow pad she kept on her night table for lists of things she had to do, found a pen beside it, and began writing down the dream frantically, before any of it could slip away.

The people the director had been shouting at were actors, but at the same time she knew they were guests. They were all in elaborate period costumes like the ones on the show, she even recognized one or two of them as gowns Elizabeth had worn. The bride in the midst of it was real, and the murder a hoax, which was why everyone laughed. And then they had all taken a tour of the castle, where scenes from the series were being played out in different rooms by the actors, but Winnie could see now that they were being played out on giant video screens. They all left the castle via some kind of museum where Rupert was selling souvenirs, cups and mugs and plates, beautiful hats and tiaras, and they were all being interviewed by reporters. She realized that the bride she had seen was Edward's fiancée, Grace, and he was with her. She'd only seen Grace in photographs so far, but she was sure it was her. Grace looked ecstatically happy, and everyone including the reporters threw rose petals at them as they drove away in Rupert's food truck with JUST MARRIED written on the back. The dream was crazy, but parts of it made sense to her. She read what she'd written over and over again, and added to it, and then divided it into sections. Some sounded more lucid than others. She tried telling herself that the whole thing was ridiculous, and turned off the light at five-thirty and tried to get another hour or two of sleep, but she was too excited to drift off, and kept thinking of more things she remembered to add to her notes. By eight o'clock, she was certain that the dream had been an inspiration, and she knew who she wanted to share it with.

She dug through some production notes and papers, and found the general number for the castle, in case of some major problem on the set, if there was an emergency like a flood or a leak, or a major power outage. She wasn't sure if a butler or a janitor or a property manager would answer, and instead she recognized the voice of Lady Beatrice Haversham. She was having breakfast and sounded surprised by the call.

Winnie explained who she was, and reminded her of where they'd met.

"Yes, yes, I know," Lady Beatrice said, sounding worried. "Do we have a leak from the upstairs master bath into the library again?"

"No, everything's fine. I know this sounds a little odd, but could I meet with you at lunchtime or after work today? I had an idea I'd like to share with you."

"If it incorporates murdering an irresponsible brother, I'd be most willing," she said crisply. "He drove my car into a pond yesterday. Odd, he never does that kind of thing with his own, or his Bugattis." Winnie laughed, but Lady Beatrice did not sound amused. "Might I ask what this is about, by the way?"

"It's too complicated to explain on the phone."

"Ah, very well. After I dispose of my brother's body and fish my car, or what's left of it, out of the pond, I'll be free at noon. Come in through the door to the family living quarters. I'll meet you in the main parlor. It's a bit dusty, I'm afraid, I haven't had time to hoover in there for three weeks, but meeting you in our boot room seems a bit rude." Winnie had seen all of it on the tour except the private quarters, but it suddenly seemed more personal going there to see Lady Beatrice. It sounded exciting, and so was her dream.

● ● ●

Edward noticed her high spirits when she got to work, but she didn't explain it to him. He guessed it was due to a romance, but didn't ask her. She warned him before he walked onto the set to play a scene that she would be leaving a few minutes before noon for an appointment. He had no problem with it. Alexander Nichols, their historical consultant, was on the set, correcting them just as intensely right to the end. He wanted everything to be perfect and was relentless to ensure it.

She left the set and walked around to the back of the castle, and wandered in through the back door the Havershams used now as their private entrance. There were two small sitting rooms for visitors to wait in, but most of the furniture and paintings had been removed to use as props on the set, and she walked past them into an enormous parlor filled with sunlight, overscale antiques and magnificent paintings, some as high as six and seven feet tall, and the ceilings were high too. It was a splendid room. They had filmed there a few times in the first two seasons, then decided there were other rooms they preferred, and the Havershams had been happy to reclaim it for their own use. It had been called the "day parlor" in the heyday of the house.

Winnie wandered around looking up at the paintings, and stood gazing intently at one of a woman riding sidesaddle on a white horse, and she jumped when she heard a voice behind her.

"That's my great-great-aunt Charlotte. She was quite mad apparently, but lovely to look at, and very amusing." Winnie turned to see Lady Beatrice in a crisp white men's shirt, tailored to fit her, jodhpurs that were obviously custom-made, and perfectly polished tall black riding boots, with her blond hair cascading down her back. She was every bit as beautiful as the woman in the painting.

"Thank you for seeing me," Winnie said, somewhat cowed by the surroundings, and feeling shy now that she was face-to-face with the lady of the house, who would surely think she was "quite mad" too, once she explained her dream, and her interpretation of it.

"Don't be silly, of course. Won't you sit down?" Winnie did, at the edge of a large antique chair covered in deep red velvet that was frayed but still impressive. "Would you like some tea?"

"No, I'm fine, thank you."

"Sorry I look like this. I got the damn car out of the pond. I'm not sure we can get it running again. My brother is an incredible nuisance." She looked as exasperated as she had sounded that morning on the phone. "No one should have to live with their siblings past the age of eight. We shipped him off to Eton and Cambridge, but he always came back. And now we're stuck with each other, trying to run this place. And there's always some little actress to chase, with the show here, although that will be all over now. He'll be bored to sobs once they leave. But so will I. And broke as well, so dreary." She sank into a velvet couch facing Winnie, with an enormous painting over it, of another of her ancestors, but didn't explain who it was. "So what did you have in mind?" She talked a lot, but was light-hearted, articulate, and funny, and very British. The series was full of people with accents just like hers, which they imitated to perfection, with the help of diction coaches to make them sound upper crust, whatever their origins. Lady Beatrice always found it amusing.

"I had a dream last night," Winnie started cautiously.

"Oh dear, not a bad one, I hope. I hope you haven't come to warn me of some dreadful premonition. I'm frightfully superstitious and shan't sleep for weeks."

"No, a good one. At least I think so. And I know it sounds terribly presumptuous, but you mentioned the other day how concerned you are about the fate of Haversham, and even the village, once the show moves on. And it worries me too. I love it here, I fell in love with the show months ago, but now I've fallen in love with the people here, the village, and the castle, and what it means to everyone. It's been troubling me, and I think that's how the dream happened. It was all an insane jumble, but I pulled it apart when I woke up, and made

some notes. I think you have some amazing possi-
bilities here to make Haversham Castle even more
important, and even more lucrative than it was as
Beauchamp Hall."

"How do you imagine that?" Beatrice Haversham
looked skeptical. "I've rattled my brain too and all
I can come up with is selling lemonade and bis-
cuits at the door after our beastly tour, which will
be even more boring now."

"It doesn't have to be. You have some opportunities you may not have explored yet. First of all,
weddings. What more fabulous place to have a wedding? Holkham Hall does them near here, and
I'm told they do very well with them. There have
been several weddings in the series, and they've been
spectacular. People will want to get married here because they've seen the weddings on the show, which
makes this a highly desirable location. You can do
less expensive weddings in the house, all carefully
organized in a package. They could be period weddings in costume, if you like. You might be able to
buy some of the costumes when the show leaves.
You could do more elaborate weddings with tents
outside. All you need is a good caterer and florist,
and this would be an ideal venue in the future. If
you can organize some of the rooms, the wedding
party could stay here." Beatrice nodded, thinking
about it.

"Getting the costumes would be a great idea.

They had five hundred extras for one of the weddings they did here," she mused pensively.

"Second, mystery weekends. Again in period costumes. People love them. They do them in the States. A group of people rent the castle for the weekend, it doesn't have to be many. Fifteen or twenty, which is manageable. They wear costumes. You have a script, and they enact a mystery, usually a murder. And they have to solve it by the end of the weekend. Wonderful for a birthday or a house party, or some sort of small corporate event. You could charge a lot of money for it. Someone would have to write the scripts they can all follow. A bit like the game of Clue, but in a real castle in real life. You could use the same script for each group, except for repeat guests.

"Third. A **Beauchamp** museum for crazies like me who love the show. You could set aside a few of the rooms that were used regularly on the show, have screens in the room with scenes playing in the rooms where they were shot. You could add that as a piece of modern history, as part of the life of the castle. And I know it's embarrassing, but a gift shop somewhere with souvenirs of the castle and the show, mugs, plates, tea services, all the things that the fans love and buy on the Internet. You can have some local girl selling them after the tour, with your book of course.

"And, lastly, you may hate it, but it's a possibility.

A reality show on television of the life of the castle today, with you and your brother. They could film weddings that happen here, and mystery weekends. Your brother with his cars and horses. They'd even enjoy your car falling into the pond. It's a vulgar idea, but could be done tastefully. People love royalty and aristocracy, and a peek into life at the castle might excite them as much as the series now. And the truth is you could make a fortune on it, if you can stand doing it. And seeing what's happening here on a reality show would make them flock here in droves. They'd be throwing money at you to get in." Winnie fell silent when she was finished as Beatrice Haversham stared at her.

"Good Lord! That wasn't a dream, it was a nightmare! You dreamt all that?" Winnie nodded. "But what an amazing lot of ideas. I have to think about it, but some part of it actually might work. Why on earth did you trouble yourself about how to solve our problems?" As she spoke, her brother walked into the room frowning, with a puzzled expression.

"Have you seen my riding crop, Bea? I can't find it. I'm going out on Comet in a few minutes. Oh, sorry, I didn't know you had a guest," he said when he saw Winnie.

"I did see it. I broke it in half and threw it in the rubbish. Thank you for drowning my car."

"Don't be silly, it'll be fine. And you should have

thrown it in the rubbish years ago. What are you doing throwing my crop away?" He glanced from his sister to Winnie as he said it. He was an incredibly good-looking man, with all the marks of good breeding, and was wearing jodhpurs and boots like his sister.

Lady Beatrice turned to her brother with a disgusted expression. "My brother, the Marquess of Haversham," she said for Winnie's benefit to introduce them. Winnie wasn't sure if she was supposed to curtsy or bow, and looked flustered.

"How do you do?" she said shyly as he shook her hand.

"Very well, thank you, other than my sister's bad temper. And Freddie will do. I hate titles, don't you?"

"I don't know, I've never had one," Winnie said meekly.

"How fortunate for you." His smile was dazzling and full of mischief.

"I have to buy groceries," Beatrice interrupted him. "Which of your Bugattis would you like to give me to replace my car? And by the way, this is Winona Farmington." Winnie had used her full name when she made the appointment, in order to sound more credible and formal. "She has a wealth of extraordinary ideas to help us stay on our feet when **Beauchamp** leaves." Beatrice stood up then, and Freddie disappeared again to find another riding crop in the boot room. "I have to think about what you said. I don't know if I'd have the courage to do any of it. But it's certainly worth a thought. I'll call you when I've had time to digest it." Winnie nodded and stood up, and thanked her for allowing her to come and share the ideas. "What part would you play in it?"

"None," Winnie said simply. "I wasn't in the dream. I just thought some of it might be helpful."

"How kind of you," Beatrice said, smiling at her. They were about the same age, and Winnie had a feeling she'd like Bea if she got to know her. And her brother was handsome and funny. They were like people in a book or a play, not real life, or not Winnie's real life at any rate. "I don't know where we'd get the manpower to pull it off," Beatrice said thoughtfully as she walked Winnie to the door.

"There will be lots of people out of work here shortly. They'd be grateful for the jobs," Winnie reminded her. Beatrice nodded agreement and Winnie left a minute later. After she left, in the distance, Winnie saw Freddie cantering toward the hills on a white horse. He looked like a good omen. She thought about it as she headed back to Edward's trailer. There were parts of her life now, in fact all of it, that felt like someone else's life, surely not hers. Titled aristocrats and movie stars, castles and hit TV shows. It still took her breath away at times. But Beatrice Haversham seemed almost normal to her, down-to-earth, and practical. She had listened intently to Winnie.

In the family side of the castle, Beatrice was pouring herself a cup of tea and shaking her head, wondering if fate had just saved them again, or was it all too absurd?

Chapter Thirteen

New scripts appeared daily on the set now to try to wind down the series to a satisfying conclusion. Viewers had to be pleased, mysteries solved, Matthew didn't want to leave anyone hanging, but to wrap everything up neatly. It took new scripts and storylines to do it, and learning all the new lines was challenging for the actors and confusing for everyone, even the crew. Nothing was going according to previous plans. Scenes were being shot in different places, costumes were changed. The costumers were going crazy trying to keep up and remaking old dresses from previous seasons. The producers wanted to maintain the same high standards to the bitter end.

Winnie was studying one of Edward's new scripts in the trailer, when her cellphone rang, it was Beatrice Haversham. She was surprised to hear from her for a minute. It was two days after their meeting, and Winnie was beginning to assume that they had decided she was crazy and had no interest in any of her ideas. It was entirely possible and she wouldn't blame them.

"Is this a bad time?" Beatrice asked her.

"No, it's fine."

"I'm sorry I didn't call you yesterday. Would you have time to come by and talk to us sometime today? My brother's going to London tomorrow, and I never know when he'll get back."

"I could come by after work," Winnie said softly, she didn't want to disturb Edward, who was trying to learn new lines, only a few feet away.

"Perfect. We'll have tea together. Six o'clock?" which Winnie knew meant a light dinner at that hour.

"See you then," she said and hung up.

She was hurrying out of the trailer at five to six when she saw Nigel coming toward her. He caught up with her a minute later.

"Do you want to go to dinner with me now?"

"I can't," she said, looking apologetic. "I've got an appointment. I don't know what time I'll be finished. I can call you."

"Never mind," he said, annoyed. "Who's the appointment with?"

"The Havershams," she said simply.

"The bloke with the Bugattis?"

"And his sister."

"What for?" He was suspicious.

"I had an idea they want to talk to me about."

"See you tomorrow," he said, turned on his heel, and left, and she didn't chase after him. She didn't want to be late for Beatrice and Freddie. She rang the bell at the door three minutes later, after she walked around the castle to their private entrance. The bell system was the same one that had existed there for over a hundred years and they used on the show. It still functioned, with occasional repairs. Beatrice opened the door a few minutes later. She was wearing jeans and a sweater and short riding boots. She and her brother both spent a lot of time on horses.

She walked Winnie into a small sitting room after following a circuitous route down a back hallway. It was the room Beatrice used as an office, and was a combination library and sitting room, with a fire-place and two comfortable couches, and several big leather chairs. The room was cozy, and her desk was piled high with papers. She handled all of their accounts with the production company, and kept track of all the schedules for the shoot, and which rooms they'd be using when, so there was never a conflict.

"Sit down," she said warmly to Winnie. "I'll be back in a flash." She reappeared a moment later with an enormous, ornate, antique silver tea tray, piled high with plates of scones and clotted cream, impeccable tea sandwiches of chicken, egg salad, cucumber, watercress, a silver tea pot, three cups, china, and silver. It looked like a scene from **Beauchamp Hall,** and worthy of the fanciest home, hotel, or restaurant. It smelled delicious, and as soon as Beatrice set it down, her brother appeared in jeans and a T-shirt.

"Are we meeting in here?" he asked his sister. "Who made the tea?" He looked impressed too.

"I did. Sit down. We have a lot to talk about." She passed Winnie the plate of sandwiches and Winnie took one of each. Freddie helped himself to several, while his sister poured tea and handed Winnie a delicate cup with a linen napkin and silver spoon. The light meal, the silver and china were a civilized relic of a bygone era.

Once they were all served, Beatrice addressed Winnie. "We've been talking about your ideas, and some of them are quite mad and positively frightening, but **very** interesting. We're wondering how much of it would really be possible, and how much manpower and expertise it would take. We don't have a big staff here. This isn't **Beauchamp Hall.**" She smiled.

"I don't think it would take a lot of people, and you could hire the ones you'd need. What part of the dream appealed to you?"

"The mystery weekends," Freddie said, smiling, helping himself to more sandwiches and his sister gave him a quelling look.

"The weddings first," Beatrice intervened. "I never thought of it before, but I think weddings could be quite marvelous here. We'd have to limit the number of guests, of course, but God knows we've got all the china and crystal and silver we'd need. And I suppose we'd have to know who the people are, so we know they're not the sort to steal the silverware."

"The bridal family could make a security deposit, as part of the price. You could design packages money-wise, depending on size and how elaborate they want it, and additional fees if they stay here or not. You could even provide a hairdresser and makeup artist, manicurist, everything they'd need. It could be very lucrative. You could hire someone just to do weddings," Winnie suggested.

"I could do it myself," Beatrice said thoughtfully. "We've all seen how they do it on the set. I think I could pull off a creditable wedding. I've never had one myself, but I've been to enough."

"I could masquerade as a priest," Freddie interjected. "Then the wedding wouldn't be legal, and they wouldn't have to bother getting divorced if it doesn't work out later."

"You are **not** being helpful." His sister glared at him. "And I loved your idea about buying wedding gowns and costumes from the production company when they leave. It could be very glamorous, and I think we have a few in the attic also."

"They might give them to you for free," Winnie

said thoughtfully. "And you should probably have an assistant to help you with the weddings, a young local girl. Do you know a good caterer?"

"Actually, I do," Beatrice said. "And they're not very dear. I think our doing weddings here is a fantastic idea. We could advertise in bridal magazines, or some newspapers. Maybe British **Vogue.** I think we should keep it high-end, so it's something people are begging to do. Their dream wedding."

"I completely agree," Winnie said, pleased that her idea had spawned something useful for them. She liked Beatrice and she thought her brother was funny. "You'll need a florist and a photographer, and a calligrapher. And catering staff of course."

"What about the mystery weekends? Do you think we could actually pull that off? I've never been to one." Beatrice was intrigued.

"I have." Freddie leapt in. "It was amazing. I loved it. I was the murderer twice, and no one guessed me." He described what it had been like, and it sounded less complicated than the weddings.

"Someone will have to write the script. I can barely write a letter." Winnie nodded in response to what Beatrice said.

"And we like the idea for the Beauchamp museum. The rooms with the video screens showing scenes from the series is brilliant. They'll eat it up, and it will keep the spirit of the show alive for tourists who come here. And the gift shop is incredibly vulgar, but they'll probably like that too. We'll likely need the show's permission to sell the merchandise, but we can split the profits with the studio if we have to. And we'd need someone in the gift shop, again some nice young girl from the village. What kind of staff do you think we'd need to do all this?"

Winnie thought about it for a minute. "Would you both be working on it?" She glanced cautiously at Freddie.

"Yes," Beatrice said immediately. "I'd do the weddings. Freddie can do the mysteries. And I can manage the museum. Freddie is good with technical issues, like the video. It would be full-time work for both of us." She glanced meaningfully at her brother, who nodded.

"You could get one girl to help with the weddings, and another one to handle the gift shop. You need a technical person to set up the videos in the rooms on the tour, but you can hire an outside firm for that. You can do a lot with independent contractors, like the caterer. I think two willing young local girls would do it at first. You can always add another person later, if you need it. If you're both willing to do the work, you don't need much staff. And someone would have to keep the costumes straight, but you could do that," she spoke to Beatrice again.

"I know a nice seamstress in the village who could do fittings for us, and her husband is a tailor," Beatrice volunteered, and then she frowned again. "I had another thought. People have been watching the show for years. There's a very convincing butler on it, and houses like this are expected to have one. I was thinking that we should hire a butler, not a real one, but someone to act as one. He could even help with the tours."

"I can play the butler," Freddie said happily. He was enjoying the fantasy immensely, and smiled several times at Winnie.

"You **cannot** play the butler," his sister said firmly. "You're the marquess, you can't be the butler. We need someone who looks the part." Winnie nodded, thinking. She agreed with Beatrice if they were going to re-enact something close to **Beauchamp Hall** and put on a real show for visitors or wedding guests, and then she had an idea.

"Do you know Rupert with the food truck in the square?" Freddie smiled when she said it.

"I went to school with him in the village for a year before I went to Eton. He's a good chap. He gives me free bangers whenever I see him. Actually, he'd be perfect."

"Brilliant," Beatrice approved. "Do you think he'd do it?"

"He was telling me last week that he's going to have to sell his food truck when the show closes, and go back to being a chimney sweep, which he hates," Winnie explained.

"I'd forgotten about that," Freddie said sympathetically. "I'm sure he'd rather be a butler than go around with soot on his face." It didn't sound like a fun job to Winnie either.

"I can ask him," Winnie said politely. She had made notes of several of the things Beatrice had mentioned. She had to hire two young girls to help her. And they needed to inquire about buying wedding dresses and costumes for weddings and mystery weekends. Haversham was a perfect venue for them. "We can also buy period gowns at auctions if we have to." Beatrice nodded agreement. They were thinking of every detail.

"And now for the horrible part," Beatrice said, looking at Winnie. "I can't even bear the thought of turning our home into a reality show, and my parents and grandparents would roll over in their graves, but I have a feeling there could be some real money in it. I hear that those shows can make a fortune. Do you suppose there's some way we could do it, without having them film us in the bathtub, or cooking breakfast in our underwear, or fighting with each other to keep them happy? We don't either of us have any 'love children' to produce to shock them. But maybe if they filmed a wedding or a mystery weekend and the preparations for it, it would satisfy them. Some of the brides might love it." She looked pained as she said it.

"From what I hear, there's some real money in

it," Winnie said. "I understand your hesitation, but commercially speaking, it would feed the wedding business and mystery weekends. People would be begging to come here, better yet if they could be on the show." Beatrice groaned at what she said, and leaned back against the couch, as her brother looked at her.

"Don't be such a snob, Bea," her brother accused her. "If we want to stay here and keep the place going, we have to be smart about it. And they can film me in the bathtub, if they insist, or driving a Bugatti naked. It's all for God and Country." He said it nobly, and all three of them laughed.

"Do you know anyone who produces those reality shows?" she asked Winnie.

"No, but I can find out. I'm sure someone on the crew knows who they are."

"I have another important question," Beatrice said, jotting something down on her list. "How soon do you think we have to start putting all this together?"

"Yesterday," Winnie said without hesitation. "I think you should try to open by Christmas. That gives you almost four months to get everything in order and ready to roll. I think you can do it by then, if you start now. There actually isn't much preparation, because you have everything right here already, and you don't need a lot of staff. And the rooms they've been using for the show are camera ready now." Both Havershams were in agreement. It sounded feasible to them too.

"And one more thing," Beatrice added, looking shyly at Winnie. "We can't do this on our own, and it was your idea. We'd like you to be our creative director."

"Me?" Winnie looked shocked. She hadn't expected to include herself in the deal when she suggested it to them. She just did it to help, because she felt bad about their being left high and dry by the show being canceled, and she liked Beatrice when she'd met her. "I've never done anything like this."

"Neither have we, and you've worked on the show. You've seen how these things work."

"So have you," Winnie said modestly. "You don't really need me. You can run with the idea without me."

"Now, hear, hear," Freddie said to Winnie in a firm voice. "You can't just hallucinate this kind of thing, dump it in our laps, and then just leave us to it. We'll muck it all up. Or I will, certainly."

"**You** might," his sister said to him. "I'm not going to muck up a damn thing." And then she turned to Winnie. "But we do need you. I think your ideas are fantastic, and we're grateful to you. Would you consider being partners with us? We could split the profits three ways." Winnie was stunned and didn't know what to say, but it sounded exciting and fun and like a whole other chapter after her months hanging around the show. It was another dream coming true.

"I did some writing in college, I could try writing the scripts for the mystery weekends," she said hesitantly, "and see if you like them."

"The whole thing is your idea. If you hadn't suggested it, we'd never have thought of it, and we'd be broke again in six months."

"We might be anyway, if it doesn't work," Freddie said realistically, but it had the potential to become a real moneymaker and they could all sense it. She looked at them both for a moment. She had nothing to lose. And all three of them were excited to try it.

"I'll do it," she said, smiling at both of them. "I'd love to! Thank you for asking me."

"And if it doesn't work, we'll sell the house and all go live in the Caribbean together," Freddie suggested.

"Let's hope that doesn't happen," Beatrice said with feeling. "So what do we do now?" Beatrice looked at her list, as Winnie glanced at her own.

"You start looking for two girls in the village," Winnie said. "Freddie, will you talk to Rupert and ask him about being the butler? And I think Beatrice and I should talk to Michael Waterman about the costumes as soon as possible. I think we should do it together. He's very impressed by you and your title." She looked at Beatrice. "Should I be calling you Lady Beatrice all the time?" She wasn't sure, and Freddie answered the question.

"Yes, and you have to curtsy to her whenever you see her."

"Oh, shut up," his sister said to him. "Of course not. Beatrice or Bea is fine. But Freddie should always be 'His Lordship' when others are around, so visitors are impressed that they're in the presence of a marquess. We can charge more for that." She grinned.

"Maybe we should tell them I'm a duke and charge them even more. 'Marquess Masquerades as Duke in Wake of **Beauchamp Hall** Scandal. . . .'"

"You don't need the producers' permission to run the museum, since the show is part of Haversham's history now, and the life of the castle. We can ask them for film clips, though."

"I think we've made some amazing progress," Beatrice said, looking pleased. It was nine o'clock at night, and they had covered a lot of ground in three hours. They had a partnership, and a plan, and a fledgling business.

"I hope it's a huge success," Winnie said sincerely, as Freddie disappeared, then returned a minute later with a bottle of champagne and popped the cork. He poured it into three glasses he'd brought with it, and they each raised a glass.

"To Haversham Castle and the three musketeers!" Freddie toasted them and they took the first sip of the champagne.

"I can't wait to get started," Winnie admitted. She wasn't even out of one job yet, and she already had another, and it was a way of holding on to the last memories of **Beauchamp Hall.** Her DVDs in the white elephant game the year before had changed her whole life. And the next chapter had just begun.

Chapter Fourteen

"What's up with you?" Edward asked her with a grin the next morning at work. "You look like the cat that swallowed the canary. New guy?"

"Better than that. New project. I met with the Havershams last night. I'm trying to help them compensate when the show wraps." It was only days away. They had just been notified that the shooting schedule for the final episodes had been extended to get all the new scenes in. All days off had already been canceled and they were doing night shoots too. They were working as fast as they could.

"And can you help them?" Edward was impressed by how resourceful she was. It was why she was such a good assistant too. She was full of energy and ideas.

"I think so. We have some promising avenues to pursue. They're fun to work with, and really nice people." And as she said it, she had another idea. "I just thought of something. They're going to start hosting weddings at the castle by the end of the year. What would you think about you and Grace getting married here? They're going to do period weddings, with costumes for those who want them, but obviously, you could wear whatever you want. Do you think Grace would consider it as a wedding location?" He looked pensive for a moment and then at Winnie with a slow smile.

"I love it. This show has meant so much to me. And the castle is exquisite. I think Grace would love it too, and so would her father. He knew the Havershams' father and grandfather. He's mentioned it to me several times. Let me ask her, and I'll let you know."

He called her that afternoon and after he did, he smiled at Winnie. "Grace loved the idea. She wants to get married at Haversham Castle. In costume!"

"Do you have your date yet?" She was so excited she could hardly stand it.

"The Saturday before Christmas, if that works for you."

"You're our first wedding customer, and we're going to keep it that way. I love that you'll be our first wedding, and you've been on the show." And it would be fantastic publicity for them for future weddings.

Winnie was so excited that she waited until she had a break in the late afternoon, and ran to the family entrance to the castle and rang the doorbell. Freddie opened it, he had just gotten back from a drive in his favorite Bugatti.

"Is Beatrice here?" Winnie asked shyly, as she walked into the hallway and was surprised to see Freddie. She wasn't as comfortable with him yet as she was with his sister. He was a little more daunting and flamboyant, and she didn't know him as well. Beatrice appeared a minute later. "Edward Smith is going to get married here the Saturday before Christmas," Winnie told both of them. "He'll be our first wedding and every magazine will want to cover it." She was ecstatic as she told them.

"Fantastic!" Beatrice was beaming. "How many guests?"

"I forgot to ask him. Do we have a limit?" The three of them looked at each other and decided they didn't in his case. "I'll ask him. And they want to do it in costume. I think he should probably keep his own, and I told him he'd be our first wedding." The three of them laughed and talked as they walked into the kitchen, and Beatrice said she'd call the caterer and wedding baker she'd already contacted to announce their new business, and they were excited about it. Beatrice had the list of everyone she had to contact. And when Winnie asked Edward, he said they wanted between two hundred and three hundred guests. She promised him a "family rate" for being their first client, and a celebrity on top of it. He said Grace's father would be delighted with the discount since he was as tight as a tick, and he had said repeatedly that he'd had some very good times at the castle in his youth. This would be one more, and great publicity for them.

Beatrice and Winnie had decided to approach Michael Waterman that evening after they finished shooting to discuss the costumes with him, now that they had their first wedding booked. He looked startled to see them both waiting outside the room he used as an office. He was always impressed by Lady Beatrice, particularly since she had a title, and thought her a lovely-looking woman. He would have loved to ask her out but had never dared.

"To what do I owe the honor, Lady Beatrice?" he asked her.

"We have something we want to ask you," Winnie said nervously. They outlined the project to him, and Beatrice added that they would be willing to pay for the costumes.

"How many do you have in mind?" Beatrice glanced at Winnie before she answered, and decided to shoot for the moon.

"As many bridal gowns as you'd be willing to sell or give us. And for the wedding guests, perhaps two hundred and fifty evening gowns and two hundred and fifty sets of tails." They both knew that they had at least that many for extras and possibly more, since some of the weddings on the show had been huge.

"Let me see what I can do," he said. He had a lot on his plate now that the show was going to close.

"We'd be grateful to buy as many as you can spare," Beatrice said politely.

"I can't give them to you until we end the show," he reminded her. But that wasn't far off now.

"That's fine." She and Winnie had already picked a room to outfit with racks for women's costumes, and a second one for men's. They had plenty of storage on the old servants' floor.

"Do you think he'll do it?" Beatrice asked Winnie as they hurried away after the meeting, giggling like young girls. She had just learned a few days before that Beatrice was only a year older than she was at thirty-nine, and Freddie was forty-one. "But he acts twelve," Beatrice said about her brother.

True to his word, Freddie approached Rupert the next day. He said he hadn't had time until then, and one of his horses had gone lame a few months before and he wanted to see the vet himself to discuss the horse's progress. But with Edward Smith's wedding date set, their project suddenly seemed very real. And he agreed with Beatrice, they needed a butler to add credibility and the right look and dignity to the house.

Rupert laughed at him when he asked him. "Are you serious? You expect me to act all la-di-da and be a butler?"

"Winnie Farmington, our new partner, said you're worried about what will happen after the show ends, and you'll have to sell the food truck," Freddie reminded him.

"True," Rupert said pensively.

"We're going to do murder weekends, and weddings, and better tours than we've been doing till now. Bea thinks we need a butler to impress the guests."

"She's probably right. My grandfather was in service at the castle. He was a footman. My father thought it was a step up to own his own business and be a chimney sweep. I never thought I'd be in service."

"You wouldn't be. We're talking about a Hollywood-style butler to impress people, open the door, and parade around in white tie and tails, not a real one to polish the silver." Rupert laughed at what he said. They had always liked each other as boys and gotten into mischief together, despite the social gap between them, which hadn't mattered to either of them, although it had to their parents.

"I'll be lucky to get a job once the show is gone," Rupert said ruefully. "You're on, mate. A Hollywood butler it is. When do I start?"

"As soon as you can sell the truck, or whenever you want to. The show will be leaving very soon. They're shooting the final episodes now at full speed. And it'll take them a couple of weeks to move out all the equipment."

"It sounds like fun. Give me until they've all left, so I can catch the last of the wave and feed the crew, and then I'll sell the truck. I should be free by the end of September."

"You've got it." They shook hands on their agreement, enjoying the same complicity they'd had as children.

Freddie texted Winnie and his sister on the way back to the castle. "Ladies, we will have a butler before September ends." His name was Rupert Tilton, and they were going to call him "Tilton," in proper form, when guests were present.

Winnie had been so busy working for Edward, meeting with Beatrice, coming up with new ideas, and making lists that she had hardly had time to see Nigel. And he was working day and night on the final episodes. He showed up late one night after a night shoot and looked exhausted. She could already feel the distance between them.

Things had been hectic on the set, and everyone was worried about their futures, calling agents and producers they knew, and unions for the crew.

"How's it going for you?" he asked her as he lay down on her couch. It was almost midnight and he had just finished work.

"It's been crazy," she said, smiling at him. "I'm starting a wedding business with the Havershams." It was the simplest way to explain it.

"What do they need you for? They've already got the castle." He looked surprised.

"It was my idea. Sometimes it takes an outsider to see the obvious." She mentioned her idea of having video screens in some of the rooms on the tour, with film clips of the show, as a kind of museum tour. She asked him who he thought she should speak to on the set for technical advice of what to buy. He told her who to see on the video team, and then he told her that he'd been busy too. They hadn't spent a night together all week. And at least he hadn't asked her about Freddie again, or Edward.

"I've had an offer to work on a show that shoots in Ireland, and another that spends a lot of time on location in Italy. The food would be better in Italy, but Ireland would be easier. I speak the language, and I lived there for a year. I'll probably do it, Winnie. I'll have to live in Dublin. Any chance you'd come with me?" He knew the answer before he asked her. It was obvious since she was starting the wedding business and all the rest. And they'd been drifting apart inexorably, and neither of them was trying to stop it. They knew they couldn't.

"I can't leave them stranded. We're just getting started," Winnie said quietly. But they both knew she wouldn't have gone with him anyway, their relationship had gone flat in the last month or two. His jealous fits had cooled her feelings for him, and she'd have nothing to do in Dublin if she went with him.

"I figured you wouldn't," he said sadly. "We're kind of done, aren't we?" She hesitated and then nodded. "I told you it was like that. It's like a family while the show lasts, and when it's over, everyone goes their separate ways. I'll be lucky if you remember my name a year from now." He looked sad as he said it and she touched his hand. His obsessive jealousy had ruined it for her, not the end of the show. But she didn't say it to him.

"Don't be silly. I've loved being with you, but I can't see how it would work for the long run. Sooner or later I'll go back to Michigan. Your life is here. I can't see myself in Dublin now. And I want to stick around Haversham for a while." He nodded again. He understood, or thought he did. He didn't ask to stay with her that night. They both knew it was over. Like a summer romance, autumn had come, sooner than expected. He kissed her one last time before he left. She watched him as he walked to his Jeep and he turned to look at her, as though to engrave her in his memory. She stood in the doorway and watched him as he drove away. They both knew their time had come and gone, and it was better that way.

Michael gave them an answer about the costumes the next day. Decisions had to be made quickly now. He called Lady Beatrice to tell her, and she was stunned when he told her that she could have the five hundred extra costumes she'd requested as a gift. They were going to sell her the wedding gowns for the equivalent of five hundred dollars each. There were five of them that had been prominently featured in the show. She was welcome to choose any of the other costumes for considerably less. He was doing it as a gesture to thank her for how gracious she and her brother had been for the past six years. He told her to make an appointment with the costumer, and they could collect them as soon as they wrapped the show. She was breathless when she called Winnie to tell her.

"We'll have five wedding gowns to offer brides!" Gowns well-known actresses had worn, which gave them even more cachet. Winnie told Edward about it that afternoon, in case Grace wanted to wear one of them, and he thought she might, since she loved the show too. But he had another gown in mind for her.

Beatrice and Winnie spent an evening setting up racks for the costumes in two of the old maids' rooms in the attic, and a separate room just for wedding gowns, and the accessories that the producers were giving them too.

"Should we set up a fitting room?" Winnie asked her.

"I think we should recarpet my mother's old dressing room. It's very elegant and has mirrors everywhere, and would make a perfect fitting room for our brides." The two women smiled at each other. Everything was falling into place, and had since the beginning. The fates had been smiling on them since Winnie's dream. "I don't know how to thank you. You turned a disaster into a miracle for us." Just as **Beauchamp Hall** had six years before by coming at just the right time.

"I'm loving it too," Winnie said. "I've never enjoyed anything so much in my life." It was the best job she'd ever had. And it had all happened because she'd had the courage to leave Michigan, come to see the making of the show she loved, and follow her dream. In spite of what had happened with Rob and Barb and her job, it had turned out to be the best year of her life, even though the show was ending. They had found a way to keep it alive, for the people who had been so devoted to it, and for themselves.

"I found a source for the **Beauchamp Hall** souvenir china, by the way," Beatrice told her. "The show has a licensing agreement on it, but we can buy it from them at a discounted rate."

"Is it very expensive?" Winnie looked concerned. She was going to commit some of her savings to their project. At least they would be saving a lot on costumes. She was prepared to put in some of what her mother had left her. And Marje had just rented her house in Beecher, which was additional income too. Every penny mattered, although it was not a very costly business to start. They had so much of what they needed on hand.

"It's not too bad," Beatrice said about the china, "and I think it will sell like crazy." Winnie agreed with her, which was why she had suggested it in their initial plan. Beatrice had hired a nice woman for the gift shop, Bridget Donahue, who was thrilled with the job, and a bright young girl, Lucy, as their assistant. She had done a year at university, was working as a maid at Mrs. Flannagan's B and B, wanted to better herself, and was willing to do whatever they needed. Lucy was starting in two weeks. They weren't opening the gift shop until December when they were fully up and running, so Bridget could start a week before to organize their inventory.

"The guy who handles the video equipment on the show is coming over tomorrow, by the way, to give us advice and tell us what we need," Winnie said, and Beatrice nodded as Freddie walked in. They had just come down from the attic and setting up the racks, and he'd been in the stables with his horses, which he was keeping now, hoping their business would be a success. He could always sell them later if he had to. He hoped not.

"What are you two tittering about?" he asked them. It was easy to see how well the two women got along. Beatrice was the closest friend Winnie had made in a long time. It was nice having a woman to talk to again. She had missed Barb.

"We were agreeing on how ridiculous you are," his sister teased him.

"We need another man around here," he complained. "Thank God Rupert will be here soon. I don't know what I was thinking, starting a business with two women. You're always ganging up on me."

"Sorry, Your Lordship." Beatrice grinned at him.

"You may call me Your Majesty," he said haughtily to his sister. "Where are we on the reality show?" he asked Winnie seriously.

"Edward is talking to someone he knows in London. He says they're all pretty rough, but it's a sure moneymaker. People like the scandalous stuff better, so we may have to come up with some sexy angle for them. Or maybe your titles will be enough," she said hopefully.

"Maybe we'll have to include your flock of girl-friends," Beatrice said seriously.

"Or your illegitimate children," he tossed back at her.

"I don't have any, just for your information," she told Winnie again.

"She's a virgin," he added, and Beatrice took a swat at him with the notepad that never left her hand.

"Seriously, though," Beatrice said pensively, "maybe they do expect us to have lovers on the show or a boyfriend or girlfriend. We're not a very interesting lot." Even Freddie hadn't had a girl-friend in months. There was no one local he was interested in.

"I don't have one at the moment," Freddie said practically, "but I can start auditioning if you want. All for the good of the cause, of course."

"What happened to the last one? The girl from Brazil?" Beatrice asked, surprised.

"She ran off with a race car driver and is living with him in Monte Carlo. We could tell the producers we're a ménage à trois. That might be interesting."

"Maybe they won't care about our sex lives," Beatrice said hopefully. "I haven't had a serious man in my life in years."

"It's your own damn fault," her brother reproached her. "The village has been teeming with actors and movie stars for six years, you could have made some effort to pick one up, or a few of them."

"They're all spoken for, or gay, or cheaters," Winnie corrected him. "To be honest, most of them would rather have you," she said, looking at Freddie. "The one I work for is terrific, but he's been with the same woman for thirteen years and he's faithful to her."

"How depressing for him. Fidelity is so overrated," Freddie said and both women laughed. "But thank God he's marrying her, since they're our first wedding. What about you?" he asked Winnie. "No boyfriend?" They were all three getting to know each other and curious about their lives.

"No, I dated a sound technician for a while when I got here, but it fizzled out, and now I don't have time. I've got two jobs and a business to start."

"You two should have been nuns," he scolded

them both. "But I'm not much better these days. At forty-one, you've seen it all. I'm beginning to like my horses better."

"I might as well have been a nun," Beatrice complained, "locked up with you all my life. And don't tell me you're reformed. I don't believe you."

"You should go to London more often," he said seriously. "You'll never find a man hanging around here. Unless you want Rupert. He's perfectly nice."

"Our butler?" she said, putting on airs. "Don't be ridiculous!" But Rupert had never appealed to her, and wouldn't. She was sophisticated despite her country life.

The three of them got along well and were becoming friends. Building something together was a strong bond. Beatrice said privately to Winnie that her brother hadn't been this busy in years, or as happy. He didn't do well when he was idle and always got into mischief that didn't serve him well. "Women, mostly," she explained to Winnie, while they waited for a carpet layer to measure the dressing room one night after work. They had decided to do the carpet in pale pink and have the room repainted so it looked fresh. The room hadn't been used in years, since Beatrice still slept in her childhood bedroom, which was huge. Freddie had his own, with a library and sitting room attached, and a dressing room that had been their father's, paneled in mahogany, at the opposite end of the castle.

Winnie loved discovering more and more about the house, and seeing things she hadn't been able to see on the tour, since their living quarters weren't on it.

It struck her as odd that neither of them had ever married. Beatrice told her in confidence one day, when they were going through the guest room to see what, if anything, they needed for mystery weekenders or bridal party guests, that her brother had been very much in love with a French girl ten years before. She had run off with someone else and broken his heart, and he had become a determined womanizer after that, and seemed intent on staying that way.

"I don't think he'll ever marry at this point, he enjoys variety too much, and they all bore him after a while. And I suppose by now I've missed that boat too. When I go to parties in London, all the sweet young things are twenty-two, and thirty-nine looks quite elderly in comparison. One can't really compete with that." She was matter-of-fact about it and didn't seem to care. "The only unfortunate thing is that the bloodline, the name, and the title will die with us. We don't have any cousins. And if Freddie doesn't have children, then it's all over. My father would have been disappointed by that. So we're the last Havershams." That mattered to her more than any regret about not having married or having children herself, but it was important to them. "Maybe Freddie will marry when he's eighty and produce an heir," she said with a grin.

"Who produced an heir?" Freddie asked, as he walked through the room.

"No one. I was saying to Winnie that you should one day."

"I'd rather wait till I'm ninety, I don't want to miss all the fun before that. Are the brides fair game while their husbands are getting blind drunk on their wedding night?"

"I forbid you to touch any of the brides, you'll put us out of business. You can have all the brides-maids you want, you have my permission for that," his sister told him.

"Excellent. Don't accept any brides with ugly bridesmaids. I'll vet them for you, with full approval rights." He smiled at Winnie as he said it.

"And why aren't you married? Beatrice is much too outspoken for any man to put up with her, and I can't seem to stay with any woman for more than three months, six at best. But you seem quite normal and easy to get along with. I would have thought someone would have snatched you up years ago." It was a backhanded compliment for Winnie and she smiled, and he seemed to expect an answer.

"I had a bad boyfriend for eleven years. He slept with my best friend, so that was that."

"How rude," he said disdainfully, "and not very imaginative of him. So tiresome. You're well rid of him."

"I think so." She smiled back at him. She could guess the kind of women he went out with, very young and very beautiful, debutantes or maybe models. "I came here when I left him, so it worked out very well for me."

"And for us. You've turned out to be our fairy godmother," he said, and went off to do something in the wine cellar. They were going to have to stock more wine for the weddings, especially Edward's, who wanted Cristal. Freddie was in charge of that.

They had another good surprise when the video technician from the set came to look at the rooms where they wanted to set up the screens with film clips from the show. They wanted to install three large screens, with scenes shot in the rooms they were placed in. He measured the spaces Winnie and Beatrice indicated, and made note, and then called them back two hours later to tell them that the production company had five screens they would be getting rid of when they left. He'd been told he could give them away, and offered them to the Havershams for free and said he would set them up for them in his spare time before they left. The show was like a retreating army, giving out bounty to the village, but it was going to save them money to have the screens. He set them up just exactly the way they wanted them, and Winnie knew just which episodes she wanted to play in each room while people took the tour. She had watched the DVDs dozens of times. The producers said they had no problem with it.

Rupert came to check out what they'd been doing right after the screens were installed, and he was impressed. It was beginning to look very professional and Beatrice and Winnie had freshened things up and moved some things around, but not too much. Freddie had selected a set of tails for Rupert, and had them dry cleaned, and Rupert looked the part of a butler once he was dressed. He put on a stern face and they all laughed. He was perfect in the role, and very convincing.

"I should have had this for the food truck. I could have doubled the prices," he said and they all teased him and played around with him.

The four of them had a light dinner one night in the kitchen, when Winnie finished work, and on her way home, she stopped in to see Mrs. Flannagan in her cottage. She told her what they were doing at the castle.

"I'm so pleased you're staying here with us." She'd been happy to hear it. "It's such a shame they've decided not to go on with the show," she said sadly. "I'll miss it." But their weddings and mystery weekends were going to generate business for her too.

"So will I," Winnie agreed with her. "I'll be watching the DVDs for years." She still watched it at night now that she was alone. Nigel had stopped coming over after they broke up. She had glimpsed him on the set, but they hadn't spoken. She knew he would be moving on shortly, and going to Ireland. And her DVDs of the show populated her nights alone. She didn't really miss him.

She promised Mrs. Flannagan she'd come to dinner soon when she wasn't so busy. And despite everything they had to do at the castle, she was trying to focus on the final moments of the show and be helpful to Edward. They were all feeling emotional about the end of **Beauchamp Hall,** and there were frequent tears on the set. It seemed to heighten everyone's performances, and they wanted to make the last episodes as memorable as they could.

"How's it going at the castle?" Edward asked her one afternoon as he waited for the production assistant to call him for his shot. He was about to get engaged to the woman he had loved all his life on the show. His cold, nasty wife had died and he was going to marry his true love, the mother of his other, clandestine children. His mistress could come out of the shadows now. Matthew had done a masterful job with several very emotional scenes to wrap up Edward's story on the show. And there wasn't a dry eye on the set during Edward's performance with the girl who played his mistress and future wife.

Matthew had outdone himself in his rewritten scripts for the end of the show. Many of them were very poignant, and even brought tears to the crew's

eyes as they watched. And the actors were giving it
their all.

"We're getting ready for your wedding," Winnie
told Edward with a smile. "Your real one."

"We're both excited to be doing it at Haversham.
I think what you're planning to do up there sounds
wonderful. I guess your days as an assistant are
over."

"For now. You never know what will happen.
They won't need me around forever. I think the
whole operation will run itself eventually, they won't
need a creative director. Just in the beginning."

"Maybe you'll marry the marquess," Edward said,
and she laughed at the suggestion. She knew Freddie better than that now, and had heard the stories
from his sister, about all the mischief he got into,
and the women in his life.

"Not likely. He has a whole lineup of women."

"You're a very special woman," Edward said.
"I hope you know that, Winnie. You're a powerful positive force to have around. I've been lucky
to have you. Now they are the lucky ones." She
was touched by what he said, and cried when she
watched him propose to his true love on the show.
It was a perfect ending for their characters. And
they were going to show his wedding in the last
episode, which was a secret, but he had told her. He
had an eye on the wedding dress for Grace. It was
spectacular, an antique the costumer had bought for

a fortune at a Sotheby's auction and well worth it, with a thirty-foot-long antique lace veil and train. It had been made for a princess.

Winnie was making room for more racks in one of the old maids' rooms on a Sunday, when Freddie came to find her upstairs.

"Beatrice says she's busy and won't come riding with me. Do you want to take a break and come with me? Do you ride, by the way?" She was startled by the invitation, but he looked restless and bored.

"I haven't in years. I used to ride on a friend's farm when I was a kid. I love horses."

"I'll give you an easy horse, if you want to join me." She'd never thought of it before, she'd been too busy working, but it seemed like a good excuse to get some air. The weather had been unusually hot and muggy. And she was caught up on her work, for Edward and for them.

"Okay." She was wearing jeans and lace-up shoes with low heels that she could ride in.

"Do you ride English saddle?" She nodded, and didn't tell him she liked to ride bareback too. A few minutes later, she followed him out to the stables, and he had the stable boy saddle up a mare for her, who looked as tame as he had promised. She heard him ask the stable boy about a horse called Black Magic. And then he mounted the white stallion she'd seen him ride before, an elegant Thoroughbred with a lot of spirit. She stepped up on the block and got into the saddle, and followed him on the mare at a slow trot. It was a beautiful early fall day, and they headed toward the nearby hills, on a path on their land. It was a wonderful change of pace from the show and their work in the house.

"I come out here to get sane again." He looked calmer than she'd ever seen him, and at peace once he was riding. "I get cabin fever in the house."

She laughed at what he said. "You would hate my cottage, it's about the size of your boot room."

"I know, we're spoiled," he said, faintly embarrassed. "What really brought you out here, Winnie?" He was curious about her. She had a strong creative streak, and a practical side. It was an interesting combination. There was no pretense or artifice about her, which he found pleasant to be around and refreshing. He knew so many arrogant, ambitious women who always wanted something or had an angle and thought they were clever, but were never as clever as they believed.

"An old dream," she answered him honestly. "I always wanted to get out of my hometown. It was just as small, but not as charming as this. In fact, it's not charming at all. Most people there settle for jobs they hate, men they don't really love, or not enough, and a life I never wanted. I was hoping for a job in publishing in New York, as an editor. My mother got sick, I dropped out of college to take care of her, and it never happened. I did what everyone else did, got stuck in a job I hated with a bad boss, and a boyfriend I didn't want to marry, who turned out to be a bigger jerk than I'd thought. Then one day, it all fell apart. The job, the man, my best friend. I felt sorry for myself for a while, and then on the spur of the moment, I came here to watch them film the show. I learned a lot from it, about good people and bad people, and having the courage to go after what you want. That's what they do on that show." Matthew wrote the plot and characters so well, which was why people loved it.

"You're lucky you knew what you wanted. I never did. We're supposed to protect our land, our history, and our homes, and follow a lot of traditions that are meaningless now. The old ways don't work anymore, but I never found new ones that work any better. I hate fakery and dishonesty and there's a lot of it in the way we live. Beatrice isn't good at it either, which is why she seems to be winding up alone. We're both allergic to all the nonsense that goes with who we are. She's too honest, and I just run away all the time. Except when I'm here. I come out riding, and it all makes sense again. I love it here. This land and our home mean everything to me. Thank you for helping us to keep it. It probably seems foolish to you, to hang on to an old house like this, but all of our history, our values, the traditions that matter to us are here."

"I can feel it when I'm in the house. It's what I

love about the show. Matthew captured that in the scripts. I fell in love with **Beauchamp Hall** and everything it stood for."

"Matthew isn't a particularly warm person," Freddie commented. "But he's a wonderful writer, with an amazing instinct for people," he added, with surprising insight. And she realized as she listened to him that there was more to Freddie than she'd thought. He hid behind the jokes and the banter, but he was just as thoughtful, deep, and kind as his sister, and observant. He just didn't like to show it, although he just had to her.

They rode on in silence, and got to the top of the hill where they could look out over the land, most of which was still his. "If we have to sell something one day, I'll sell some of the land. I would hate to give up the house."

"I hope you never have to," she said sincerely. "What we're planning to do now should shore things up for you, hopefully for a long time. You could make some real money from it." Some very big money in fact, and the whole franchise was theirs, other than what they'd offered Winnie. But no one would be telling them what to do.

"It's a bit of prostitution," he admitted ruefully, "especially the reality show, but if it works, so be it. It's worth it." They rode back down the hill then, and took another path toward the stables, past the stream, and under the cover of ancient trees in fields of wildflowers. She could see why he loved it. "Will you go back to Michigan eventually?" He was curious about it. She seemed so at home here in England, and reluctant to go back where she came from.

"Probably. I don't really want to. I'm loving it here, especially now that I'm involved in our project, it's like a continuation of the love I have for the show, only in real life. But I have a sister and two nephews in Michigan. They're my only family and I suppose one day I should go back." He nodded, and she added, "I have no valid reason not to."

"Maybe what we're all doing together will be that reason. It's ample justification to stay here. We need you," he said simply. "You made it all happen, and saved us, just like the show did. But your concept may last longer."

They rode past a small elegant house on the property then, with gardens around it, where his grandmother had lived, and Freddie pointed it out to her. "That belongs to my sister, and the land around it. I gave it to her when I inherited the rest. She owns some of the tenant farms as well. It seemed only fair. She'd rather live in the castle now with me. But she'll have the dower house, whenever she wants it. No one can take that away from her." Winnie nodded. It touched him that the castle meant so much to Winnie, the land, and the village and all it stood for. It was as though she had been drawn to exactly where she was meant to be, and she felt it too.

"It's funny how you find your right place accidentally," Winnie commented as they rode. "I thought
New York would be it for me. But it turns out to be
here." He smiled at her.

"It's damn lucky you found us. Lucky for us,
that is."

He helped her dismount when they got back to
the stables, and she thanked him for the unexpected
treat of riding with him. She liked getting a deeper
look into who he was. She was getting to know Beatrice and felt a bond with her, but Freddie was more
elusive and harder to get to know. He joked and
played all the time, and stayed hidden.

She was thinking about it as the stable boy led a
spectacular-looking black stallion out of the stables
and took him toward the ring where Freddie said
he and his sister had been taught to ride as children.
The horse looked skittish and took off at a gallop
around the ring once he was in it, and then switched
directions as Freddie watched him intently.

"He got spooked a few months ago," he told her.
"He slipped when I had him out riding and he fell
near the river. His leg has healed but no one's been
able to ride him since. It was my fault. The bank
was too steep, and slippery from heavy rains. It
lamed him for a bit, nothing serious and he's fine
now, but he still won't let anyone ride him. He's
a fabulous horse but he's not himself now." They
were standing at the railing watching him, as he

stopped running and pawed the ground. Without hesitating Winnie hopped the fence as Freddie tried to grab her, but she was already in.

"What are you doing, you mad girl? Come out immediately." He didn't want her to get hurt, and Black Magic was watching her from the center of the ring, with a look of panic. Winnie had already made eye contact with him as she ignored Freddie and walked slowly and confidently toward the black stallion. "Winnie, come back here!" Freddie said and headed toward the gate, but he didn't want to frighten the horse any more than it already was.

Winnie looked totally at ease as she walked toward him, speaking softly, as Black Magic continued to watch her and Freddie was mesmerized by what he was seeing. She walked right up to the horse, patted his neck, and then gently touched his muzzle, still talking to him. You could see the tension go out of him, as he leaned toward her and nuzzled her, and then rested his head on her shoulder. They walked around the ring together for a few minutes, the horse totally relaxed as he followed her. Freddie watched with fascination.

She stayed with Black Magic for ten minutes, still talking to him, and then she patted him again and left the ring. Freddie was in awe of what she'd just done.

"Do you realize I've spent hours with him since we fell and couldn't get near him? Who are you, Winnie from Michigan? You have an incredible gift with horses." Freddie was floored by her gentleness and her courage.

"I just like horses, and they know it."

"You're some sort of magician." They walked back to the castle then in silence. Freddie was too stunned to say more about it, until he saw his sister, waiting with tea for them, and he described the scene to her, as Winnie looked casual about it.

"He was just scared, that's all," she said gently.

"He's been half mad for two months, no one's been able to ride him or get near him until you today."

"We had a nice time riding before that and saw your house," Winnie told her as Beatrice handed her a cup of tea. She had prepared one of her wonderful tea trays, with elegant little sandwiches and scones with clotted cream and jam.

"I'm saving the dower house for my old age, or for when Freddie marries some intolerable girl who hates me, and has ten children with her. Until then, I'm happy here," Beatrice said, smiling.

Freddie still wanted to talk about Winnie's extraordinary handling of the black stallion. "You're a woman of hidden talents," he said with open admiration as Winnie smiled at him. She knew she had won him as a friend that afternoon, for her innate ability with horses. He couldn't wait to go riding with her again.

Winnie and Beatrice started talking about the wedding dresses they were acquiring, and the evening gowns Winnie still wanted to buy. Freddie left them then, in awe of Winnie's performance with Black Magic. One thing was for sure, she was indeed a woman who loved horses. He was beginning to think there was nothing she couldn't do. And he was suddenly absolutely certain that their joint venture was going to be a stunning success. She was a totally amazing woman.

Chapter Fifteen

When the reality show producers Edward had recommended came to talk to the Haver-shams and Winnie, their suggestions for the format of the show made all three of them shudder at first. But Beatrice was very direct with them, and told them it wouldn't fly. She told them what their boundaries were, what they were willing to show and what they weren't, and what their goals were in doing the show, as publicity for the castle. It was the first show of its kind. No titled aristocrats had opened their homes to reality TV. The weddings and mystery weekends had the potential to make it a fun show for the viewers. Both sides had something to gain, and Beatrice handled the meeting well and took control of it while Winnie and Freddie watched. She had been equally good with contacting magazines and getting them PR. She was fearless about getting what she wanted, and a great spokesperson for their project.

The reality producers agreed to modify their plan and send them an outline more in keeping with what Beatrice said. Their main producer, Paul Evans, was deeply impressed by her. And true to their word, they sent an outline for the show that respected most of Beatrice's parameters, though not all. They showed it to an attorney, and after two more attempts at negotiation and compromise, all three of them were somewhat anxious but satisfied with the results. Beatrice had done a good job defending their interests. They were all discovering their hidden talents and covering new ground.

The producer of the show came to Haversham for a final meeting and called Beatrice "Your Ladyship" every time he addressed her, and she didn't tell him not to. Freddie teased her about it after they left, after their final meeting.

"You are such a bitch, Bea, you had the poor guy terrified. He acted like he thought you'd send him to the Tower of London."

"Good. It will keep him in line." They had agreed to an introductory show, with a tour of the castle, with all three of them present. They liked that Winnie was American, to balance the Havershams' titles. And the second show would take place at Edward's wedding. Winnie had asked his permission and he thought it was fine. It would add spice to the wedding, and it was good publicity for him too.

It was a factor he had to consider as an actor, to be kept visible at all times, and Grace understood it, although her father undoubtedly wouldn't.

There was a big article in the **Mirror,** in the 3 A.M. column, about Edward's engagement, and a photograph of Haversham Castle, where the wedding would be held. Beatrice got them to say that the castle could be rented for weddings by select guests. And each bridal couple was carefully chosen, to make it seem even more exclusive. They had five inquiries for weddings the day after the article appeared.

"Yes!" Beatrice shouted when she hung up after the fifth one. "We just got our second booking, and we might get two more. This is so wonderful! It's working!" She hugged Winnie, and Freddie looked delighted too.

He and Winnie had taken to riding together whenever she could spare an hour, although she didn't have much free time now. He had let her ride Black Magic, who was now back to his old self.

They were working double time on the set, with night shoots that went very late and all weekends. The show was drawing toward its dramatic close. The final episode would be two hours. Everyone was working hard.

Winnie was on the set most of the time now and could only come to Haversham at night. They had three weddings booked by then, including Edward's, two of them in January, Edward's right before Christmas. A mystery night for a party of twenty was booked on New Year's Eve. It would be their first. The reality show was filming all four events, and the introductory show that would be more about the Havershams and Winnie than the guests. After that, the guests would be heavily featured.

Marje was fully aware of what they were doing now, and kept telling Winnie how proud of her she was. She was the creative director of Haversham Castle, and the co-producer of a reality show.

"We want to come over and visit," Marje had said.

"Wait till we're up and running and have all the kinks ironed out, then I'd love it." Winnie knew they were going to be insanely busy from the time the show wrapped for **Beauchamp Hall,** and for three months after, through January. They were nervous about it, but exhilarated too. This was a new world for all of them. Rupert had taken to strutting around the house in his white tie and tails, practicing his role, and got quite good at it. He was a very convincing butler and very proud.

The final days on the set were unbearably stressful, bittersweet, and agonizingly nostalgic, as people who had appeared in earlier seasons and episodes came back for final appearances. And each character and plot twist on the show was brought to its

final denouement to tie it all together in the final
two hours.

Predictably, the last day was the hardest. Beatrice
and Freddie had come to watch discreetly from the
sidelines, but with less sadness now that they had
something to look forward to. Winnie did too, but
it was painful for her, watching the last scenes and
knowing that there would be no more after this.
Beauchamp Hall would be syndicated and shown
for years, but there would be no new episodes. It
made Winnie's heart ache to think about it.

She and Nigel had a few minutes to talk on the
set, and he said he was leaving for Ireland in a few
days.

The final scenes were achingly beautiful. Matthew had outdone himself with the script and so
had the costumer. The costumes in every scene
were remarkable. And Edward's wedding to his true
love was the last segment they shot, with a wedding
gown that took everyone's breath away, and was
now earmarked for Grace to wear at their wedding.
Michael had given it to them as a gift.

The very last shot was of Edward and his bride,
and there were tears in their eyes as they were de-
clared man and wife and kissed, as everyone on the
set was crying openly, and so was Matthew. Winnie
wondered if he regretted now having the show end
here, but if so, it was too late. The die had been
cast.

When the director shouted "Cut! That's a wrap!"

for the last time, there were sobs all over the set. People were hugging and crying, congratulating each other, and wishing each other luck. A family was being disbanded, and friends would never meet again, except by chance one day on another soundstage.

Edward hugged Winnie after he kissed his co-star, and thanked her for the time she'd spent with him, and how helpful she'd been. But they knew they would meet again in December at his wedding. He had already signed to be the star of a new show and was excited about it. He had two weeks off and then he was starting again. He was to have top billing and be the main character on his new show. **Beauchamp Hall** had helped him get there.

Freddie and Beatrice came over to hug Winnie as the chaos started to die down. And almost as soon as people stopped hugging and kissing, the crew started tearing down the sets and packing up the equipment. It would be days before it would all be dismantled and removed.

There were already moving vans outside and in the square to take costumes and props and equipment to studios and storage to London. A whole world was being dismantled, one that would never come again. **Beauchamp Hall** would only be a memory now in the hearts and minds of the millions of fans who had loved it, Winnie among them. It had changed her life forever and that of so many others. Its subliminal message had revived her dreams. She owed a lot to Matthew, whether he knew it or not.

When the cameras stopped rolling, the stars packed and left quickly. By that night, only the crew remained, and Winnie had dinner with Freddie and Beatrice in the castle kitchen reserved for their use. The main kitchen had been part of the show, and would be on the tour now, with one of the screens they'd been gifted with set up there, with clips of the lovable cook and kitchen staff from the show. The actress who played the cook had decided to retire. In an interview, she said that nothing could match **Beauchamp** for her.

"I feel like I left home forever today," Winnie said sadly, as Freddie poured them each a glass of wine. "It's so sad knowing it's over."

"But it isn't over," he reminded her. "Now you're part of the real story, and the family, and its future, not the fake one. You're part of Haversham now." Not **Beauchamp Hall,** which had faded into the mists that night. By morning the sets would be gone, the costumes and hats and wigs would have vanished, the familiar faces would disappear as if they had never existed. She was woven into the future of Haversham now, but the past was a tender memory for her, and had brought her here in the first place. **Beauchamp Hall** was an important piece of the Havershams' history too now, a turning point for them, and had led them to the next chapter with Winnie. It was all intertwined, like the roots of a tree that had been planted, and had grown to maturity on the show.

"You can't get maudlin now," Freddie told her. "We have too much to do." They had to focus fully on Edward's wedding, and their first night of the reality show before that. Beatrice was trying to decide if she wanted to wear one of the costumes they'd been given, or a dress of her own, and said she had nothing decent and hadn't shopped in ages, nor had Winnie. And Freddie couldn't decide whether to wear a suit or jeans.

They sat and talked late into the night, and drank a lot of wine. Freddie walked Winnie back to her cottage afterwards. He would have driven her, but knew he'd had too much wine. They saw the crews working straight through the night breaking down equipment and packing up.

When they got to her cottage, he looked surprised. "It looks like a dollhouse, but it suits you. I didn't realize it would be so small." He smiled at her. He'd never seen her cottage before. He had talked to Beatrice about offering Winnie the dower house to live in since it was empty, but she thought Winnie might not want to live on the property so close to them. She suggested that Winnie might want to have some distance and independence, but Freddie didn't see why. And he hadn't gotten around to asking her about it yet. He thought it would be convenient to have her even closer than she was now. They would have so much work to do together. "I think you need a bigger house," he said cryptically.

"No, I don't. This is fine. Do you want to come in for a nightcap?" she asked. It had been a special day. One chapter was ending, and another one starting.

"If I do, you'll either have to let me sleep on your couch, or call a cab to get me home and there are none at this hour." It was two in the morning.

The reality show technicians were coming the next day to decide on the path the house tour would take on the first show. They wanted the contrast between the private quarters and the more public ones. Freddie and Beatrice had agreed to show certain rooms, but not all. It was still in negotiation.

Freddie decided that he wanted to see the inside of Winnie's house and would have a glass of water. He walked in and she handed it to him, as he looked around. It was comfortable and cozy. He peeked around the ground floor and didn't ask to see her bedroom upstairs, although he was curious about it, and sat down on the couch with her.

"I like it," he admitted, "it's like a pair of comfortable old slippers that are nice to come home to." She nodded, it was how she felt about it too.

"My sister and I have been talking about selling my mother's house, where I live in Michigan. If I do, I might buy something here, maybe this cottage or something a little bigger."

"I have an idea about that. We can talk about it tomorrow. I like the idea of your being closer to us.

You belong at Haversham now." She was startled by his saying it, and she didn't see why.

"I'm only a short walk away."

"I'd feel better if you were under our wing. If you ever need anything, we'd be right there." He felt suddenly protective of her, and she felt as though she had acquired a brother. He had his own wing at the castle, at the opposite end from his sister, so they both had privacy, though neither of them took advantage of it. Whatever dalliances he had, he had in London when he went there, and stayed in his pied-à-terre. When Beatrice went to London, she stayed with friends, and preferred it that way.

He swayed slightly when he stood up, but other than that, he seemed sober. He hugged her when he said good night, and told her he'd see her in the morning.

After he left, he had a mad impulse to turn around and go back to the tiny cottage and spend the night with her. He just wanted to be close to her, but he was sure they'd both regret it in the morning, so he didn't, and walked back to the castle alone.

The trucks were still there in the morning when Winnie walked past, and let herself into the castle kitchen. It was her first day of not going to the set and it felt strange. Beatrice was drinking a cup of coffee and looked up at Winnie with a rueful smile.

"Was I drunk last night or do I have a brain tumor?"

"I think we drank a lot." Freddie had brought out some very good red wine to mark a special night and the end of the show.

He came down half an hour later and looked fresh and rested and in good spirits. He had slept off the wine more successfully than his sister.

Two hours later the reality show crew showed up with Paul Evans, the producer, who looked respectable and serious, and was still nervous around Beatrice. Edward had told Winnie that he was the most successful reality show producer in the business, and everything he touched turned to gold. She hoped it would be true in this case.

He walked the suggested route with Beatrice, and they debated which rooms to use, and agreed on all of it. Not knowing what else to do, she invited him to stay for lunch, and he sent his crew to a restaurant in the village. During lunch, Winnie was surprised to learn that he had gone to Oxford and to Eton, like Freddie, but he was four or five years older. Freddie said he actually remembered him, although he looked different then, and now he had a beard.

"How did you get into doing reality shows?" Freddie asked him.

"Money," he said simply and they all laughed. "I started doing reality with rock stars, which was pretty grim, and moved on to movie stars, which was a little more civilized, but just a little. And then real people, which is actually very interesting. The others are so predictable, and you know what it's going to be about, sex, drugs, and rock and roll, which gets old very quickly. The real people always surprise you, and the viewers like them better. They can identify with them. You're going to be an intriguing case, because you're real and you're not real, like the royals. People love them and want to reach out and touch them, but they know they're different. Your titles and this house make you special. And Winnie is a commoner and American, which they'll love, because she's like them, but she's with you, which makes them feel they could be too. Then you'll have movie stars and the rich and famous in for weddings, and mystery weekends. This show has every ingredient it needs to be a smash hit. Aristocrats, real people, stars, a castle, a young American woman. It's pure gold." He smiled as he said it.

"Thank you for the 'young,'" Winnie said, laughing.

"You look even younger than you are," Paul said kindly, then turned to Freddie. "It's too bad there's no marchioness in the mix, but that also makes you an eligible bachelor. Every woman in England is going to want to show up here and meet you, and be your fairy princess."

"Now there's a frightening thought," Freddie said, looking worried.

Paul left shortly after lunch to join his crew and drive back to London, and the three of them went to pick up the costumes waiting for them on racks at the set. They rolled them around to the back of the castle, and spent the rest of the afternoon carrying the clothes upstairs. It was exhausting, since many of them were heavy. Freddie called Rupert to come and help them. He came over quickly, and carried armloads of them to the rooms Beatrice and Winnie indicated and had set up for them. There were day clothes, evening gowns, morning coats for the men, and all the suits of tails they needed for Edward's wedding. They had a separate room set aside, with sheets on the floor for the five wedding gowns they'd purchased for very little money. There were veils and headpieces to go with them, and every dress had a long train, which would look magnificent going down the stairs.

Beatrice had developed a checklist for Edward's wedding, and they already had several items ticked off. And they had three months to complete the rest.

After they put all the costumes on racks upstairs, Winnie was about to leave at six o'clock when Freddie stopped her and asked her to take a walk with him so he could show her something. She had no idea what he had in mind but assumed it was for the tour for the reality show. He led her down a path she hadn't noticed before. There was a narrow gate and a garden, and then she saw the small elegant stone house with dark-green painted shutters. He had told her when they were riding that it had been his grandmother's. She hadn't paid much attention to it, other than that she knew it belonged to Beatrice now.

He took a key out of his pocket and walked to the front door. "Traditionally, when the marquess died, and his son inherited the title and took over the castle, his widowed mother would move to a smaller house on the property, and live out her days there. The tradition is a bit sad and very British. In France, they live the rest of their lives in their chateaux, but here we put the widow in a small house, and her daughter-in-law takes over the castle. But some dower houses are very pretty. I rather like ours," he said as he led her inside to gracious rooms of livable proportions that managed to be both elegant and not too daunting. "It's a bigger version of your cottage, by quite a bit." He smiled at her.

"It's a lot bigger." She looked around, not sure why he had shown it to her except for its historical value. She wasn't sure it would be interesting for the tour.

"No one lives here now. I thought you might like to try it, Winnie. It would be nice to have you close by."

"Have me move here?" She looked shocked for a moment. "Wouldn't Beatrice mind?"

"I asked her, she likes the idea too. You're part of our family now. You've protected our home, so now we want to protect you."

"But I'm safe where I am." She liked her cottage, although the dower house was truly lovely and very elegant.

"I'm sure you are, but you'd be more comfortable here. And you could come and go as you want at the castle. We have my grandmother's furniture in storage in one of the barns. Will you let me set this up the way you want it?" He looked gentle as he said it, and he put an arm around her, as she sank against him. It was a comfortable place to be, like the house, under his wing.

"Are you sure?" She felt like an intruder or an impostor, but she didn't want to hurt his feelings and refuse. She could see that it meant a lot to him, and was a gesture of his thanks for everything she was doing, and had done for them.

"Yes, I'm sure," he said, smiling at her. "I'll have it up and running for you in a few days. I had it cleaned up for you last week. And I want to get a few things painted." She had never known him to be so organized and serious since she'd met him. It wasn't like him. "I think my grandmother would like knowing you're here. You've become the family savior."

"With a reality show? I doubt she'd be happy about that."

"True," he said with a laugh, "but these are modern times. We all have to adjust." And he liked the producer a great deal more since he'd learned he'd gone to Eton. He knew it was small-minded of him, but he found it comforting none-theless. Surely he wouldn't betray or embarrass one of his own. He hoped he was right about Paul Evans.

"So do we have an agreement, and you have a new home?" She nodded, overwhelmed. He looked happy as they left the house together.

"I don't know how to thank you," she said softly.

"Oh, we'll figure out something. Tithing maybe, or you can give me your firstborn when you have a child," he teased her, "or call me 'Your Grace,' so people think I'm a duke. Or 'Your Majesty.'"

They were laughing as they walked back to her cottage, and she saw that there were only a few trucks left. The last of **Beauchamp Hall** had almost disappeared. But they still had the best part, with the castle.

He walked into her cottage again as he had the night before and it looked familiar to him now. "Well, it won't take you long to pack up. I'll tell Be-atrice you've agreed, she'll be pleased." He seemed very satisfied with the arrangement.

At the end of the week, she moved into the dower house and found an enormous bouquet of white roses from the garden in a vase in the living room, with a note: **Welcome home. Love, Freddie and Beatrice.** She texted photographs of the house inside and out to Marje, who sat in her kitchen looking at them, frowning, and handed her phone to Erik. "She'll never come home now," she said unhappily, and he nodded.

"No, maybe not," he agreed when he saw her new home. It was impossible to compete with that.

Chapter Sixteen

The first episode of the reality show was a two-hour special, and took a week to film. They did it in the first week of December. Freddie showed off the stables, with a great many explanations about the horses. Then he showed his car collection, which included the Bugattis. There was no mention of what they were worth, which was one of Beatrice's conditions and they stuck to it. So far, Paul had kept all his agreements with them.

They began the tour of the house then, with Beatrice in the lead. They walked the path of the rooms that had been most used by **Beauchamp Hall,** and then explored the family rooms, and some of the most stately rooms of the castle, including the ballroom. Freddie and Winnie joined her eventually, and they talked about the history of the house, who had stayed there and when, all the way back to Queen Victoria, who they explained had been a frequent visitor and a cousin of the Havershams, which Winnie hadn't known.

They showed some film clips of **Beauchamp Hall,** and the important actors who'd been in it, Winnie handled that part of the interview. It saddened her for a moment that it was only history now and no longer the present. Then she told them of their plans for Haversham Castle, and Edward Smith's wedding, although they didn't give the date to protect his privacy, and so they wouldn't be besieged by paparazzi. They described the mystery weekends they were planning, and how they would work, showed off the costumes, and described what a weekend would include. They also interviewed Winnie about her life in Michigan.

Paul stayed with them for the week. They set him up in a guest room and he ate dinner with them every night. He was good company and had a great sense of humor, and seemed fascinated by Beatrice, and continued to call her "Your Ladyship" for the entire week, even after she'd asked him not to.

Rupert played his role perfectly, looming throughout as the dignified butler. He thoroughly enjoyed it.

Paul invited them all out to dinner at a pub the night before he left. He walked ahead with Beatrice on the way back, and Winnie tucked her arm into Freddie's and pulled him back and whispered to him.

"I think he likes her."

"So do I." It amused him.

"Do you think she likes him?"

"You can never tell with my sister. She can be a terrible snob, or she can like people, and men, who have absolutely nothing in common with her."

"Like me," Winnie added.

"I wasn't thinking of you. You two get along like two peas in a pod. I was thinking of men. I can never figure out who's going to strike her fancy. But he's smart, has a good job, and seems to be crazy about her, although if he calls her 'Your Lady-ship' one more time she may slap him." They both laughed at that, and then Freddie walked her to the dower house so she didn't trip in the dark. He usually took her home at night to make sure she got in safely. She had given up her cottage by then.

When the show aired, it was a mind-boggling success, with fantastic ratings, and they had over a hundred inquiries about weddings and mystery weekends, and sixteen firm bookings, with deposits in the mail. And their rates weren't cheap.

"We did it! We did it!" Beatrice said when they got the first check, and she waved it in their faces at breakfast. "Take a look at **that**!" she said to her brother and Winnie. "And that's all thanks to Win-nie's dream!"

"Thank God you listened to her," he said seriously.

"I thought she was mad for a minute," Beatrice confessed, and they laughed.

Edward's wedding was two weeks away by then, and Beatrice wanted every detail to be perfect. She went over it again and again with Winnie to double-check everything and make sure they hadn't missed a single detail.

The bridal party showed up on schedule on Friday morning. British **Vogue** and assorted members of the press were staying at nearby B and Bs and the village's best hotel. Grace had a maid of honor and two bridesmaids. At his insistence, Beatrice gave Grace's father the room he had occupied at the castle sixty years before, and Rupert helped him up and down the stairs so he didn't fall. Winnie had given up the dower house to Edward so he would be comfortable, and wouldn't see Grace on the morning of the wedding. His family was in Australia, and couldn't come, so the wedding party wasn't large. A parade of masseuses, manicurists, and a yoga instructor came to minister to Grace and her attendants, and the morning of the wedding, the press appeared in earnest, and makeup artists and three hairdressers got to work, while Winnie and Beatrice orchestrated all of it, with Lucy, the young girl they'd hired from the village who came in as needed. She remained mostly in the background but came running when they called her. And Bridget came to pitch in.

The caterer had been serving delicious meals for two days.

Edward had his own exquisitely tailored set of

tails, Freddie had the ones that he'd worn since he was twenty, and Grace's father had his. The guests began arriving on schedule. The music Grace had chosen was being played by the orchestra Beatrice had hired from London. There were flowers throughout the house, fabulous white orchids and fragrant lilies of the valley. The minister was there on schedule, and Freddie went to get Edward from the dower house at the appointed time. His best man was staying at Mrs. Flannagan's along with the photographer from **Vogue.** Every single detail came off without a hitch. The bride came down the grand staircase just as Miranda Charles and Elizabeth Cornette had on **Beauchamp Hall,** and the wedding gown from the last episode of the show was a masterpiece and perfection on Grace. Her father had tears running down his cheeks when he walked her down the aisle, and Edward's eyes were damp when he saw her.

The valets had dispensed with the cars for all three hundred guests, and Winnie and Beatrice agreed it was the most beautiful wedding they'd ever seen. They had both worn black dresses so as to be unobtrusive. The reality show filmed every moment of it, and interviewed the guests afterwards, particularly the famous ones. Edward had invited a number of fellow actors that he had worked with, all of whom were major stars. It was an extraordinary wedding.

Halfway through the evening while the guests were dancing and before the bride and groom cut the cake, Beatrice and Winnie slipped into Beatrice's office for a break, and found Freddie sitting on the couch with his shoes off, drinking champagne.

"What are you two doing here?" he asked, pleased to see them.

"Same thing you are," his sister said. "My shoes are killing me." She took them off and Winnie sat down in a chair, relieved not to be on duty for five minutes. She had been watching every detail, as had Beatrice and Freddie. Their future depended on the success of the first event, which could make or break them.

"I'd say it's a great success, wouldn't you?" he asked them, and they all agreed that it was fantastic. And Edward and Grace were a particularly lovely couple. They looked like a fairytale prince and princess.

Winnie, Beatrice, and Freddie went back out among the guests ten minutes later, and after Edward and Grace cut the wedding cake, Freddie asked Winnie to dance, and Paul stepped forward and invited Beatrice to dance with him. He said the filming was over, and he had stayed to enjoy the rest of the evening. He had been seated with them at their small table for dinner.

The wedding went on until 4:00 A.M., with a buffet breakfast of eggs and oysters, lobster, and caviar before everyone left and the wedding party went to bed. The bride and groom had reluctantly left at 2:00 A.M., after tossing the bouquet, and departed in a shower of rose petals to be driven to London in a Bentley, and catch the plane Edward had char-tered to take them to Tahiti. Every single moment of it had been gorgeous and exactly what Edward and Grace hoped it would be. Edward had left them a huge additional check to thank them. Paul had gotten his crew going again to film the bridal getaway, and the **Vogue** photographer had stayed until the bitter end too. And in the morning, they were going to put Grace's father in a Rolls and send him home, and the bridesmaids in another, after they shared a hearty breakfast of eggs and crêpes.

When the last guest and bridal attendant had left, Freddie, Beatrice, and Winnie danced around the front hall and hugged each other. There wasn't a single detail that had backfired or been overlooked.

"It was **unbelievable**! You did such a great job," Freddie complimented his sister and Winnie.

"We all did," they both said generously. Their suppliers had proven to be reliable and skilled and had done their jobs well.

"I've never been so tired in my life, but it was worth it," Beatrice said, collapsing on a couch in the main living room. "I'm not sure how often I can do that."

"A lot more," Winnie said to her. "We have eleven more weddings booked, and six mystery nights. And twenty-six calls I haven't returned yet." And when Edward's wedding turned up in **Vogue,** and the reality show of the wedding aired, their phone would be ringing off the hook.

"Oh God," Beatrice groaned at the thought. "I'm going to wear orthopedic shoes to the next one."

"We're going to become the primo location for weddings after Las Vegas," Winnie said happily.

Their cleaning woman from the village had come in early and cleaned up the dower house by then, and Freddie walked Winnie back to reclaim it. He walked in with her and she smiled at him.

"Do you want a drink or a cup of tea?" she offered.

"A transfusion . . . actually, tea." She made him a cup of Earl Grey and handed it to him. "How did you ever come up with this idea, and why didn't we think of it before? It was so obvious," he said to Winnie, "to have weddings here."

"It was all in that crazy dream I had." He was smiling at her as he set his cup down. He had changed in the last few months, Beatrice had noticed it too and mentioned it to Winnie. He was more serious and reliable. He was just as funny, but they could count on him to do what they needed and he promised. He was very much a functioning member of the team, and took care of both women. "Did you see your sister with Paul last night, by the way? I thought he was going to kiss her on the dance floor." Freddie looked amused at what she said.

"I think he might have. Or she might have kissed him. She won't admit it because she's such a prude around me, but I think she likes him, quite a lot in fact. I like him too."

"So do I," Winnie agreed. "I can't believe we've

got the mystery night coming up in ten days. And a wedding two weeks later. This is positively athletic!"

"We can do it," he said confidently. And then he looked at her in an odd way, and she had the feeling he was going to ask her something, and then his mood changed and he didn't. "Do you want to go for a walk later?" he asked her.

"Yes, if you carry me."

"We can take turns."

In the end, he stayed for an hour while they talked about the wedding and the upcoming mystery night. Then he went back to the main house, and she promised to come over for dinner. She had the option to eat by herself or with them, but most of the time she went over to join them. It was always warm and friendly being with them.

When they met up for dinner in the kitchen, they were all wearing jeans and old sweaters and running shoes, and helped themselves to whatever they wanted from the neatly organized leftovers arranged by the caterers. Edward had sent them a text saying it was the most beautiful wedding he'd ever been to, and they were thrilled.

"Did you see the check Edward left us last night as a bonus? I nearly fainted," Winnie commented.

"Me too," Beatrice agreed, munching on a perfectly trimmed lamb chop left over from the wedding. The food had been superb.

"So tell us about Paul," her brother teased her and she gave him an evil look.

"Mind your own business. And yes, I like him. But he's divorced and has two children I haven't met yet, who will probably hate me. Both teenage girls."

"At our age, most people have been married and are divorced with kids," Winnie said practically. "And if they haven't been married, they're weird." Freddie looked insulted the moment she said it.

"I've never been married and I'm not weird," he defended himself.

"You're just crazy, that's different," Beatrice said easily.

"I'm not crazy or weird, I just haven't found the right woman."

"Well, you've certainly auditioned enough of them," his sister reminded him.

"I've reformed," he said weakly. "I don't think I'd want a big wedding like that if I got married," he said, thinking about it.

"Neither would I," Beatrice agreed. "I think I'd elope to Las Vegas, or somewhere else vulgar and fun. I don't want all that formal stuff, hundreds of guests and a white dress trailing down the stairs. I'd probably trip and fall flat on my face. But it was certainly pretty. They're stars, so people expect all that, and after thirteen years, she earned it."

"Her father looked happy," Winnie commented, enjoying rehashing the wedding with them. It was like having roommates, which they were in a way.

"If you drank as much as he does, you'd look

happy too," Freddie added. "And he had a flask in his pocket."

They sat in the library afterwards, and Freddie poured them each a glass of port as Winnie groaned.

"I think I'm becoming an alcoholic. Are we drinking too much?"

"I don't think so," Freddie reassured her. "I wonder what the footage for the reality show looks like."

"Gorgeous, I hope," Beatrice said, and stood up when she finished her drink. "I'm going to bed before I pass out. I'm sleeping till noon tomorrow."

Winnie and Freddie sat talking for another hour after that. He made her laugh, telling her stories about Eton, and the pranks he used to play on his teachers and friends.

"Were you and Beatrice always close?" she asked him.

"We hated each other growing up, and then I turned around one day and we were best friends. Especially after our parents died. We were both very young, and she needed a big brother to protect her. And once she grew up, I could go back to being an adolescent," he said, and she laughed. "But lately, I'm growing up or getting old. This business of ours has forced me to be responsible. I think I rather like it." He seemed surprised.

"I've noticed. It suits you. I like you as a grown-up," she commented.

"I think I do too." He looked at her for a moment, and held her hand. "You're a brave woman,

Winnie. I admire that about you. It took guts for you to come here all alone."

"Brave or foolish, I'm not sure which. But it's worked out well. I've been very lucky." She smiled at him.

"So have we," he said gratefully.

He walked her back to her house then, kissed her on the cheek, and looked serious when he left. After that she got into bed and watched an old episode of **Beauchamp Hall** before she fell asleep. It was almost Christmas, but with the success of their first wedding, she felt as though she'd already had the best Christmas gift of all.

Chapter Seventeen

Christmas was a quiet affair, and anticlimactic after the excitement of the wedding. They shared a simple dinner in the kitchen, reminiscing about their childhoods, when their parents were alive, and they relaxed on Christmas Day and Boxing Day. Winnie called Marje and Erik and spoke to the kids, and the day after Boxing Day, they got to work, to get everything ready for the first mystery weekend.

The preparations were almost as complicated as those for the wedding had been. They were doing it on New Year's Eve, so everyone's expectations were heightened.

Winnie had written the script for the mystery with Freddie's help. Beatrice and Winnie organized the costumes. There were maps and clues to hand out. The food had to be flawless, the rooms perfectly prepared. They had put appropriate accessories with each outfit. The evening was going to be black tie, evening gowns for the women. The murder was to occur the night they arrived, and be solved by the time they all left late the next day. The weapon, cleverly concealed somewhere in the house, was used as part of the guessing game and would have to be found and identified.

The whole process was intricate, and the three partners worked hard on it before the guests arrived. Not all of them spoke fluent English. There were twenty people in the group, among them a couple of Italians, a very exotic-looking French woman, a Turkish man, and the rest were English. The reality show crew was on hand to film it. Paul had come with them, and Beatrice looked pleased to see him, especially since it was New Year's Eve.

Everything went off smoothly during dinner, while Winnie and the Havershams supervised and Paul hovered near the guests, offering to help. After dinner, the guests were sent off to various locations in the castle to do errands they'd been assigned as part of the mystery, which was confusing for the film crew, who weren't sure which group to follow. Paul instructed them to stay with each group for a short time.

And then a scream rang out, according to the script, when a body was found in the main salon. It was the French woman, who was supposed to be dead, but was actually lying in an enticing position, smoking a cigarette.

"You're supposed to be dead," Beatrice reminded her. She spoke no English, so Beatrice repeated it in French.

"I am dead," she assured her. "I am smoking in the afterlife." The others circled around her, trying to guess how she had died.

"From smoking," someone suggested, and Freddie and Winnie tried not to laugh. They were a group of friends who had all chipped in for the evening, as a fun way to spend New Year's Eve. And the price they were paying was appropriately steep.

The guests were offered after-dinner drinks from a large silver tray that was a Haversham heirloom, and the smoking corpse ordered a cognac.

It was finally decided, per the script, that she had been strangled with her pearls, and there were lengthy interrogations about where they had last seen her alive and when.

Beatrice put music on then, and the murdered French woman got up and wanted to dance.

"Is it a language problem?" Freddie whispered to Winnie. "Or is she just difficult?"

"Both, I think," Winnie whispered back, as Beatrice gave them pleading looks to rescue her. Freddie took over as the police detective, and narrowed it down to nine possible murderers, which was several too many. The guests were all dancing by then, and put the murder on hold.

"They're not following the script," Beatrice complained with immense irritation. "Who has the script? Do you have it?" she asked Winnie.

"I gave it to Freddie," she explained.

"I don't have it." He looked blank.

"Sorry," Paul said, pulling it out of his pocket. "I forgot to give it back to you."

"I'm not sure they care who killed her," Freddie commented.

"I don't blame them," Beatrice said. "I'd like to kill her myself." And Paul laughed.

"It's going to make a great show, so don't worry about it," he told them. "Murder goes awry at Haversham Castle. Do you want to dance?" He had finally stopped calling Beatrice "Your Ladyship," which was a relief. They all began dancing to the music Freddie had set up on the sound system. The guests were dancing too. A few minutes later, Freddie and Winnie joined them. It was almost midnight. As the hour approached, Freddie began a loud countdown to warn them, and at the stroke of midnight, he blew a horn and put "Auld Lang Syne" on the sound system, and all the guests kissed each other, far more ardently than he had expected. They were still kissing when the song ended, several with their tongues halfway down each other's throats and their bodies pressed together.

"Now what do we do?" Freddie asked his support group. "They're still kissing."

"At least they haven't taken their clothes off yet,"

Paul said and kissed Beatrice with equal ardor. And they didn't come up for air for a long time either.

"Oh, sod it," Freddie said, took Winnie in his arms, and kissed her.

"What are you doing?" Winnie said, shocked for an instant. She hadn't expected it, and thought he was kidding.

"Don't worry, it's in the script," he insisted.

"No it's not, I wrote the script."

"Yes, it is, I added it," he said, and kissed her with all the pent-up passion he'd felt for her since he'd met her, and she melted into his arms and kissed him back. They were still kissing when Beatrice and Paul stopped and looked at the scene around them, which the film crew was recording diligently. The mystery guests were starting to grope each other. Winnie and Freddie had come apart by then, as Beatrice stared at her brother.

"Do you realize you just kissed Winnie? Are you drunk?"

"Not yet, but I'm considering it. And yes, I do know I kissed her. It was intentional, not an accident."

"That's like kissing your sister!" she said, looking outraged. "She's family!"

"Not exactly. Although I hope you kiss like that, for Paul's sake." As Freddie and Beatrice were discussing it, the guests hurried up the stairs in pairs to disappear into their rooms, the murdered woman among them, her arm linked through the arm of one of the Italians, whom she hadn't arrived with. His wife was with the Turk.

"Wonderful evening," they all murmured as they rushed past their hosts. "Great party! . . . So much fun . . ." And with that, the last of them disappeared, their doors closed, and Freddie, Winnie, Beatrice, and Paul were left alone in the grand salon and started laughing. It was obvious what the guests had gone upstairs to do, to celebrate the New Year, hopefully in pairs, not in groups.

"Maybe they're a sex club of some kind," Freddie suggested.

"Aren't they a little old for that?" Beatrice responded, as Paul's film crew came over and asked if they should continue filming.

"I don't think so, they all went to bed. You can stop now," Paul told them.

"Should we film you?" they persisted.

"No, that's fine." Freddie suggested the crew each have a glass of champagne, which they did, conferring quietly with each other, as Freddie looked at Winnie intently, dropped quietly to one knee in front of her, and gazed at her lovingly as she stared at him, and Beatrice looked at him in astonishment.

"Freddie, **what** are you doing, for God's sake?"

"I'm proposing to Winnie," he said, never taking his eyes off her face, and she started to smile and look shy.

"Now?" Beatrice scolded him. "Are you mad? You've never been married before."

"No, I haven't, so I'm free, which is a good thing. If I weren't, this would be awkward. It's already hard enough." Realizing that he was serious and something major was happening, Paul signaled frantically to his camera crew to get the cameras rolling again.

"Winona Farmington," Freddie said in a louder voice, as he reached for Winnie's hand and held it, "I'm totally mad about you, and have been from the first time I laid eyes on you, and I can't wait a moment longer to share my life with you. Will you marry me?"

"Freddie, for Heaven's sake," Beatrice complained. "Can't you do something like that in private?" She saw the cameras rolling then and shrieked. "Oh my God, you just proposed on a reality show. What's wrong with you?"

"Nothing," he assured his sister. "Winnie, will you?" he asked the woman he wanted to marry in a gentler voice, oblivious to the cameras rolling, and Paul was beaming. It was the best show they'd filmed in years.

"Yes," Winnie said in a hushed voice. "Yes, I will." Freddie stood up and kissed her then, as Paul's crew got the kiss and their smiles afterwards, and Beatrice rolled her eyes.

"I can't believe you just did that. How can you be so undignified? You proposed on a reality show, Freddie." Her feathers, and her nerves, were seriously ruffled by the entire evening. "Congratulations of course, and best wishes to the bride." She kissed Winnie on the cheek and glared at her brother. "You're incorrigible, and I thought you'd finally grown up."

"I think I have," he said, undaunted by his sister.

"Now we can be sisters," Beatrice said, smiling at Winnie. "And you will be the Marchioness of Haversham." The thought of it suddenly hit Winnie like a lightning bolt.

"Oh my God. How do you do that?"

"It's easy," Freddie said, still holding her hand. He looked over at his sister then. "I tried to get Grandmama's ring out of the safe to give her when I proposed, and I couldn't get into it. Did you change the code?"

"No, it sticks," she informed him, as Paul told the cameraman they could stop rolling film. They had everything they needed. The newly engaged couple then retired to a quiet corner and he kissed her again, more discreetly, as Paul walked Beatrice to one of the other couches.

"I need a drink. This has been a ridiculous evening. We have to work on these murder evenings a little more," Beatrice said, looking exhausted.

"They were a tough group," Paul said comfortingly, and then kissed her, and both couples sat lost in their own worlds for a while until Beatrice said good night to Paul, announcing that she was going to bed. He left without bothering Winnie and Freddie, and a little while later, they got up, Freddie found her wrap, and walked her to the dower house. The cameraman had disappeared with Paul.

"Do you really mean it?" she asked as he walked her home. The proposal had been so crazy and theatrical, she wasn't sure if it was a joke. It didn't feel real yet.

"Of course I mean it. I wanted to propose to you on New Year's Eve. I decided weeks ago. Tonight just got a little out of hand. The delivery was not as smooth as I would have liked. When do you want to get married? Let's do it soon. And where?"

"Here," she said without hesitating. "Just us and our sisters. I want to get married in this house. That's my dream." They had reached the dower house by then and it was cold outside. They were both shivering. "Do you want to come in?" She looked at him lovingly. He nodded in answer to her question, she opened the door, and he followed her in, to finish what he had started.

Their first murder group appeared at noon on New Year's Day and ravenously ate breakfast. They left as soon as they had finished, although they weren't supposed to leave till that afternoon. But they all seemed very happy. They thanked their hosts profusely, and said it had been perfect, just what they'd hoped for. They added generous tips to the bill, and looked delighted when they left. The mystery remained unsolved and the designated murder victim looked hale and hearty, with a cigarette pressed to her red lips when she left.

"I think we need to work on that script some more. She was the most uncooperative murder victim I've ever seen," Freddie said.

And with that, Beatrice came up to her brother and put something in his hand discreetly. "I think that's what you were looking for." He glanced at it, and recognized the beautiful rose-cut oval solitaire diamond that had been their grandmother's. He nodded and smiled at his sister and slipped it on Winnie's left hand. She looked down at it in amazement.

"I love you," he whispered to her and kissed her, as Beatrice walked away quietly, smiling.

They called Marje a little while later and told her the news, and she laughed and cried, and couldn't believe what had happened.

"And you're going to be a marchioness. I can't even pronounce it."

"Neither can I," Winnie said happily.

"I'll teach you," Freddie whispered, and they smiled at each other, as Winnie thought how incredible it was.

It had started with two DVDs in the white elephant game at Christmas in Michigan a year before. They had turned out to be the best gifts she had ever received and the key to her future. The dream had become a reality once she had the courage to pursue it. Who could have known? Who could have dreamed it or imagined it? **Beauchamp Hall** had changed her life. And in turn, she had come to Haversham and changed the lives of those who lived there. Reality had turned out to be so much better than her dreams.

About the Author

DANIELLE STEEL has been hailed as one of the world's most popular authors, with over 650 million copies of her novels sold. Her many international bestsellers include **In His Father's Footsteps, The Good Fight, The Cast, Accidental Heroes, Fall from Grace, Past Perfect, Fairytale,** and other highly acclaimed novels. She is also the author of **His Bright Light,** the story of her son Nick Traina's life and death; **A Gift of Hope,** a memoir of her work with the homeless; **Pure Joy,** about the dogs she and her family have loved; and the children's books **Pretty Minnie in Paris** and **Pretty Minnie in Hollywood.**

Daniellesteel.com
Facebook.com/DanielleSteelOfficial
Twitter: @daniellesteel